Kate and the Soldier

Kate had been warned by the man she was supposed to marry that David Merritt was a scheming and penniless fortune hunter who would prey on an heiress such as she.

She had been warned by the noblewoman who had raised her that David was an outcast of society whom all decent women shunned.

She had been warned by David himself that he hid guilts and shames that would make her despise him if she ever learned the naked truth about him.

But the one thing that no one warned her about was how she would feel when he took her into his arms. . . .

Kate and the Soldier

Barbara Bell

ROBERT HALE · LONDON

© Barbara Yirka, 1993, 2009
First published in Great Britain 2009

ISBN 978-0-7090-8434-1

Robert Hale Limited
Clerkenwell House
Clerkenwell Green
London EC1R 0HT

www.halebooks.com

2 4 6 8 10 9 7 5 3 1

Typeset in 10½/13¾pt Sabon
by Derek Doyle & Associates, Shaw Heath
Printed and bound in Great Britain
by the MPG Books Group

To Carol Smith, *critiquer extraordinaire*

Acknowledgements

I wish to express my thanks to Mr Peter Davenport of the Bath Archaeological Trust for his inestimable and very kind assistance. Any mistakes I have made regarding the period of the Roman occupation in Britain are mine and not his.

I would also like to thank Marion Dodd, the present owner of Mrs Vivier's at 32 Brock Street. Her charming John Wood town house, and her gracious hospitality, greatly enhanced my visit in Bath.

My thanks go also to Dr Don Wright of St Paul for his advice on matters medical.

Prologue

Thomas, the third Earl of Falworth, lay still and silent in his darkened bedchamber, listening for the sound of footsteps along the corridor outside his room. Regina and Lawrence would be here soon. Lawrence – his son and heir, thought Thomas. wearily. God, how had things come to such a pass? He was preparing to face his Maker. One would have thought that the burden he'd carried for so many years would have lightened by now, worn away by time and the passing events of life. Yet it remained heavy as death itself, and, he smiled bitterly, no doubt as permanent.

Too late – too late. The words rustled slyly in his mind like the whispering of mourners at a grave side. But was it? Could he still make reparation? His breath, frail and spasmodic, caught in his throat. No, he had made his choice those many years ago, and he had reaped its dubious reward.

A sound outside the door made him turn his head slightly, and he watched as his valet ushered in his wife and son.

Lawrence entered the earl's bedchamber in some trepidation. The room had always intimidated him, with its huge, canopied bed and oppressively dark hangings, and he entered it as seldom as possible. Assuring himself that his mother stood at his back, he approached the great bed. God, the old man looked awful. Lawrence could hardly bear to look at the drooping eyelids and the thin line of spittle that ran from a sagging mouth.

To his consternation, the earl waved his mother out of the room.

'But, Thomas. . . .' she cried in protest.

'Go, Regina!' His slurred voice growled petulantly. 'I would be alone with my son.'

Regina's lips tightened, but she bowed her head and left the room. Lawrence remained near the door, and it was only when his father beckoned with some impatience that he approached the bed. He perched uneasily on a chair covered with faded damask.

For some moments the earl stared at him. His gaze traveled from the glowing Brutus of which the young man was so proud, to the carefully arranged cravat, past the satin waistcoat, and down to gleaming Hessians, their silver tassels atremble. Raising his head, Thomas peered into the somewhat protuberant, rather vacant eyes that blinked anxiously at him.

He sighed.

'Earlier, you and I were discussing the River Farm.' He mouthed the words slowly.

Lawrence nodded.

'If I should give it to you, what would you do with it?'

Lawrence's features relaxed in pleased surprise.

'Why, sell it, of course. Been sitting there for donkey's years, might as well get some good out of it.'

'I see. And the Farside acreage. Pettigrew says we should marl it and put it into oats next year. What do you think of that?'

'What? Oats? Well, how should I – that is, it seems to me Pettigrew has been getting above himself lately. What do we have there now?'

'Barley.'

'Ah. Well, barley is good, isn't it? I think we should leave it in, er, barley.'

'You think Pettigrew an unsatisfactory bailiff, do you?' Thomas spoke softly, but his breathing was becoming labored. 'It does not seem to me that you have ever taken the trouble to acquire enough knowledge of estate matters to enable you to make such a judgment.'

'Good God, Father,' cried Lawrence, genuinely shocked. 'Gentleman's son, and all that. Pretty cake I'd have made of myself slogging about out in the mud. M'friends would have laughed themselves sick to see me.'

The earl sighed once more.

'Was it I who taught you it's beneath a gentleman to concern himself with his own land?'

'Well, indeed, Father, *you* never did!'

Thomas flinched.

'Does it not bother you that the estate is in dire financial trouble? Did you know that I had considered selling the River Farm to an outside buyer, for the money it would bring?'

'No! That is, I knew things were a little tight, but – surely, Father, we'll come about, won't we? We've always come about. You'll see. A few good runs at the tables, and we'll be all right and tight again. You've told me that a hundred times.'

As he spoke, Lawrence's expression lightened, as though he had vanquished with his words the moment of discomfort that had sent a frisson skittering along his spine.

His father knew an urge to throw back his head and give utterance to his grief and rage in a primal howl. In the same instant, he was swept with the cold realization of the futility of such an act, even were he capable of accomplishing it. He had never known such desolation.

He looked into the eyes of his son, and saw mirrored there his own failings. Before him, slumped in a worn chair, sucking on the end of his quizzing glass, sat the hope of his house. Dear God, what had he done?

He sank back into his pillows, closed his eyes, and waved his hand, which Lawrence correctly interpreted as a sign that the audience was over. With relief, and some puzzlement, the young man tiptoed out of the room.

Thomas lay for some minutes, only the faint, erratic rasp of his breathing and the painful rise and fall of his chest indicating that life still burned, albeit faintly, within his wasted frame.

However, when his man came to inform him some half an hour later that Mr George Smollett had arrived, he was sitting up in bed, his thin cheeks flushed, and a rare expression of determination on his face.

'Send him in,' he barked, with a semblance of his former vigor. 'But first, Pargeter, I want you to do something for me.'

Beckoning the servant to his bedside, he issued a short but precise series of directives, and when he had seen his puzzled valet from the room, he permitted himself a chuckle.

He had done a terrible thing many years ago, but perhaps it was not too late after all to set matters to rights.

'Ah, Smollett,' he cried, and a strange sense of release swept over him. 'Come in. I hope you've come prepared to stay awhile. I have matters of import to discuss with you.'

Chapter One

Major David Merritt, late of His Majesty's Peninsular forces, had nearly reached the limit of his endurance. White-lipped, he clung to the side strap of the carriage in which he had been jolting across southern England for the last several hours. When the vehicle lurched in and out of yet another cavernous pothole, he could not suppress the groan that seemed to well directly from the wound that throbbed in his hip like a living entity.

'David? Are you all right?'

The young man seated opposite him in the luxuriously appointed carriage was slight and neat in aspect and action, with brown eyes that affirmed the concern in his voice. He turned to a third passenger, whose servant's garb contrasted with rough-hewn features and a fierce, canny stare. He, too, had turned to David, and was attempting to help him to a more comfortable position.

'Damn it, Curle,' said the neat gentleman, 'I told you we should have stopped for the night in Bath.'

'Yer talkin' t' the wrong man, guvn'r,' grunted the servant. 'It's 'is bloody, stubborn 'ighness, 'ere who insisted we keep on the march.'

Gasping with the effort it took to speak, David shifted his body restlessly.

'I wish you two old hens would cease talking about me as if I weren't here. Bath is hardly more than two hours from Westerly, and we've come almost that far now. See?' He gestured with a thin hand. 'We are just passing through Bitton. We'll leave the main road in a moment and will soon reach our village. In another five miles, we'll be home – at Westerly.'

He sighed the word, as though he had just uttered an 'Amen' at the end of a prayer. His two companions glanced at each other.

David noticed the look that passed between his friends, but remained silent and continued to gaze at the increasingly familiar landscape that flashed by the window.

He was not a large man, being only a little above-average height, but his presence seemed to fill the interior of the coach. He might have been handsome once, but deep lines had been graven in a face already harshened by sun and storm. Hair of crow's-wing black had long since grown out of its military cut, and now fell just past the back of his collar in shaggy tendrils. His eyes glinted darkly against the pallor of gaunt cheeks and a broad brow, and his clothes, though they had been purchased after he sold out just a few months ago, hung loosely on his thin frame. He turned to face the man opposite him, and his mouth lost some of its rigidity.

'I understand your concern, Lucius, and I'm grateful,' he said, 'but you must understand my desire to make this journey.'

'No, I don't,' replied Mr Lucius Pelham with some irritation. He paused to remove a speck of lint that marred the pristine contours of his sleeve. 'I don't understand at all why you'd ever want to set foot in Westerly again. I know your father's message was urgent – and I am sorry to hear that he is so ill, but after the way your precious family has treated you, I'd think you'd make steering clear of them your life's work. Although,' he continued meditatively, 'there is your cousin, Kate, of course. I suppose you'll be glad to see her. She was, what – fourteen when you left? From what you told me of her, she must be a rare handful by now.'

Oh God, thought David. Kate. The image of his childhood play-mate had sustained him in many a black moment, but now – how was he to tell her. . . ?

He shifted uncomfortably, then winced at the pain. Curle once again made as though to aid him, but David waved aside the efforts of his erstwhile batman.

'Lucius, my friend, I cannot sponge off your good nature forever. Besides, you've been telling me for weeks that what I need is a good dose of country air. The air hereabouts is as outstanding a product of the countryside as you're liable to find.'

'David,' Lucius replied severely, 'I have repeatedly asked you to stop talking fustian. Good nature, is it, by God? Have you forgotten why you carry that nasty little chunk of metal in your bones?'

'No, but. . . .'

'You did save my life, you know. That may not seem like a worthy accomplishment to you, but I regard it as a feat of major importance.'

A look of anguish flashed in David's eyes, and he flung up a hand in a defensive gesture. Lucius continued, unheeding.

'And, in case you hadn't noticed, my family has all but adopted you. Father thinks you're as clever as you can hold together, you know. Now that you've finished your recuperation, you have only to say the word and he'll put you to work.'

But David was not listening. He had turned to the window once more, and now he cried out softly.

'There, can you see, Lucius – Curle? See that hill, beyond the village? Just on the other side, in a fold of earth, lies Westerly.'

The remainder of the journey passed quickly, and soon the carriage swept through gates of Bath stone and up a long, curving drive. In another moment, the manor house came into view. It was an imposing building, built of the same material as the gates, and for an instant it seemed as though the rays of the setting sun had been captured to warm its rough-hewn blocks. A gracious Paladian facade spread on either side of a pillared entrance. Though David's angular features now glinted with a sheen of perspiration, he barely waited for the carriage to come to a halt under a spreading portico before flinging open the door to begin his painful descent. Bolting from the other side of the vehicle, Curle grasped his arms just in time to prevent him from falling to the ground in an awkward heap.

Lucius leapt down as well, supporting his friend as a second carriage drew up, laden with luggage, under the supervision of Fellowes, Lucius's manservant. Curle ran up the steps to wield the knocker with imperious abandon, and within seconds, the great door swung open to reveal an august personage who could only be a butler.

'Fleming!' croaked David, remaining upright only through a supreme effort of will.

'Mr David!' The butler hurried forward, blank surprise written on his features. 'Welcome home! We did not expect you until the morrow!'

15

David's grin was ghastly.

'Don't you know, Fleming, that bad pennies not only turn up where they're not wanted, but also when least expected?'

The butler's shock at the young man's appearance was obvious, but he hastened to assist him into the house, nodding to the others.

'Nonsense, Mr David,' he replied, 'you're surely welcome here, for this is where you belong.'

Then, as though ashamed of having given vent to such unbutlerlike sentiments, he beckoned peremptorily to a footman, ordering him to summon the housekeeper.

'Her ladyship,' continued Fleming, 'is with his lordship. You did know of his lordship's illness?' he queried anxiously. At David's nod, he continued.

'I shall have her informed of your arrival at once.'

The little party, minus Curle, who had been dispatched belowstairs, had by now reached one of the saloons opening off the entrance hall, and David sank gratefully onto a faded brocade settee. He was relieved that his stepmother was not among those present.

'Please don't disturb her ladyship, Fleming,' he said. 'We will greet her at dinner. In the meantime, this is my friend, Mr Lucius Pelham. He will be staying with us for a few days. Can you find a place for him to lay his head?'

'As if you need to ask such a question, Mr David!'

The words were spoken in warm feminine tones, and David turned to discover that Westerly's housekeeper, Mrs Seagrave, had entered the room. Evidently she had been warned of his present disability, for she waved a minatory finger as he struggled to rise.

'And you'll stay just where you are, if you please.' She paused to give him a measuring look. 'It's about time you came home, young sir. You look like a death's head on a mop stick, if I do say so, but we'll have you all right and tight in no time. Cook has been baking since word came yesterday that you'd be arriving soon, so you'll have fresh scones for tea.'

David's dark eyes lit with laughter.

'Ah, Siggy, you have not forgotten my addiction! Come here then, please, so I may greet you properly.'

The housekeeper bent to receive a hug and a hearty kiss on the cheek. Mrs Seagrave let her hand rest a moment on the shaggy head, then turned, her eyes bright. She bobbed a curtsy to Lucius.

'If you'll follow me, sir, I'll show you to your room.'

'Yes, but . . .' His eyes were still on David. 'You'll need help getting to your own room. Shall I. . . ?'

'No.' David waved his hand. 'Thanks, but I believe I'll just sit here for a moment, and then make my own way. Really,' he added, as his friend hesitated. 'I shall do very well now that I am not being shaken from stem to stern over every boulder and pothole in the county. I would like to walk for a bit before I go upstairs.'

'That doesn't seem like . . . Oh, very well,' Lucius concluded, recognizing only too well the thrust of that very determined jaw.

After the group had left the saloon, David sat in silence and looked about him. At last he sank back into the settee and closed his eyes wearily, remembering the last time he had been in this room. His step-mother, Regina, Countess of Falworth had stood at that window over there, and it seemed as though her words still echoed from the walls, settling as they had six years ago, in the pit of his stomach where they churned in a maelstrom of humiliation and rage.

'*I've stood this long enough, Thomas. How many other women would have allowed the presence of her husband's by-blow in such close proximity for so many years? Is the boy to remain here forever, leeching off an estate that can barely maintain itself as it is?*'

The tirade had continued at some length, but David, now sickened anew, closed his mind to the painful memory and rose from the settee. He limped from the room and crossed the entrance hall, fleeing toward the rear of the house and out to the stables.

'Mr Davey!' The head groom hurried across the stable yard. 'I couldn't believe it when they said you was here. Lord, but it's good to see you, sir.'

David stared at the grizzled form before him.

'Moody! Josiah Moody!' He enveloped the man in a fierce hug. 'Are you still here, you old reprobate? Good God, you haven't aged a hair!'

'Go along with ye now, Mr Davey. I'm gettin' by, don't ye know?'

The two chattered for several minutes, reliving old times that David had not allowed himself to think of for an eternity.

17

'And do ye mind the time,' Moody said, 'when Miss Kate's cat had her kittens in the stable, almost beneath the feet of his lordship's stallion? And do ye think we could keep her. . . ?'

David stiffened, and a sick feeling settled in his stomach.

'Where is little Kate?' he asked hesitantly. 'I haven't seen her.'

Moody seemed taken aback.

'Little Kate? Well, I guess I wouldn't be knowin' that, Mr Davey. She took her mare out some two hours gone. Wouldn't hear of takin' a groom with her, o' course.'

'I wonder . . .' mused David, a faraway look in his eyes. His desire to see his old playmate overcame the dread he felt at what he must tell her. 'Do you have a mount available for me, Moody?'

'Well, of course, sir, but. . . ?' he trailed off, his glance straying dubiously to David's lame leg.

'I do all right on a horse, as long as I don't try any steeplechasing. I'll need a leg up, but then I can manage.'

The pain was bad, but, David assured himself, manageable when he cantered out of the stable yard a few minutes later. He made his way slowly toward where the sun's rays gleamed low in the sky. What would be Kate's reaction on seeing him, he wondered idly. She had certainly been in the devil's own temper at their last encounter. He could not even remember the childish slight he must have inflicted on her to inspire her anger, but she had raged at him like a young virago, hurling her spite at his head. And she had gotten to him. Even then, she had known how to use words as a weapon, and she had made him furious. He, a wholly mature, superior eighteen-year-old! He had been tempted to take her over his knee and give her the paddling she so richly deserved, but he had been hurt beyond childish retribution. He had simply swung away from her, and had not spoken to her again before he left.

He smiled, remembering the stiff little notes tacked onto Father's letters to him. She had obviously been trying to apologize without letting her uncle know that she'd called him an 'overbearing toad' – among other things.

He allowed his glance to roam over the gently rolling land of the Home Farm, and his throat tightened. He'd thought never to see the fields and coverts of Westerly again. Now that he was here, the sight was almost more than he could bear. Why had he been cursed with such an abiding love for this piece of earth? He, who had no place here and no right to cherish it.

His attention was caught by a grainfield in the distance, its growth only half what it should have been. It looked as though it had not been fertilized for several years. As he rode, he noticed other signs of neglect – tenants' houses in poor repair, woodlots in disarray. He should not have been surprised, he mused ruefully. Even when Father had ruled here in good health, the estate had not been productive. The earl readily admitted he had no head for management. Nor, apparently had he a talent for hiring others to manage for him. Pettigrew, the bailiff, was a good man, but not forceful in persuading Lord Falworth to spend money on land improvement, which he preferred to spend on gambling, horses, and all the other essentials to the life of a gentleman.

He crested a craggy hill. He was far out of sight of the manor house now, and, ignoring the smooth slope that fell to a meadow on the other side, he turned into a tangled little ravine that dropped precipitously to a rocky mound overlooking the River Avon, shining in the distance. He saw no one, and disappointed, began to turn back. He had gone only a few yards when an odd sound caught his ear. It was the chink of metal colliding with stone and earth. Someone digging? Reversing course, he moved cautiously past an outcropping of rock, and there he saw a little mare tethered. Beyond, the chinking sound continued.

'Hello?' he called.

The sound stopped abruptly, and phased into a clatter of skittering pebbles. A small, grimy hand appeared over another outcropping, followed by a cloud of fiery red hair and a pair of enormous hazel eyes.

'Oh dear,' cried the owner of the flaming mane. 'I did not realize it was so late. Aunt will be furious that she had to send someone . . . Oh!'

Having clambered into full view, the girl stopped and lifted a slender hand to shade her eyes from the sun glaring on the horizon. She pushed her hair back from her forehead, and so flamboyant was its color that one might have expected sparks to fly as a result.

19

'Who. . . ?' she murmured uncertainly. Then . . . 'David?'

David sat motionless as a wave of apprehension washed over him. The moment he had looked forward to for so long with a mixture of longing and dread had arrived.

For a moment, Kate Millbank stood still while the world rocked about her. How many hours, she reflected wildly, had she spent curled on this sunny knoll, dreaming of his return – reliving memories – and now – right before her. . . .

But what was he doing here? He was not expected until tomorrow, Aunt Regina had said. Kate recalled the displeasure on her ladyship's thin face as she had called her into the crimson saloon earlier this morning.

'It's David,' she had announced abruptly, waving a note that had evidently just been handed to her.

At the sound of her cousin's name, Kate's hand had flown to her throat, and she lowered her eyes to hide the gladness she knew must shine there.

'David?' she echoed blankly. 'But, I thought. . . .'

'Yes,' replied her aunt in a voice of controlled irritation. 'It came as a surprise to me, too. I had thought him tucked snugly away in that little village in Kent, sponging on his friend.'

'Wrotham,' said Kate, her voice brittle. 'He is recuperating in Wrotham at the home of a man who owes him a great deal.'

'Yes, yes.' Her ladyship broke in impatiently. 'I have heard quite enough of his gallantry at Toulouse and how he was wounded in the hip – or leg, or whatever – saving his friend's life, and all that.'

'But he could have been killed!' Kate cried.

Lady Falworth's penciled brows rose.

'That would have been unfortunate, of course, but you must remember, my dear, that David is no longer considered part of the family.' She continued hurriedly, observing the tightening of Kate's mouth. 'It was to be expected, of course, that he would leap at Thomas's invitation to come ho – to Westerly. He's always been obsessed with the place. I wonder if he knew of Thomas's paralytic stroke when he decided to scurry back.'

Kate stared at her aunt in growing wrath.

'Are you implying that David is coming home in order to take advantage somehow of Uncle Thomas's illness?'

'Of course not,' replied her ladyship calmly. 'What could he hope to gain? David was informed long ago that he can expect nothing more from your uncle. What is left of the estate resources must be husbanded for the heir to the title. Lawrence has little enough to look forward to as it is.'

Kate struggled for composure, repressing the urge to scream her anger at the countess. For perhaps the thousandth time, she tried to understand Lady Falworth's enmity toward David Merritt. Perhaps it was not to be expected that she would accept the presence of her husband's by-blow in her home with any degree of equanimity, but merry, dark-eyed David had never wished harm to anyone. He had not asked to be born a bastard. It was Uncle Thomas who had decided to raise him here at Westerly – and that was long before Aunt Regina had come to reign as the Countess of Falworth.

Her ladyship was speaking again.

'I, of course, cannot be expected to make the necessary preparations. You will have to take care of getting his room ready, and you will have to find a manservant for him. I suppose he will need someone to care for him. I gather that he cannot manage for himself yet.'

'It is possible, Aunt Regina,' Kate replied calmly, 'that David will bring his own servant. He is a major in the army, after all, and not a pauper. As for caring for him, I shall be glad to do that myself.'

Lady Falworth's narrow features sharpened in displeasure.

'That would be unseemly,' she said, clipping her words.

'Unseemly! But, I have known David all my life. He was like a—' she choked suddenly, remembering – 'a brother.'

The older woman lifted her hand in an impatient gesture.

'Yes. You and David and Philip were close, too close I always thought. However, just because David was with Philip when he was killed, I fail to see why we should grant him any special attention. We will find someone besides yourself to nurse him. I must go to your uncle now – he becomes restless when I am gone from him for long.'

Kate stood aside, biting back the angry words that sprang to her lips, as Lady Falworth swept from the room. She turned to the fire and stood staring into the flames for some moments.

David. Coming home. His image had stayed with her all these

years, but she had thought never to see him again. Certainly, he had seemed relieved to depart Westerly. Why, the last time she'd seen him ... Dear God, the last time she'd seen him, his eyes had been filled with anger and pain – all directed at her.

Now, returned to the present, she straightened, thrusting the unpleasant memory from her mind. The important thing was that he was home. She leaned the shovel she carried against the outcropping and was surprised to note that her hand trembled. She drew a deep breath, then plunged over the rocks toward him. But, why did he not dismount? Why did he remain astride his horse, with that strange expression on his face?

She stopped suddenly, her hand flying to her mouth. He still remembered! He remembered and had not forgiven her for her inexcusable outburst. Her heart sank to the soles of her scuffed walking boots, and she pushed her hair back with a self-conscious gesture. Her steps slowed and then, seeing David's outstretched hand, she lifted her own to be enveloped in his warm clasp.

Chapter Two

'Kate!' David cried. 'Little Kate, indeed.' How stupid of him. Of course, she would not have stayed forever the wild, independent child he had held in his heart all these years, an image crystallized by affection. Little Kate had grown into a splendidly beautiful young woman! The setting sun caught her in its brilliance, highlighting her delicate features and outlining curves that had matured to lissome fullness. Her hair was a fiery halo.

'Please forgive me,' he continued a trifle breathlessly, 'for greeting you like this. As you may have heard, I suffered a slight, er, indisposition during the late fracas in Spain, and now the only way I can dismount a horse is to simply fall off. Then it takes a helpful passerby or two to reinstate me in the saddle.'

He had maintained his hold on her hand, but now released it. Kate hastily thrust it behind her, blushing like a schoolgirl, her heart pounding jubilantly. There had been laughter in his voice, and a smile in his eyes – he had forgiven her! A weight that had burdened her for six years melted in the warmth of his gaze.

'Oh, David,' she cried, 'I was so sorry to hear of your wound. Are you recovering?'

He had shifted his position slightly, and now she could see his face clearly in the sunlight. She almost gasped as the horror of his appearance struck her. Dear Lord, was this really David? The smooth-faced, smiling boy she had known had been transformed to a gaunt, harsh-featured, infinitely weary man.

A silence stretched between them, until Kate, recalling herself, continued.

'I'm so glad you're here! I'll just untether Belle, and we can go.'

As she ran to accomplish this, David called after her.

'But, what on earth were you doing when I arrived? It sounded like a coal miner at work, as well it might have been, judging from your appearance.'

Kate whirled, her face alight.

'Yes, I suppose I must look a sight,' she laughed, uncaring, 'but, oh, David, wait till I show you!'

She darted behind the rock from which she had emerged a short time before, and when she returned, she carried something wrapped in an old shawl.

'Look! Just look!'

David reached down to receive the bundle and stared in amazement at its contents.

He turned the object, examining it carefully. It was the head of a young boy, carved in marble. Tousled hair curled over a smooth brow, and a turned-up nose wrinkled engagingly. His lips curled in a mischievous smile. The detail was astonishing; one could almost trace a delicate network of veins along the temples. The artist had captured all the exuberance and vulnerability of childhood.

David let out a soft whistle.

'Where in the world did you find this?'

'Back there!' She gestured. 'I discovered it several months ago. And there's so much more! Oh, David, we never dreamed – you and Philip and I – when we spent so much time playing here – there's a whole house, right beneath our feet!'

'What?'

'Yes. One day I was sitting up here by myself, and a really ferocious storm blew up. It seemed only a matter of moments, and then thunder and lightning scared me to death. I shrank back against the rock wall, trying to find some shelter. Mud and rocks began to slide from above as I made my way farther along the ledge – farther back into the underbrush than any of us had ever gone before – and suddenly, I slid. I was so frightened! I thought I was going to tumble all the way down into the valley, but I lodged against a tree, with my foot caught in a sort of crevice.

'As I tried to wrench it free, the crevice grew wider, and before I knew it, I had fallen into what seemed like a cave. The first thing I saw was the head. I scrabbled about some more, and saw that I was in some sort of room, with vases made of bronze, and what looked like part of a leather sandal.'

'Good Lord, Kate. Do you know what you've stumbled into?'

'I think so. It can only be an ancient Roman villa! A family lived in this place – a Roman family, but so far from home, and so long ago. You can see' – she pointed to the thin line of road that lay between their vantage point and the river beyond – 'the house was situated close to the old Via Julia – the road between Bath and Bristol.' She turned her attention to the sculpture. 'The marble head is, I believe, a portrait bust. He was a real child, don't you think? Look, here, he has a tiny scar at the corner of his mouth.'

David ran his fingers over the childish contours.

'This is astonishing! Yes, I believe you're right, but it's a much finer example of marble portraiture than any I've ever seen in this country.'

'Yes, it is, isn't it?' She wrapped the bust carefully in the old shawl. 'Uncle Thomas took me to see the excavations at Bignor, and . . .' She stopped at David's questioning look. 'It was, oh, three years ago, I think, when a farmer in Sussex found the remains of a whole villa in his field. It's a huge place, and two portrait busts were found, but not nearly so fine as this. I've left the artifacts pretty much as I found them – I'd better put it back now.'

She turned and disappeared again behind the outcropping. When she emerged once again, she mounted Belle, and the two began making their way back along the little ravine.

David shifted in the saddle in a vain effort to ease the pain that was beginning to gnaw at him once more. He watched Kate assessingly.

'I see you have not been spending your time in embroidery and watercolors.'

She laughed. It was a musical sound, and David found that he was looking forward to hearing it on a daily basis.

'Aunt Regina tried to make a lady of me, but I'm afraid there isn't a governess alive who could instill in me a single talent. My embroidery was fit only for dust clouts, and my watercolors for lining bird cages.'

'But how is it you are up here alone?' said David, joining in her self-deprecatory amusement. 'I should think a discovery of this

25

import would have drawn antiquarians from all over the country.'

Kate dropped her eyes.

'I haven't told anyone about it,' she said in a low voice. She looked up at him, and at the surprise she read in his face, she continued hurriedly. 'I will sometime. Well,' she amended, 'I did tell Uncle Thomas that I found what I thought were some Roman ruins, but I didn't mention the artifacts. He was mildly interested, but that was all. Oh, and I told Aunt Fred all about it, but she's the soul of discretion – if you ask her to be. I know I can't keep it a secret forever, but this has always been such a special place. It's a sort of haven for me, and it holds so many dear memories, because it was our place. I feel closer to Philip here than I do anywhere else, and to you.'

At the mention of Philip's name, it was as though a shutter had come down over David's face. The smile dropped from his lips, and his mouth curved into a thin, bitter line. His eyes grew hard.

You idiot, Kate chastised herself. *You are not the only one to grieve for Philip.* And how much worse it must have been for David, who had been obliged to watch his best friend die on that riverbank so far from home.

'Anyway,' she continued awkwardly. 'I have set aside the things I have found, and noted where I found them, as well as making sketches of them as they lay. Not,' she smiled ruefully, 'that they will be of much use to anyone, given my lamentable lack of artistic talent.'

David remained silent. Kate's thoughts had been almost visible, and, though he had known that this meeting with Philip's little sister would be painful, her clear sympathetic gaze was almost more than he could bear. He would have to tell her the truth eventually, he knew. But not now.

'How is it,' he asked, in an effort to turn the conversation, 'that you are still here at Westerly? I would have thought you married, with a home of your own, long since.'

He thought she tensed at that, and, despite an unexpected tightening the words caused in his heart, he continued in a teasing tone, 'Or could you not bear to leave?'

She smiled, and her gaze swept the gently rolling landscape that lay about them like the folds of a green velvet robe tossed on the hills from above.

'I do love it here,' she said softly. 'I think there must be no other place on earth half so beautiful. And you're right. I don't think I could bear to leave it.'

'Ah' – he nodded wisely – 'spoken like a young woman who has never been in love. I'm surprised some young buck hasn't swooped down from London and carried you off. For I should imagine,' he concluded expressionlessly, 'that you clean up fairly well.'

Kate's mouth flew open, but she recovered quickly. She blew a kiss at him with dirt-caked fingers, and, arranging the grimy folds of her old muslin dress with a bored flourish, she drawled, 'Oy, guv'ner. Aintcher never seen a laidy out t'take the air afore?'

David threw back his head and laughed. It hurt, but, by God it felt good. He could not recall how long it had been since anything had seemed even remotely humorous to him.

'Doesn't Regina ring a peal over you when you return to the house looking like you've been digging in the Mendip mines?'

Kate's eyes crinkled in a mischievous smile, and within him, a response stirred.

'I usually manage to sneak up to my room without being observed, although I may be in for it tonight, since we will probably arrive home close to dinnertime.'

'And no one suspects what you do up in the back of beyond all day?'

'Well, the place is so inaccessible – I think that was what enticed us three to make it our own – nobody knows exactly where it is, nor do they particularly care to find out. From time to time I bring Jem up with me – Jem Carver, one of the stable boys. I have been forced to build supports, else the hillside is likely to cave in on me, and I need help for that.'

'And Father permits this activity?'

Kate remained silent, brushing vigorously at a mud stain on her sleeve.

'I see,' he said. 'Father doesn't know, does he?'

'Well, he hasn't asked, after all. And I just – didn't want to bother him,' she finished lamely. She rushed on before he could speak again. 'But, what about you? Are you home for good, David?'

'No.'

He knew his answer was unnecessarily short, and as the eagerness in Kate's eyes faded, he added, 'This isn't really my home anymore. I have only returned because Father insisted that I do so – to recuperate. Even then, if I hadn't learned of his paralytic stroke. . . .'

'But where will you go?' The question came out in a childish wail.

'Oh, back to the Continent, I should imagine. I have been offered a position on Castlereagh's staff – a very lowly, minor position – to help with the preparations for the Congress. After that . . .' He shrugged, then said in an effort to lighten the moment, 'By that time I shall no doubt have made myself so valuable to the Foreign Office, they'll be clamoring for my services on a permanent basis.'

'But, how could you bear it? To go away and never see Westerly again? David, there is the River Farm. It is unentailed, and there is a lovely cottage on it already. Uncle Thomas always said you should have it someday. Perhaps. . . .'

'No!'

Her eyes widened at the harshness of his tone.

'I do not want to live,' he continued in the same voice, 'on a patch of land on the outskirts of Westerly, like a child with his nose pressed up against the toy-store window. This place,' he swept an arc with his arm, encompassing rolling hills and the lovely old manor house lying in its fold of earth, 'was my home, but I am not a boy any longer. I must make my own way.'

'But I was so looking forward to your being here,' she said softly. 'Since Philip died, I have had no one. . . .'

The pain was ripping at him now, and he interrupted savagely.

'You are no longer a young girl. Good God, Kate, you are – what? – twenty now? Have you been living in some sort of a fantasy all this time – dreaming that big brother would come back to you someday and make everything all right? Well, Philip is dead. He is not coming back, and I cannot replace him.'

Kate gasped under the onslaught of his words. A hot reply sprang to her lips, but they had by now reached the stable yard and Moody, the old groom, was approaching to help them dismount. She slipped from her horse, unaided, and averted her face so that David would not see the tears that spilled down her cheeks.

David's empty gaze followed her as she ran into the house. *This is only the beginning, little one. I have not yet told you the worst. Will you still cry when you have learned to hate me? Or will your tears harden – as your heart surely will?*

Through long practice, Kate managed to avoid anyone in her blind rush to the sanctuary of her room. She slammed the door and flung herself on her bed, sobbing among the ruins of her universe.

How could David have spoken to her so? How could he have deliberately hurt her? She had not asked him to be the big brother that would 'make everything all right.' She was perfectly capable of managing her own life. She only wanted a friend. What was there in that to make him lash out at her? Where was the David she remembered? – the merry companion of her youth, who, with Philip, had taught her how to bait a hook and how to shinny unobserved down the tree outside her bedroom window. What had become of the friend who had arranged an elaborate funeral service on the death of her kitten, and taken the blame when it was she who had stolen six damson tarts from the larder?

She was sure he had forgiven her for the childish outburst that had tormented her for so long, but the eyes that had stared at her just now in such fury belonged to a stranger – a haggard, pitiless stranger. What had gone wrong?

She shuddered slightly, and rose from the bed. Phoebe, her maid, would be tapping at the door in a moment to help her dress. Mindlessly, she reached for the pitcher of water that stood on her nightstand, splashing some of its contents on the floor. On a sudden impulse, she replaced the pitcher and fled from the room as though to let her unpleasant thoughts melt in the puddle of water she had left in her haste.

She ran through several corridors, past the main staircase that led to the Great Hall below, and up another flight of stairs. She continued down yet another hallway, reaching its end before she stopped at last before a heavily paneled doorway. She tapped lightly, and without waiting for an answer, opened the door and stepped into the room.

She might have been forgiven for assuming she'd entered Aladdin's Cave, such was the profusion of jewellike colors that greeted her gaze. However, the riotous splendor came not from precious gems, but from piles and spools and bobbins and bolts of thread, piled on the floor and cascading from tables and chairs. They were mostly of wool, but here and there glowed rich silks, and glittering among them were strands of silver and gold. In the midst of it all, at a huge loom, sat a plump, white-haired sprite.

'Aunt Fred!' exclaimed Kate. 'I thought I'd find you here. How goes your work today?'

The sprite whirled, revealing itself to be a small and unmistakably mortal old woman. She rose from her chair and spread her arms in welcome.

'Kate! My dear, I was just wishing for someone to come talk to me. The work goes well. I had run out of the cerulean, but I think this cyan works even better for the sky, don't you? Come and look.'

Kate stared at the panorama, which pictured a biblical scene – Adam and Eve being driven from the Garden of Eden, if she were not mistaken. However, unlike the manicured gardens that usually provided the background for such instructive tableaux, with perfect globes of fruit hanging from rigidly symmetrical trees, Aunt Fred's garden was a lush jungle. The fleeing mortals, eyes wide with terror, ran beneath a luxuriant canopy of trees through which birds of every size and shape swooped in iridescent splendor. Shadowy shapes with gleaming eyes prowled behind foliage that bloomed in hues never designed by nature.

'It's beautiful, Aunt Fred,' whispered Kate, her throat still tight with unshed tears.

Lady Frederica Merritt, spinster sister of the second Earl of Falworth, and aunt to Thomas, the third earl, grinned.

'It's going to hang in Ely Cathedral, you know,' said the old woman, examining several bobbins of thread that lay on the table before her. 'The dean was quite taken with the two pieces I made for Lord Dolphinton's new place in Bedfordshire, and said he had to have one. So, what about the cyan?'

'The. . . ? Oh, yes, for the sky. Just fine, I should think.'

Aunt Fred clapped her hands.

'Absolutely! Cerulean would have been too bright, and a nice, threatening sky sort of adds to the – the menace. I'm so glad it was you who came to visit. Regina would simply glance at the piece and shudder and call it lurid. You know,' she chuckled, 'I believe it pierces her to the very soul that I have met with such success with my tapestry work. Why, some are calling them works of art!'

She turned to Kate, and for the first time looked at the girl closely.

'Why, what is this? Kate, you look as though you'd spent the morning in a midden – and, good heavens, my dear, are you crying?'

'No, of course not, Aunt. I – I just returned from my digs, and I thought I'd bring some news for you. David is home.'

'So I heard,' replied her aunt, her eyes returning to the tapestry.

'But how did you know? He arrived not two hours ago!'

Aunt Fred peered over her spectacles.

'I have my own sources,' she replied in a bland tone.

'You've been bribing the footmen with toffee again, haven't you?'

'Nonsense. The servants know I like to know what's going on. Can I help it if they pop in now and then for a little conversation?'

'Aunt Fred, if Aunt Regina knew that you encourage the servants in 'a little conversation,' she'd be very displeased.'

'Never mind about that,' her aunt retorted. 'Tell me about David. How has his wound affected him'? Is he healed, or is he bedridden? Has he seen Regina yet?'

Kate flung up a hand.

'No, he is not bedridden, and he has not seen Aunt Regina. Oh, Aunt Fred, you would not believe the change in him! He is so harsh and bitter. At first, he seemed glad to see me, but then he said such cruel things.'

'War does terrible things to people, Kate. I wonder what he will have to say to Regina,' the old lady mused. 'After all, it was largely due to her efforts that David was sent away.'

'Yes, and it was so unfair. David loved Westerly more than anybody else in the family. Even Lawrence.'

'Lawrence!' Her aunt grunted again. 'His father's heir, and such a puppy.

'I remember the day David came to Westerly,' she continued, a faraway look in her eyes. Thomas had been shunted to the Falworth spice plantation in the West Indies by the family to "make something of himself." Well, when he returned to assume the title, there in his luggage, so to speak, was David, Thomas's son by a half-breed West

Indian woman. He wasn't much more than a year old, and solemn as a little owl when he stared up at one with those great, black eyes. They were a heritage from his mother, along with his straight, dark hair.

'It wasn't long, though,' ruminated the old lady, 'before he was cock of the walk. I can still see him, crowing with laughter as Thomas tossed him nearly to the ceiling. He was without fear, and he ruled us all – at least until Regina came.'

'Aunt Fred,' asked Kate on an impulse, 'why did Uncle Thomas bring David here? No one ever told us – Philip and me – the circumstances of David's arrival. I don't think David was told much, either. It all seems so odd. I mean, it's not common for a man to bring his – his. . . .'

'Bastard?' finished Lady Frederica dryly.

'Yes,' replied Kate, with a small grin. 'I've always wondered, and no one in the household has ever been willing to discuss David's, er, background. He told me once that his mother died giving birth to him, but that's all I know.'

'Mm, yes,' the old lady began slowly. 'That's about all we were told, as well. It does seem like an odd thing for Thomas to have done, settling David in here at Westerly. Particularly for someone like Thomas, who is hardly what you'd call revolutionary in his thinking. He's a good man, but, as you have no doubt perceived, somewhat weak in nature. Like many such men, however, he can occasionally turn stubborn.

'The household was in an uproar. Amaryllis, the silly widgeon, took to her bed saying that Thomas was an undutiful son and would be the death of her. My brother, Seth, spent hours in fruitless remonstrance with him, and all the other uncles and cousins and aunts buzzed at him like so many angry hornets, but all to no avail. Thomas had got the bit between his teeth. He said flatly that he had made his decision and that he was, after all, head of the family and by God that was to be the end of it. Well, it wasn't, of course, but eventually they all simply gave up. The word put out to the world was that David was the son of a friend who had died on Barbados, naming Thomas as the boy's guardian. David was supremely happy here until Thomas married Regina, and the boy was relegated to the position of an unwanted relative.'

Kate sat for a moment, absorbing her aunt's words.

'Uncle Thomas must have loved her very much,' she said at last. 'David's mother, I mean.'

'Mmm. In any event, he was left with a motherless infant and, I suppose, a load of guilt.'

'Oh, Aunt Fred, I'm sure Uncle Thomas was motivated by more than guilt. He is so kindhearted. Look at how he treated Philip and me. We were very young, too, when Papa and Mama died, but he brought us right to Westerly. And, he's not even really my uncle. My mother was only his cousin, so the relationship is fairly distant, after all.'

Lady Frederica's lips curled in an ironic smile.

'Yes, I'm sure the fact that your papa had become a nabob during his years in India, and that you and Philip were his sole heirs had nothing to do with your uncle's decision – instigated, as I recall, by Regina – to tuck you safely away at Westerly.'

'Aunt Fred!' This time Kate's gasp was audible. 'What an awful thing to say! Uncle Thomas has not indicated the slightest interest in our money.'

'Not so far, at least. We'll see what happens when you actually come into possession of your funds. For you are a very wealthy young woman, Kate, since Philip's death.'

Kate rose from where she had flung herself at her aunt's feet.

'That is unfair, Aunt. I have never known Uncle Thomas to be any other than an honest man.'

'To be sure, my dear, but even honest men will take advantage of what might be considered a windfall. Westerly is in desperate need of funds, and what could be more natural than an alliance between you, Thomas's wealthy young relative, and Lawrence, Thomas and Regina's oldest son.'

Kate spoke in a shaking voice.

'Even if what you said were true, I have no interest in marrying Lawrence, and Lawrence certainly does not want me for a bride. And – and Uncle Thomas has made only the merest mention that someday we might – that is. . . .'

Lady Frederica now rose also and extended a hand to her great-niece.

'There, child, forgive my wretched tongue. Please excuse my words as the maundering of an old lady.'

Kate shook her head, a smile lighting her clear hazel eyes.

'You need no excuse or forgiveness, Aunt. I would never want you to be less than your honest, if sometimes misguided, self, and I know you always speak from love. But,' she added as she prepared to leave the room, 'please, for heaven's sake, let us drop this particular subject. I must go and get cleaned up for dinner now.'

She brushed the top of Lady Frederica's head with a light kiss and slipped through the door. Reaching her room once more, she rang for Phoebe, her maid, and as she removed her filthy muslin, her expression remained thoughtful. For, as much as she might decry her great-aunt's sentiments, she had begun to realize some time ago that Uncle Thomas's plans for her future leaned heavily toward a union between herself and his oldest son. His oldest legitimate son, that is. She sighed, then brightened a little at the thought that this, at least, was a problem she would not have to face in the near future.

David, however, was something else.

Chapter Three

David paused for an instant at the doorway of his father's chamber before quietly approaching the great bed. For another long moment, he stared at the figure sleeping there. Lord, he thought, the change in the older man was appalling. Though his brown hair lay thick above eyes of the same color, and was scarcely touched by gray, his illness had taken its toll. Lord Falworth looked twenty years older than his forty-five years. His features were touched by a deathly pallor and as he opened his eyes, the hand he stretched forward was thin and trembling.

'David!'

The earl made a spasmodic attempt to lift himself on his bed. 'Ah, Davey, my boy, you have come!'

For the first time, David realized the seriousness of the earl's condition, and he moved to cover the older man's hand with his own.

'Of course, I have come,' he smiled. 'How could I refuse your invitation. I – I have missed you, Father.'

Thomas writhed in agitation, his mouth working and his hands clinging to those of his son.

'David, I have something to tell you,' he whispered with an effort. 'I did a terrible thing. . . .' He broke off in a paroxysm of coughing.

'Did a terrible thing,' he began again breathlessly.

'Father, you are tired,' said David, smiling to conceal his anguish. 'You must rest now.'

'No!' The old man's voice sounded as though it were coming from a great distance. 'Must tell you. . . .'

'Later, Father.' Gently, David touched his father's shoulder. 'We will talk later when you are stronger.'

The old man lifted a trembling hand in protest, but could not speak. He sank back among the pillows, tears of exhaustion making their way down the seams in his cheeks. His eyes closed, and David fled the room so that his gathering tears would not be seen by the man who lay fighting for his life.

Some minutes later, with Lucius in his wake, David entered the gold saloon, the customary pre-dinner gathering spot, and was relieved to see that only two other members of the family had preceded him. He knew a moment of gratitude that his friend stood at his side as reinforcement.

He became conscious of the faded splendor of the room. The silk hangings, already gone to a dim yellow at the time of his departure, were now even more pale, and noticeably threadbare. The gilt on some of the armchairs had begun to peel, and the chandeliers, though clean and sparkling, were missing several lusters.

A young man crossed the room with outstretched hand.

'David! Welcome home!'

David grasped the hand in some surprise.

'Crawford! It's good to see you.' He looked beyond the young man to where a slender girl stood near an old-fashioned pianoforte. 'And Cissy! I see your brother has far outstripped you in height.'

He turned and gestured to his friend.

'Lucius, these two very handsome young people are Lord Crawford and Lady Cilla – Cecilia – Merritt, my half brother and sister. They are twins, and I must say they have improved vastly over the grubby brats I remember. They were twelve when I left.'

Crawford chuckled, but Cilla's smile was faint. She still had not moved, but remained standing stiffly by the pianoforte, a determinedly cool expression on her face.

'We are eighteen, now,' said Crawford, a trifle importantly. 'I shall be coming down from Oxford next year, and Cilla made her come out last Season.'

He was a tall young man, loose limbed and angular. Brown hair fell over a rather meager forehead and appraising brown eyes. His smile, however, was open and unaffected.

Cilla, as might be expected, bore a strong resemblance to her brother, except that she was slight in stature, and small of feature. Her hair, a lighter brown than that of Crawford, tumbled artlessly about her shoulders, confined only by a slim thread of pink ribbon that matched her sarcenet gown.

Lucius shook Crawford's hand, then bent low over Cilla's. There was speculation in her young ladyship's brown gaze as she accepted his polished courtesies.

'Ah, so you have arrived, brother mine,' a voice drawled near the door, and the four turned to face the newcomer.

He was younger than David by a few years, and though of nearly the same height, was narrow of face and form. His looks were not displeasing, despite a faint touch of petulance about his mouth. Pale blond hair curled modishly about his thin cheeks, and the high points of his collar and the elaborate arrangement of his neck cloth announced a tendency toward dandyism.

David paused a moment before moving toward him.

'How are you, Lawrence?' he asked quietly, clasping the hand offered him.

'Oh, tol-lol.' Lawrence, Viscount Standing, was Thomas's heir, and the oldest of David's half siblings. He raised his quizzing glass. 'Better, at least, than you, my boy. You look decidedly down pin.'

David made no response to this, but introduced Lucius, who shook Lawrence's hand with a marked lack of enthusiasm.

'I'm surprised to find you at home, Lawrence,' said David. 'I expected you would be savoring the delights of the metropolis.'

'Ah, well,' yawned Lawrence, 'London's pretty thin of company just now, y'know. Besides, dibs not in tune, and thought I'd be better for a spot of rustication. I'm no less surprised to see you here. Hardly the return of the conquering hero, but, welcome home, none the less.'

An insulting sneer accompanied these words, and Lucius started forward. David put forth a restraining hand, turning a bland smile on Lawrence.

'You've become quite the sophisticate since I left, but I see your charm of manner remains as it was.'

Lawrence blinked uncertainly, then made his way to a settee in a far corner of the room.

David turned to converse once more with the others, but his attention was arrested almost immediately as another person entered the room.

Regina, Lady Falworth, stood in the doorway for a moment, one hand raised to the rigid sculpture that was her coiffure, her rather flinty blue eyes surveying those already in the chamber. She had been an accredited beauty in the fast-receding days of her youth, and she still comported herself in such a manner as to keep the aura alive. It was her habit to sweep into a room, pausing on the threshold for a few moments to allow those gathered to become aware of the diamond in their midst. The length of the pause was in direct proportion to the number and importance of the persons present to witness the spectacle.

Thus, on this evening, she hesitated for only an instant before moving into the room in the flowing motion that had taken years to perfect.

Lawrence had stopped in his progression to the settee, and now hastened to his mother. Regina, as though oblivious to everyone else in the room, grasped his hands in hers.

'Dearest,' she cried in delight, 'I did not know you would be dining with us tonight. Were you not engaged with a party to spend a few days in Bath?'

'Um, yes, Mother, but two of the fellows were forced to cancel out at the last minute, and I thought—' Lawrence sent a sidelong glance to the group near the fire – 'I thought perhaps I should be at home when. . . .'

Following the direction of his gaze, Regina allowed her own to rest on David. As though at that moment becoming aware of his presence, she smiled. It was a very thin smile, and might easily have scratched glass, but David returned it with a bow.

Regina did not move from her son's side, but said only, 'I was told you had arrived. I trust your wound is improving?'

'Thank you for your concern, my lady. Yes, I am getting on very well.'

He then made Lucius known to her, and at the sound of his name, a small furrow appeared on her still unlined brow.

'Pelham? The name is familiar. Are you related to William Pelham, the Marquess of Alconbury?'

She smiled sweetly, and David realized instantly that she knew the answer full well.

'No, ma'am,' responded Lucius, who had come to the same conclusion. 'My father . . .' He shot a glance at David. 'My father is a farmer. We live in Kent.'

'Well, then . . .' Her laugh was high-pitched and flavored with malice. 'Now that we all know one another, shall we go in to dinner?'

David's glance raked the room.

'But where is Kate?' he asked.

Lady Falworth swept past him to the door.

'Kate will join us momentarily.' She threw the words over her shoulder. 'I spied her coming from her room as I descended the stairs.'

David glanced down the corridor and caught his breath as he observed Kate hurrying down the massive staircase that led to the entrance hall. Earlier, with her hair a tangled tumble of curls and dressed in her tattered muslin, she had still managed to look appealing. Now, wearing a gown of clinging amber silk, her flaming locks contained in a graceful Clytie knot, she looked like a youthful autumn deity. She had grown taller. She would just about reach his chin now, he reflected irrelevantly. Her eyes had always been huge, too big for her face, really, but now they seemed to gather the candle glow from the wall sconces into their sparkling hazel depths. He shook his head dazedly and watched as she fell into step with the group, apologizing to Regina for her lateness.

Last to join the procession was Aunt Fred, who bounced down the stairs garbed in a gown composed of floating, multi-hued gauze panels, looking like some sort of renaissance elf. On catching sight of David, she hurried to him and stood on tiptoe to envelop him in a warm embrace.

After a delighted exchange of greetings, the old lady grasped the young man's hand in her own and chattered to him all the way down the corridor.

Kate, after casting a single glance at David, had confined her conversation to the ladies of the group, and now, entering the stately scarlet-hung dining room, she found to her dismay that she had been placed next to him.

After introducing her to Lucius, who sat on her other hand, David had little to say, addressing himself assiduously to his portion of roast beef. Kate was conscious of his nearness, and she knew an urge to reach out to touch him – to feel the warmth of his fingers beneath her own. Suppressing this unsettling idea, she attempted a few scraps of bland dinner conversation, meeting a noticeable lack of response. He had, she concluded miserably, set a wall around himself that she could not hope to penetrate. With one more unhappy glance, she turned her attention to his friend.

'Is this your first visit to Somerset, Mr Pelham?' she inquired, forcing her voice to cordiality.

'No, Miss Millbank,' Lucius replied with meticulous courtesy. 'I accompanied my mother here when I was just a sprout, to take the waters in Bath. Had a perfectly wretched time, to tell you the truth.'

'I should imagine,' said Kate, smiling, 'that the Pump Room and the Abbey do not provide much diversion for a boy. Did you drink the waters?'

Lucius's face screwed into an expression of distaste.

'Once. It tasted like tepid salt water in which someone had been soaking rusty nails and old boots.'

Momentarily abandoning her despondency, Kate laughed aloud, thereby gaining the attention of Lady Falworth, seated at the end of the table. She frowned at the girl, but addressed herself to her guest.

'Tell me, Mr Pelham. How did you and David meet? Were you in the same regiment?'

'Yes, ma'am. We were in the Fourth Division – The Enthusiastics, we were called,' he said with a deprecating laugh.

'Oh, yes,' cried Kate softly. 'My brother was very proud of being one of their number. Perhaps you knew him. Philip Millbank?'

'I met him a few times – with David,' Lucius replied gently. 'He was in the Twenty-third foot, and we were in the Twenty-seventh – different brigades, you know, so we did not see all that much of him. I was sorry. . . .'

'By Jove,' interrupted Crawford. 'Did you say the Fourth Division? You fellows saw some action at Toulouse! Were you part of the storming of Mont Rave?'

Lucius glanced at David, before answering shortly.

'Yes.'

'What a show that must have been,' cried Crawford, his voice bright with enthusiam. 'Don't I just wish *I'd* been there!'

'Only a fool would wish to have been at Toulouse.'

David's voice was little more than a growl, but it caught the attention of all at the table.

'Really, David,' began Regina.

'Did you think it a glorious siege?' continued David, as though she had not spoken. 'With banners flying and bugles trumpeting?' He laughed harshly. 'No, halfling, it was blood and screams and the groans of boys no older than you, dying in unspeakable agony.'

An appalled silence followed this speech, and Kate could only stare at David.

'Well, really!' gasped Regina again, and Cilla hiccupped in shock behind her napkin. Lawrence snickered uneasily.

'I say . . .' began Crawford. 'I didn't mean – that is, I'm sure it must have been quite wretched,' he trailed off unhappily.

'David,' snapped her ladyship, 'I'll thank you to remember that you are in a polite home now, not in some low Spanish tavern drinking with your disreputable cronies.'

David whitened, and for a moment, Kate thought he meant to leave the room. But, after a slight pause, he turned a brilliant smile on his stepmother.

'Please forgive me, my lady. I had forgotten that while it is perfectly permissible to die for one's country, it is not considered de rigueur to bring the war home with one, so to speak.'

Lucius, who had half risen at Regina's words, sank back into his chair.

'Bitch!' he muttered into his wine, and Kate, while breathing a comment of her own in agreement, pretended she did not hear.

From across the table, piped the voice of Aunt Fred at her most fey.

'What an odd thing to bring home for a souvenir. I would prefer something prettier, like one of those lovely mantillas so many of the young men brought for their ladies.'

The tension that had gripped those at the table relaxed suddenly, and Kate smiled in gratitude at the old woman.

David stared down at his plate once more. He felt Kate's gaze return to him, but he steadfastly refused to look at her. He could sense her concern, and shame at his outburst warred with a deep sadness at her unguarded affection for him. He was dismayed by the desire he experienced, as fierce as it was unexpected, to bathe in the warmth of that affection. No, he had ruined any chance he might have had to keep Kate for a friend. He would have to do something about Kate very soon, he thought wearily.

Or perhaps not. When Lucius left a few days hence in that elegantly appointed carriage, he would simply hop aboard. He knew he would be welcome to resume his stay with the Pelhams, and surely it would not be too long before he was well enough to make his way again to the Continent. God knew this trip had been a mistake. What had possessed him to accept Father's invitation? Some vision of himself as the prodigal son, welcomed into the bosom of his family with the love that had never been shown to him before?

No, that was not true. Kate and Philip had shown him kindness, and he knew his father loved him. It would be base of him to return that love with any further displays of self-pitying petulance.

He heaved a troubled sigh, and turned once more to Kate.

'My wretched temper prohibits me from tendering an apology to my beloved stepmother, but I will offer one to you. I must be possessed of a demon of ingratitude to have spoken so. And,' he continued, his eyes searching hers, 'I must apologize for this afternoon as well. God knows I am in no position to reject an overture of friendship from anyone, let alone someone who is as dear to me as a sister.'

For some reason this graceful little speech did not please Kate as it ought to have, but her eyes warmed as they returned his gaze.

'Is the pain very bad?' she asked softly. 'I – we were never told the precise nature of your injury.'

David stiffened, and through habit, a casual response formed on his lips. To his surprise, however, he found himself answering in a like tone.

'To be truthful, it hurts like the very devil – constantly,' he confided. 'The ball entered my leg just under the hip. The doctors feared to remove it, since it lies deep and very close to a major nerve, and there it remains, hence the limp and the pain. They removed some damaged tissue, but they say that's all they can do – they would not go farther for fear of paralysis. I'm lucky to be walking, they say, and they don't promise much improvement. I'll just have to wait and see. No, no,' he added hastily, observing the anguish in her face, 'it is much better than it was, and – and the pain is usually manageable. It's just that today – with the traveling and all. . . .'

He shifted in his seat, uncomfortable at having revealed so much of his ordeal. He had never spoken so before, even to the doctors at whom he had sworn and, finally, cried during those first long weeks after his injury.

In swift understanding, Kate placed her hand on his arm and forced a smile she did not feel.

'I shan't plague you anymore, for I have an apology of my own to tender.'

At David's lifted brows, she paused a moment and twisted the napkin that lay in her lap.

'Before you left, I said some awful things to you. No, let me finish,' she said as David raised his hand in a gesture of negation. 'Uncle Thomas and Aunt Regina have been at me all my life about my temper, but I never listened. Every time I became angry at someone – or thing – I simply let fly with the most vicious things I could think of, never giving a thought to the hurt I was inflicting. That day with you was no different. I don't even remember what you had done to make me so angry, but I flew into a tantrum and spewed out the words I knew would wound you the most. Dear Heaven, David, what a terrible child I was!'

'Must be all that red hair,' he murmured, amusement in his eyes. 'But that is. . . .'

'In the past. I know,' finished Kate. 'But, I used to think my temper really could be blamed on my hair. You've heard the expression "seeing red"? Well, I actually did! When I'd fall into one of my rages, I looked out at the world through a red mist. I thought there must be some connection. Until the day of that final outburst at you. Then, I realized, finally, the fault lay, as Shakespeare said, within myself.'

'You refine too much on it, Kate. I was well acquainted with you, if you'll remember. I knew you must have repented in horrible agony almost the minute I left the room. I'm only sorry we parted on such terms.'

'Oh, David, I was, too,' she said. 'And you're right about the repentance. I vowed that I would never again allow my emotions to goad me into causing pain to another. I can't say my temper never gets the better of me, but I've never again lost control.'

David smiled at the vivid face before him, her earnest expression reminding him of the child he had known in his youth, when he'd been all too aware he dwelled at Westerly on sufferance. Then, she and her brother had been a beacon of light and warmth in an otherwise rather bleak life. Philip had not cared that he was a bastard, and Kate – well, Kate hadn't known what the word meant. The three of them had been inseparable. Or, rather, he and Philip had been inseparable; Kate, years younger, had been merely tolerated. And that was due only to her fierce insistence that she be included in their adventures.

He glanced about the table as conversation flowed around him. Watching Regina insinuate herself into each conversation, he chided himself that he had been in her company for less than half an hour before he had allowed her to get under his skin. He was more than ever determined to cut his visit to Westerly short.

Chapter Four

The meal progressed, and David returned to the grim contemplation of his future. It was not until dessert was served that he became aware that Regina was addressing him. Good Lord, she must have been reading his mind.

'I plan to stay for a few days only, my lady,' he replied in answer to her pointed question. Beside him, he heard Kate gasp in protest.

'My recuperation is almost complete,' he continued smoothly. 'I came at Father's invitation because he wished to see me, not because I planned to make an extended visit.'

'But where will you go?' asked Regina, her tone indicating that his ultimate destination must be the gutter.

'Since I am no longer of any use to His Majesty's army, I plan to go into the Diplomatic Service.'

Regina said nothing, but lifted her brows disbelievingly.

'David has been asked to join Lord Castlereagh's staff,' interposed Kate, her face rather flushed. 'He will be assisting in the preparations for the Congress, in Vienna.'

Regina's brows flew into her hairline, and Lawrence laughed unpleasantly.

'Well, it looks as though you learned to curry favor in the army, if nothing else,' he said.

This time, David's only response was a bored smile. Lucius, however, took issue.

'Not all, my lord,' he snapped. 'The major already spoke fluent French by the time we came to the Peninsula, and thereafter, he picked up quite a bit of Spanish. Since he was also one of the most intelligent and well-informed officers in Beresford's command, he was chosen on several occasions to handle local negotiations. With marked success, I might add.'

David's smile was genuine now.

'You'll have to forgive that totally objective report from a good friend.' His laughter was warm.

Kate's attention was still focused on her aunt's rudeness, and an imp of anger took possession of her.

'I've been trying to convince David to remain longer – perhaps to make his home here.'

Regina's reaction was all that Kate had hoped. A furious flush spread to her cheeks, and she lifted her hand in a gesture of protest.

'Yes,' continued Kate serenely. 'Uncle Thomas has promised for years that he should have the River Farm. The cottage – well, it's a small mansion, really – has been sitting empty for a long time, and Mr Pettigrew says it's a valuable piece of property that could be made to turn a profit if it were properly administered.'

For a moment, Regina simply gabbled, but Lawrence flushed in fury.

'Never mind what Pettigrew says. He's always been on David's side! Whose agent is he, anyway? David has no right to so much as a pebble of Westerly land.'

Kate could have bitten her tongue for indulging her temper – and just after she had made that self-important speech to David. Now, she had brought about another spiteful attack on him.

Her eyes met those of Aunt Fred, who only smiled and dropped one eyelid in a slow wink.

David had gone rather white around the mouth, but he answered calmly, 'I've already explained to Kate that I have no plans to install myself at the River Farm, even if Father were to deed it to me – which, as far as I know, he has no intention of doing.'

Regina had by now regained her composure, and rose to signify that the meal was at an end.

'But of course, it would be impossible.' She smiled as she made her way from the room, gesturing to the females in the group to join her. 'Lawrence will need every available asset at hand for his future. As a matter of fact, I believe Thomas plans to assign the River Farm as a personal bequest to Lawrence when he and Kate marry next year.'

Regina's thin laughter drifted back into the room as she shepherded the ladies into the corridor, leaving the gentlemen to their port and brandy.

It seemed to David that his brain was extraordinarily slow in functioning. Kate and Lawrence? No – it was impossible! He glanced down the table to where Lawrence sprawled in his chair, twiddling the stem of his wineglass. His face bore an expression of self-satisfaction mixed with embarrassment and – what? Uneasiness?

Kate could not possibly be considering marriage to that insufferable little popinjay! But she had not denied Regina's statement. Why had she said nothing to him?

His gaze moved to Crawford. Certainly that young man seemed unsurprised, but he, too, seemed uncomfortable. What was afoot here?

Only Lucius seemed unperturbed.

'So we may wish you happy, my lord?' he said to Lawrence, lifting his glass.

Lawrence squirmed in his seat.

'Yes – well, nothing's been announced formally, of course. M'father's illness and all that. Been his dearest wish for years, though.'

'And Kate?' asked David quietly.

Lawrence wriggled even more agitatedly.

'Well, as I said, nothing settled yet.'

'Ah.' David leaned back in his chair.

The ladies gathered in the gold saloon to await the gentlemen, except for Lady Frederica, who retired immediately to her rooms as was her habit. As soon as the doors closed, Kate whirled to face the countess.

'Aunt, what in the world can you have been thinking of? Lawrence and I betrothed? What madness is this?'

'But my dear,' Regina answered smoothly. 'You know it has always been anticipated that you and Lawrence should marry?'

'Anticipated by whom?' gasped Kate.

'Why, all of us.'

With a rustle of silken skirts, Lady Falworth seated herself on a settee by the fireplace.

'What could be more natural?' she continued with a complacent smile. 'You and Lawrence have loved one another for years.' She ignored the titter that arose from Cilla and the muffled snort from Kate's direction. 'It was only to be expected that your affection should culminate in – in a permanent union.'

'But nothing has ever been said,' cried Kate, 'at least, not in so many words. Aunt, I do not wish to be married! And, I'm sure Lawrence does not, either. As for love . . .' Kate paused helplessly. 'We have been raised almost as brother and sister, so I admit there is some family affection, but. . . .'

'My dear child,' interrupted Regina gently, 'there is no need to fly up into the boughs. You will soon grow, er, accustomed to the idea. I know you have not been used to look at Lawrence in such a light, but now that the seed is planted. . . .'

An idea struck Kate.

'Does Uncle Thomas know of this?'

Regina's reply was swift. 'Of course, he does. In point of fact, he and I were discussing the matter just before I left him to change for dinner. You must know, he has been uneasy in his mind of late that your future is unsettled.'

'Aunt Regina, I can take care of my own future. I must ask that you drop this absurd notion.'

Regina's lips thinned, but she merely smiled.

'We'll see,' she said softly, then turned quickly to another subject.

'I must say that I was somewhat relieved to discover that David will not be staying long. I cannot conceive what possessed him to make the trip here at all.'

'Because Uncle Thomas asked him to,' retorted Kate. 'He can certainly have had no other reason for returning to a family that has treated him so shabbily.'

Regina opened her lips as though to reply, but Cilla was before her.

'I do think his friend is nice – that Mr Pelham.'

Regina sniffed.

'I wish you'd try for a little more discrimination, Cilla. A farmer's son?' she continued with some asperity. 'One would think that David would aspire to a higher station in his friends. I'm surprised he would bring such a person here.'

'But he was an officer, Mama,' replied Cilla, with unusual boldness. 'And I sense nothing of the barnyard about him.'

'I shall admit that to be true.' This, accompanied by a gracious nod. 'Perhaps a wealthy patron bought him a pair of colors. However, he is still hardly fit to be invited to the Earl of Falworth's residence.'

Kate bit her lip. She had no wish to enjoin in a brangle with her aunt. She cast about in her mind for a less volatile subject.

'I visited the conservatory this morning, Aunt. I see your acidanthera is about to bloom.'

'Yes,' said Regina in a pleased tone. 'I have been caring for it most assiduously. I have promised several of the ladies in the neighborhood the opportunity to see it when it blossoms. Perhaps. . . .' She was interrupted by the entrance of the gentlemen.

'You were not long!' exclaimed the countess in surprise. 'But, where is Lawrence?'

David and Lucius shot a glance at each other, but it was Crawford who answered.

'Oh, his precious lordship went into one of his miffs. He and David got into another bicker, and when David started to leave the room, saying he planned to visit Father, Lawrence pushed ahead of him, saying, no, *he* was going to go up. What a clunch!' he finished with a derisive chuckle.

'That will do, Crawford,' snapped Regina. She turned to David. 'I had hoped, since your stay here is to be brief, that you could manage to refrain from venting your ill nature on my son. It was always your way, of course.'

'On the contrary, ma'am,' Lucius interjected, unable to help himself. 'It was your son who discharged his spleen – at considerable length, I might add.'

'What a good friend you are, Mr Pelham,' purred the countess, her eyes narrowed to two points of steel.

David flung up his hand.

'Handsomely over the bricks, Lucius,' he said. To Regina, he added only, 'I'm sure Lawrence will be down shortly.' As if to turn the subject, he continued, 'Tell me something of Father's illness, my lady. Is he recovering as the doctors said he would? I was shocked at his appearance.'

For a moment Kate thought Regina meant to ignore her stepson, but finally she sighed.

'No, he does not go on at all well. He rallied immediately after his paralytic stroke, and we were hopeful at first, but he seems to have fallen into a decline. It's as though' – her voice fell to a whisper – 'he doesn't care.'

Her concern was obviously genuine, reflected David. But then, she had always seemed truly affectionate toward his father. It was only his father's love child whom she could not abide.

Lawrence strode into the room. He was obviously in a towering rage, and he trembled as he spoke to David.

'Father wishes to see you.' He turned to the countess. 'Mama, he practically threw me out of his room! Are you going to allow that – that upstart' – he pointed a trembling finger at his half brother – 'to come here and twist Father around his finger again?'

Regina hurried across the room to place a hand on her son's arm.

'But, what happened, my dear?'

'I told Father that David is angling for the River Farm and that he should order him to leave at once. He became furious, Mama – at me!' He swung to face David, his face contorted in a snarl. 'I suppose you think you have a sinecure here, but when my father is gone, then – well, be assured you'll never set foot in Westerly again!'

'Lawrence!'

It was his mother's voice that spoke in a tone of outrage. He stopped abruptly, and his eyes dropped.

David moved swiftly to the door, his limp pronounced.

'I hope' – he flung over his shoulder – 'that you did not phrase your displeasure in those words to Father.'

Lucius followed David from the room, murmuring of his fatigue from the journey and his intention to retire.

'Whew!' he said to David, once they were in the corridor. 'What a hellhole this place is! Were you serious about returning to the Court with me? It certainly seems advisable. Why in God's name does that little snerp hate you so?'

'I don't know,' sighed David. 'As youngsters, we got on fairly well, but Regina was always there, dropping her poison. "Never mind that he beat you in the race, my dearest. He only does it to show off, of course – so that your Papa will praise him. He is jealous because Papa loves you more than he does him." '

'The woman is incredible,' said Lucius, shaking his head. The two parted at the head of the main staircase, Lucius repairing to his room, and David turning toward the earl's chambers.

Later, Kate sat before the fire in her room. She had long ago ceased to notice that the primrose silk hangings were beginning to fray, and that the furnishings were growing increasingly shabby. She stared into the dying embers and reflected dismally on the events of the day.

David, home at last! It had seemed at first that it was not David at all who had returned, but a mean-spirited stranger. Then, at dinner, he had warmed her with the crooked grin that had won the heart of a small, red-haired termagant so long ago. He was still David. But how changed he was. Such bitterness was reflected in his dark eyes, and the pain he lived with spoke from every line in his face.

And there was Aunt Regina's announcement. Kate admitted to herself that she was not as surprised as her words might have led her aunt to believe. She could not remember when the hints first started. Her schoolmates at the exclusive seminary in Bath where she had spent several fruitless years trying to learn deportment, giggled and sighed over various beaux. When she had perused the current crop of dandies for a young man of her own to sigh over, Uncle Thomas pursed his lips and said, 'But you have Lawrence!'

Kate frowned. Lawrence? How ridiculous. Yes, they had grown up under the same roof, but he had drifted in and out of her universe like a minor planet, moving in his own orbit, seemingly utterly unconscious of Kate in hers. If Lawrence had any thought of marriage to anyone, let alone the tiresome cousin whom he saw rarely and thought of even less, she would be prepared to eat his highly polished Hessian boots, tassels and all.

With a yawn, she dismissed Phoebe, her maid, and prepared to climb into bed. She was stayed by the sound of commotion in the corridor outside her chambers. The next instant, Phoebe had thrust her head inside the room.

'Oh, miss, you must come! It's his lordship – they say he's dyin'!'

Chapter Five

When Kate tiptoed into the earl's chambers, she found the rest of the family assembled there. Regina sat near the head of the bed, holding her husband's hand. Lawrence hovered diffidently behind her, and Cilla and Crawford stood together on the other side of the room. The only sound to be heard was the stertorous breathing of his lordship.

Thomas lay unmoving against a mound of pillows and bolsters. His eyes were closed, his face an ashen gray, and the silken quilt that covered him trembled spasmodically with each labored breath.

Kate moved swiftly to David.

'What happened?' she asked softly.

'I'm not sure. I had just entered the room, and Father was trying to tell me something. He lifted himself and reached out to me. He said the words, "terrible mistake" several times. Then . . .' His voice faltered. 'Then, he cried out suddenly, and sank back on his pillows. He has been as you see him ever since. We have sent for the doctor, but he is away from home on a call. A servant was sent after him, and he should be here momentarily.'

David moved to the other side of the bed and knelt to take Thomas's hand in his own.

'Father,' he whispered. 'Come back to us.'

Kate, watching from the foot of the bed, felt her eyes fill with tears. It seemed to her, that at the sound of his son's voice, the old man stiffened slightly, and his head turned, almost imperceptibly.

David glanced down at his father's hand in his. God, it was like holding cobwebs. He closed his eyes, willing the dying man to take strength from his own handclasp, and held his breath as he felt the

52

earl's grip tighten slightly. The pale eyelids fluttered, but did not open, and the flaccid mouth worked, as though trying to form words. David bent his head to listen.

'Davey.' The sound of his own name came so faintly, that at first David thought he had imagined it. But, the whisper came once more.

'David. You're – here. Glad—'

'Don't force him to speak, David.' The voice was Regina's, sharper than he'd ever heard it. 'He's ill enough already.'

David did not so much as look at her, but spoke softly to his father.

'Don't try to talk, Father. Just rest now. We'll speak later.' A spasm crossed the sick man's face.

'No. No time.' Again, his mouth worked in an effort to speak. 'Davey – must tell you – I've made it all right. Did a terrible thing – but now. . . .'

'Hush, Father. You must not tire yourself.'

Suddenly, Thomas's eyes flew open, and for an instant, David recognized in him the vigorous man who had bade him good-bye six years ago.

'David – take care of. . . .'

The words were a mere murmur, and now his eyes closed for the last time. Thomas drew a long, shuddering breath, and was still.

It seemed to Kate that the next few days passed in a suspended blur. She had little to do with Thomas's funeral arrangements, except to see that everything was made ready for the guests who would soon arrive for the obsequies. Regina managed the details of the service and interment with her usual efficiency.

Kate knew that Lady Falworth truly mourned her husband's passing. For months she had sat by his side, uncomplaining, performing the most menial tasks for him with her own hands and setting aside her own pleasures to see to his comfort. She displayed, however, few outward signs of the depth to which she felt her loss. Only her reddened eyes and the sounds of distress that emanated from her room at night indicated the dimensions of her grief.

But, of all the family, Kate's heart went out to David. To her utter disbelief, Thomas's last words had scarcely died away when Regina uttered a harsh order, seconded by Lawrence, that David leave the room. Glancing about in a dazed fashion, David had departed, silent as a shadow, and Kate had run from the chamber after him.

'It doesn't matter, my dear,' he replied gently in answer to her storm of indignation at his treatment. 'There is nothing she can say anymore that matters one whit.'

The next day was a confused blur, and dinner the following evening was an unrelieved disaster. Regina sat silent, staring at the empty chair at the head of the table, and eating little. Lawrence, on the other hand, made a good meal, interspersed with comments on the correct attire to be displayed at the funeral by the males of the family. To these, Cilla and Crawford listened with a marked lack of attention. Aunt Fred, to Kate's disappointment, had remained in her room with a tray. The only other persons at the table were David and Lucius, who conducted their own muted conversation.

'I shall have to have black tassels for my boots, of course,' Lawrence was saying, waving his fork in punctuation. 'Silver won't do at all. Don't know if I can procure any in Bath, and it's too late to order any on such short notice. Perhaps. . . .'

'Curse it, Lawrence,' interrupted Crawford at last. 'Can't you think about anything except your wretched wardrobe? Is that all Father's death means to you – a chance to rig out?'

'But,' replied Lawrence in affronted surprise, 'merely showing Father the respect due him, don'cher know. I mean, how would it look to show up at his services dressed just anyhow? Like David,' he finished with a sniff.

David, hearing his name, turned to face Lawrence.

'Beg pardon?' he asked mildly.

'Lawrence was just expressing the hope that you won't disgrace the family by showing up at Father's funeral dressed – just anyhow,' responded Crawford dryly.

'Crawford, for heaven's sake,' interjected Regina in a taut voice. She bent an icy stare on David. 'Lawrence was talking of trivialities merely to take his mind off his sorrow, I'm sure. Be that as it may, perhaps we should discuss what you will wear, since you obviously brought nothing suitable with you.'

Kate watched in dismay as David's anger spread visibly across his thin cheeks.

'Oddly enough, my lady,' he snapped, 'my plans for this visit did not include attending my father's last services. Nonetheless, I shall try to dredge up something suitable from my wretchedly inadequate wardrobe, so that I shan't bring shame upon the noble Falworth name.'

At this, Lawrence set his wineglass on the table with such force that several drops spilt onto the tablecloth.

'By God,' he cried. 'If that ain't the outside of enough! Since you have nothing to do with the noble Falworth name, do you think we care what you wear?' He paused for a moment as a new and apparently pleasurable thought struck him. 'For that matter, I think we would be much better off if you did not attend the funeral at all. In fact' – he shot a sidelong glance at his mother – 'you may depart the premises first thing tomorrow morning,' he concluded regally. He settled back in his chair, sending a second, more belligerent stare at his half brother.

David sat motionless for a moment, his face white. Lucius placed a hand on his arm and murmured something inaudible. Kate, who had been dreading this moment, half rose as though to shield David from Lawrence's childish malevolence.

David opened his mouth to reply, but Kate's motion caught his attention. His eyes flicked to hers, and he relaxed suddenly. He turned to contemplate Lawrence's glowering countenance.

'But, my dear brother,' he said calmly, 'I fully intend to leave. Right after Father's funeral.' He spoke the last sentence slowly, with a deliberate pause between each word.

'Look here,' Lawrence fairly squeaked in his rage, 'I'm running things here now, and I say. . . .'

'Lawrence!'

Regina's voice sliced through her son's incipient tirade, but she continued in a mild tone.

'While I'm pleased to see you take the reins of Westerly into your own hands so promptly, I think we must make allowances for appearances.'

'Of course, my dear fellow,' interposed David lazily. 'Do you intend to throw me out bodily? Think how it would look! But, never fear,' he continued, his eyes glittering behind shuttered lids, 'directly after

Father is laid to rest in the earth of Westerly, I shall depart.'

Regina put a handkerchief to her mouth and rose from the table. Lawrence, too, took his departure. Mother and son fled the room in mutual commiseration, leaving those remaining to pass the remainder of the meal in an awkward silence.

Thus it was, some three days later, as the last of the carriages of the guests who had come to partake of the funeral meats was wending its way down the long driveway, Lucius Pelham's smart traveling coach could be seen approaching the house from the stable. Inside the manor, David descended the wide staircase into the entrance hall, where Kate awaited him.

After a sleepless night, agonizing over his departure, she had resolved not to plague him by pleading with him to stay. She knew that nothing she could say would stay him. Why did she feel such a sense of loss at his imminent departure? He was no longer, she told herself for the hundredth time, the David she had loved as a child. *But, no!* The silent cry came from deep within her. She felt that in the last few days she had begun to crack the shell of bitterness in which he was imprisoned. And now she was not to be given the time to try to free him completely.

Observing her wide, anguished gaze, David's heart lurched within him. Lord, he hadn't realized it would be so hard to leave Westerly again. No, that wasn't it, of course. He was finding it difficult beyond his imaginings to leave Kate. How could she have become so important to him in just a few days? His affection for her had always been strong, as it had for Philip, and seeing her again, he told himself, had brought the happier days of his childhood back to him.

It was too bad he had to leave her in Regina's scheming hands. The thought of her wed to Lawrence was – well, best not to dwell on that. Besides, Kate would surely not be forced against her will. She could handle her own problems. Couldn't she?

Reaching the bottom of the stairs, he stood for a moment, absorbing the sight of her. In her severe gown of black crepe, flaming curls catching the candlelight, she looked like a slender taper herself, set alight to relieve the dismal aspect of the house.

'Come to see me off, have you, Midget?' he asked, smiling. He chastened himself silently. It had been donkey's years since he'd used that name for her. Why did he find it necessary to remind himself that Kate's only importance to him was as a cherished symbol of the past?

At the sound of the name she hadn't heard since she was a child, Kate stiffened. Then, she shrugged inwardly. Why should she be surprised that David still thought of her as the tiresome infant who used to plague him and Philip? He had made it abundantly plain that, to him, she was still the sister of his best friend, whom he had adopted for his own so long ago. And, after all, that was what she wanted, wasn't it? A not-quite-brother – a confidant with whom she could share her joys and her troubles?

'You will write, won't you, David?' she asked, with a shy smile. 'I would so love to hear about all your doings in Vienna.' She fought to suppress the tears that thickened in her throat, and forced herself to a light, inconsequential tone. 'How exciting it will all be! The ladies in all their finery – the balls. And, of course, all the important person-ages gathered together!' She listened to her own brittle laughter, and felt the tears rise higher.

'Of course, I shall write. And you will tell me of your own doings, I hope?' David found he was having trouble with his voice. 'Tell me more of your diggings and scraping. Or perhaps I shall read about you in *The Gentleman's Magazine*. They always feature the latest anti-quarian news, you know. And when. . . .'

'Ah, David! All ready to be on our way, I see.'

Dressed impeccably, as always, in a dove gray traveling costume, Lucius Pelham ran lightly down the great staircase toward them.

'I just passed Curle in the hallway upstairs with your luggage, and Fellowes has already stowed my gear in the other vehicle, so we can be on our way at your convenience.'

He paused to take Kate's hand in his and bestowed a warm smile on her.

'Most happy to have made your acquaintance, Miss Millbank. My only regret, if I may say so, in leaving this place is that we shall not have a chance to further our acquaintance.'

Kate smiled in return, but her reply was cut short by the entrance into the hall of the remainder of the family, moving toward the library for the reading of the will. They were led by Lady Falworth and

Lawrence, followed by Crawford, Cilla, and Lady Frederica. Mr Smollett, the attorney, drew up the rear, followed by those family retainers who expected to be remembered in his lordship's last testament.

On catching sight of the little party in conversation at the foot of the stairs, Regina halted abruptly. Lawrence, too, paused, and raised his quizzing glass in a languid manner.

Taking his mother's arm, he advanced toward the smaller group. The rest of the procession waited respectfully in position.

'Shaking the dust of Westerly from your boots are you, David?' he asked in a muted, but unpleasant tone of voice. 'And high time, too. Don't mind telling you, we'll all be glad to see your back.'

Crawford snickered self-consciously, and Cilla raised her black silk handkerchief to her mouth. Aunt Fred, a small, plump wraith in her black silk draperies, said nothing, but her eyes flickered brightly between the two young men.

'Since you've been telling me that on a regular basis for the last three days,' replied David in a quiet voice, 'your sentiments do not come as a surprise, brother.'

'Oh, for Heaven's sake, Lawrence,' snapped Kate angrily, 'can't you mind your wretched tongue for once in your life?'

'That will do, Kate,' interjected Regina. Turning to David, she smiled and extended her hand. 'You must forgive my son's, er, impetuosity. We do, of course, wish you well on your endeavors. Our good wishes go with you to – Vienna, is it?'

Of course, growled Kate inwardly. Now that she is about to be rid of David forever, she can afford to be magnanimous. No 'do come back to see us,' of course. No 'our house is your house' will we hear from my lady.

David simply blinked at Regina's words, uttered with what could almost be taken as warmth, but Lucius took the opportunity to bend low over the countess's hand.

'So very happy to have met you, my lady,' he murmured smoothly. 'You are everything David led me to expect.'

Before Regina could reply, Lucius grasped David's arm, and with a nod to Kate, led him toward the door.

'And now,' he said, 'if you will. . . .'

He was interrupted by Mr Smollett, who placed his short, plump form directly in David's path.

'But you're not leaving, Mr Merritt! Were you not informed . . . that is, there must have been some oversight. You must stay, sir. For the reading of the will, you know.'

Regina gestured impatiently.

'I'm sure that won't be necessary. Thomas assured me last week that he settled what he felt was his financial obligation at the time he purchased David's commission. There can be nothing. . . .'

'I'm afraid there has been a – a slight change, my lady,' replied Mr Smollett, with an air of suppressed tension. 'It will indeed be necessary for Mr Merritt to attend the reading.'

David glanced questioningly at Lucius, who sighed and began to divest himself of his superbly tailored greatcoat.

Lawrence, who apparently had at last grasped the significance of the attorney's words, hurried to his mother's side.

'What? What? David in the will! Mother, I thought you told me. . . .'

Lady Falworth clicked her tongue impatiently.

'I'm sure it is nothing, my boy. David apparently once more importuned your father to grant him some favor. Let him stay.'

'I know!' Lawrence howled in rage. 'It's the River Farm! David managed to wheedle the River Farm out of Father. Well, I won't stand for it! That place is mine, and David can't have it.'

'My lord!' gasped Mr Smollett. 'Please, restrain yourself.'

Regina gripped her son's arm and, fairly dragging him in her wake, began to make her way again to the library.

'Enough, Lawrence,' she said from between tight lips. 'Come along. It will all be over soon.'

The servants' bequests were soon dispensed with, and those of the staff who had been remembered by his lordship departed the library, with much sniffling and flourishing of handkerchiefs.

Seated at the large Sheraton desk belonging to the late earl, Mr Smollett gazed about the room from beneath a pair of spectacularly bushy brows. His rather prim mouth was curled in a slight, unaccustomed smile, and an oddly expectant expression sat on his plump features as he allowed his piercing stare to rest on each member of the family in turn.

Lady Falworth sat nearest him, in a regal attitude. Next to her, as usual, slouched Lawrence, sucking on the end of his quizzing glass. Farther back, Crawford and Cilla murmured together, their eyes wide with the unaccustomed solemnity of the occasion. David sat apart, glowering and uncomfortable. Kate watched him from the other side of the room, and Lady Falworth gazed at her black-gloved hands, occupied with her own unfathomable thoughts.

Mr Smollett rustled the papers before him to gain the attention of those remaining in the room.

'My lady,' he began, 'my lord – ladies and gentlemen. If we may get started?'

'By all means.' Lawrence yawned. 'Let's get on with it. You've already been prosing on for hours.'

'We have been here for only forty-five minutes, Lord, er, Standing,' said the attorney, drawing his watch from his waist-coat, 'and one cannot rush these things.'

'Fudge,' said Lawrence. Then he added importantly, 'But you really should address me as Lord Falworth, you know.'

Mr Smollett opened his mouth, but immediately closed it again, and contented himself with a sour smile.

'Before we discuss the various bequests,' he said, 'I must read a document signed by his lordship only a few days before he passed away. It is of, er, some significance . . .' Here he glanced at Lawrence, who was boredly leafing through a copy of the *Racing Journal* he had picked up from the table beside his chair. '. . . So I ask that you all pay close attention.'

Mr Smollett adjusted his spectacles and began reading.

' "I, Thomas Merritt, third earl of Falworth, Viscount Standing, Baron. . . ." '

'Please spare us the embroidery, Mr Smollett,' interjected Lady Falworth. 'We are all familiar with my husband's titles. Is this to be a very long document? Perhaps you could paraphrase it.'

Mr Smollett stiffened, and his already formidable brows beetled alarmingly, but his voice was controlled as he replied.

'No, my lady, it is not a long document. If I may proceed?'

He lowered his eyes again to the paper in his hands.

' "I, er, Thomas, do affirm that while in the West Indies, in the year 1790, I became acquainted with Miss Felice Wharburton, a young woman living on the island of Barbados in the West Indies. Miss Wharburton's mother was the former Dominque Le Fevre, a native of the Indies. Her father, George Wharburton of Great Shelford, Cambridgeshire, was a clerk in the governor's office there. I fell in love with Felice, and. . . ." '

'Good God!' It was Regina who spoke, fairly quivering in her outrage. 'Are we to be subjected to a chronicle of my husband's youthful misdeeds? How dare you, Mr Smollett!'

'I'm sorry for any discomfort you may be caused, my lady,' replied the little attorney, who did not look sorry in the slightest, 'but this reading, as you will see, is necessary.'

Referring again to the paper, he continued. ' "I fell in love with Felice, and in the course of our relationship, she became pregnant. I wished to marry her, but feared the reaction of my family. Felice died giving birth to our son, David, on November 15, 1791, but I am happy to say that shortly before that event, I overcame my reluctance. I now affirm that on August 10, 1791, Felice Wharburton and I were married in the Church of Santa Clara, on the island of Carriacou, a dependency of Grenada, where I lived at the time on my family's spice plantation. Our vows were repeated later in a ceremony performed by a British cleric on the same island. Felice, therefore, was my first wife, the Viscountess Standing, and, had she lived, would have become the Countess of Falworth." '

Mr Smollett smiled benignly, first at Regina, who had shrunk in her chair as though struck, her face a ghastly white, and then at Lawrence, who sat, quizzing glass at the ready, a puzzled expression beginning to spread over his features. The attorney's gaze then moved to David, who had risen to face him, thunderstruck.

Mr Smollett, too, rose, and extended his hand. 'Allow me to be the first to congratulate you on the accession to your father's title, Lord Falworth.'

Chapter Six

M r Smollett smiled benignly at the scene of chaos before him. Lady Falworth had now also risen from her chair, and she advanced on the attorney as though he, personally, were responsible for the crack that had just opened in her world. Her eyes glittered darkly in her white face.

'This – this is monstrous! What kind of hoax are you trying to perpetrate?'

Ignoring her completely, Mr Smollett stood and moved toward David, who still seemed rooted to the spot.

'My lord, you are understandably, er, bewildered by this turn of events, but if you will read this. . . .' He handed the bemused young man a sheet of paper, covered in a thin, precise script and embossed with the seal of the Earl of Falworth. 'It is a letter your father dictated to me the morning of his death, and I believe it will explain matters more fully to you.'

Blindly, David accepted the letter from Mr Smollett. He felt as though he stood alone on a teetering precipice, watching the universe rearrange itself around him.

He must be dreaming! He, David Merritt, a bastard all his life – now the master of Westerly? The fourth Earl of Falworth! The words, reverberating in the suddenly hollow cavern that was his stomach seemed the gibberings of a madman.

Kate could scarcely comprehend what she had just heard. David – Uncle Thomas's legitimate son! She watched his hand close over the letter. Observing his dazed expression, she unconsciously put a hand out to him, though he was across the room from her. As if some pull emanated from her fingertips, David turned to look at her, and it seemed to Kate that beyond the shock, past the utter astonishment in his eyes, there shone a spark of something else – something she could not define.

She jerked her attention back to Mr Smollett, who had wheeled about to deal with Regina. She clawed at his arm, almost babbling in her rage. Kate caught the words, 'ridiculous' and 'madness' and 'fraud,' but Mr Smollett remained calm.

'There is no fraud, my lady, and Lord Falworth was in complete possession of his faculties. He provided me with certificates documenting his marriage to the lady in question, as well as Mr Mer – that is, the fourth Earl's birth certificate. Everything is quite in order, madam, and there is nothing more to be said.'

As it turned out, there was a great deal more to be said, nearly all of it on the part of Lady Falworth and Lawrence. It was a full hour before Regina could be convinced of the legality of David's claim to the title, and even then, she fumed impotently, threatening to have the will overturned and to insure Mr Smollett's disbarment from the legal fraternity.

Lawrence merely squeaked, 'It can't be!' and 'It's not fair!' over and over in a number of variations until Lady Frederica grasped Kate's arm and said in a loud whisper, 'If I have to listen to this uproar for another second, I shall go round the bend. Come, we'll have a cup of tea in my room.'

Kate cast one last glance at David, who had gone to stand at the window, apart from the storm, where he gazed unseeingly at the unkempt landscape spread before him. With a sigh, she allowed the older woman to lead her from the room, and in a few minutes they were seated before the Adam and Eve tapestry, steaming cups in hand.

'I cannot comprehend this, Aunt Fred,' gasped Kate, as breathless as though she had been running. She loosened the high, restraining collar on her mourning gown.

'It's a stunner,' agreed her aunt, removing her veiled bonnet, with which she began to fan herself briskly. 'Who would have thought Thomas to have so much spunk in him? To marry his inamorata!'

'And to keep it such a secret all these years.' Kate paused, then continued with indignation, 'One doesn't wish to speak ill of the dead, of course, but how *could* Uncle Thomas have kept silent for so long, when it caused David so much unhappiness. If Aunt Regina had known he was the true heir. . . .'

'Her enmity would have been none the less virulent,' finished Aunt Fred. 'But she might have concealed it a little more adroitly. What I want to know, is how he managed to keep the news of the marriage from the family. The wedding of a member of the peerage must always gain attention, even in the Indies!'

Kate could only shake her head, her thoughts with the solitary figure belowstairs, who stood at a window looking into his future.

In the library, the strident sounds of protest behind him went largely unnoticed by David. He felt remote, somehow, as though all the chaos had nothing to do with him. David Merritt, the Earl of Falworth? The words simply had no meaning.

Yet, they carried an undeniable ring of exultation. Westerly was his! He need not leave, but could stay to cherish it forever. He would work, he vowed, and use every ounce of wit at his disposal to transform the lovely old estate to its former glory. And at his side . . . No. He had received a gift from Heaven, and that must be enough.

The rest of the day passed in a state of suppressed pandemonium. It did not take long for the momentous news to circulate among the servants' quarters and thence to the stables and gardens and the tenants' cottages. Soon the entire estate was humming with surmise as to the course the lives of 'the grand people in the House' would take. Speculation ranged from the immediate departure of Lady Falworth to the Dower House to the dim future ahead for Mr Lawrence, who in one afternoon had gone from Viscount Standing, to Lord Falworth, and then, ignominiously, to a mere courtesy title of Lord Lawrence Merritt.

David remained closeted for several hours with Mr Smollett, and the two were served dinner on a tray in the library. Regina dined in her chambers, as did Aunt Fred. Lawrence had stormed out of the house some time earlier, and had not as yet returned home. Crawford, sensing that the atmosphere at Westerly might not be conducive to good digestion, rode out to 'take his mutton' with a neighboring friend. Cilla, in a rare display of filial duty, dined with her mother.

When Kate, prepared to eat alone, entered the gold saloon, she was startled to find Lucius Pelham awaiting her. She blinked at him in consternation. Having almost forgotten the existence of the young man in the turmoil of the day's events, she had told Cook to prepare a simple meal for her of meat and fruit.

'Why, Mr Pelham!' she said, feeling extremely foolish.

'Ah, Miss Millbank,' he replied with his usual calm courtesy. 'It appears we dine *à deux* this evening. I am not sure this is quite proper, but if you can bear my company for an hour or two, I shall be honored to dine with you.'

'Mr Pelham, I'm so sorry. You have been treated abominably – first left to cool your heels in the hall earlier today, and now – well, I'm afraid you'll find you've been condemned to a horribly inadequate meal. It's just that—'

'Everything is quite at sixes and sevens,' finished Lucius, his eyes twinkling. 'Perfectly understandable. And no meal, I am sure, could be considered inadequate when taken in your company.' He sketched a graceful bow, and Kate smiled with relief.

'I suppose,' she said hesitantly, 'you've heard about David?'

'That my erstwhile comrade-in-arms is now the Earl of Falworth? Yes, he took a moment before he began his conference with the attorney to tell me his news. What an astonishing turn of events!'

Kate nodded abstractedly. 'It has taken us all by surprise. Tell me, Mr Pelham,' she said, suddenly glad to have this opportunity to talk to David's friend alone, 'how did he receive his injury? He won't talk about it to me, and he doesn't seem to think he will ever really recover from it. Do you think that's true?'

Lucius was silent for a long moment.

'The Battle of Toulouse lasted only one day,' he began finally, 'but it was a day that seemed to go on for an eternity. David had volunteered for the Forlorn Hope, of course, but. . . .'

'The what?' asked Kate in puzzlement.

'Before every battle,' explained Lucius, 'a contingent of volunteers is sent ahead of the main body of troops to get things started. Their purpose is mainly to draw the enemy's fire, thus revealing their positions. As a rather painful example of our famed dry, British wit, this force is called the Forlorn Hope, wherein very few men survive duty. There are, however, always plenty of volunteers, because if one does get through the engagement, he is virtually assured of promotion.'

'And David was a part of this – this Forlorn Hope?' asked Kate in appalled accents.

'No, as I said, he volunteered, but he was refused. Generally no one above the rank of lieutenant is allowed to participate.'

'But why would he *wish* to go? He had already risen to major in a remarkably short time.'

Again, Lucius hesitated.

'Yes – yes, that's true – but – he had his reasons. Not very good ones, to my mind, and not,' he added pointedly, 'ones that he would want discussed. At any rate, David had his own company, of which I was a member. We were ascending the slopes of the Mont Rave, just outside Toulouse. It was a long ridge, really, rather than a hill, and the enemy was securely entrenched. Our target was the Sypière redoubt. Ten of our lads and myself had attracted fire from a single rifleman perched on the heights. He had us pinned down, and was picking us off like hens in a barnyard. There were only three of us left alive when David spotted our predicament. He was a good two hundred yards away, but he simply stood up, grabbed a rifle from a nearby enlisted man, and walked over to us, ignoring the fire that showered down on him. When he got within range of the sniper, he took careful aim, for all the world as though he were at a firing range. The sniper, seeing him, shot first, and that's when David was wounded. He didn't fall, though, until he fired his own rifle. The Frenchie went down, and we were safe.'

'Dear Lord,' breathed Kate. 'And the doctors say there is nothing they can do to alleviate the pain? Or to lessen his limp?'

'I sometimes think the sawbones at the front did more damage than good. They cut out a lot of tissue, but they didn't want to touch the ball itself. I brought him to my home at once, and my family took him to their hearts. Father made sure that he had the finest treatment available. David underwent four operations, at the end of which, the doctors said they had cleaned up the area as much as possible, and that was all they could do for him. One of them did suggest a program of therapeutic exercise, but David would have none of it. Future surgery, possibly to remove the ball, after the healing process had gone forward was also suggested, but David rejected that, too.'

'That's what I don't understand,' said Kate anxiously. 'It isn't like him to just give up. The David I know would walk on hot coals if there were the slightest possibility. . . .'

'I'm afraid the David you knew no longer exists,' Lucius interjected in a sharp voice.

'I know' was Kate's miserable reply. 'Oh, Mr Pelham, what happened to him? Was – was it Philip's death?'

Lucius seemed to withdraw into himself.

'I really don't know, Miss Millbank,' he said slowly. 'Certainly it was after Badajoz that he seemed to – change.' He sighed. 'I'm afraid I can't say any more.'

They had by now adjourned from the dining room to the music room, Lucius declining to sit in solitary state over the port decanter.

'And you, Mr Pelham,' she began, 'what made you decide to sell out?'

'Oh, with Boney *rompu*, there seemed little point in staying. I can't tell you how tired I was becoming of bread and beans. By the by, do you think we could dispense with Mr Pelham and Miss Millbank? I find I'm growing a little tired of them, as well. May I call you Kate? I have heard you spoken of by that name for so many years, it seems much more natural.'

'Indeed, sir,' she dimpled, 'if I may call you Lucius.'

'I'm not sure I approve of all this unchaperoned fraternization of the troops,' said a voice from the doorway.

'David!' cried Kate, as she and Lucius leaped to their feet. 'I'm so glad to see you at last. You must be exhausted!'

'Well, it's certainly been an interesting afternoon,' he replied as he accepted Lucius's assistance in settling into a wing chair by the fire. Lucius drew chairs for himself and Kate, and they sat watching David expectantly.

'What has Mr Smollett been telling you all this time?' asked Kate. 'Have you spoken to Aunt Regina yet? Oh, David how could this have happened? I mean, for Uncle Thomas to. . . .'

'And how about Lawrence the Dreadful?' put in Lucius. 'I could hear him squealing all the way up to my room. You've made an enemy there, David.'

David nodded wearily. 'Not that we were ever what one could call close,' he added.

He pulled from inside his coat pocket the letter Mr Smollett had given him.

'This pretty much explains everything,' he said quietly. 'But I still find it hard to believe. You see. . . .'

'Perhaps I should leave you two,' interrupted Lucius in a diffident tone.

'No, please.' David laid a restraining hand on his friend's sleeve. 'I very much need all the counsel and advice I can get right now. In fact, I was just going to ask if you would mind remaining here for an extended length of time.'

'Absolutely, old man. Father would give me the finest trimming of my life if I left while I can still be of use to you.'

'That's all right, then. Now, about the letter. As you know, Father dictated it to Mr Smollett a few days before he died. He tells of his meeting with Felice Wharburton, the daughter of a minor government functionary on Barbados. Her grandmother was pure Carib Indian, so Felice was very much a product of the Islands, and beautiful beyond imagining, according to Father, with dark, uptilted eyes and skin the color of wild honey. They began to see each other, much against the wishes of her father, who saw in the interest of Thomas, Lord Standing, as he was then, only the dalliance of a wealthy, young peer.

'Felice was a devout Catholic, and she was overcome with guilt when she conceived Thomas's child. She was afraid to tell her father. At about that time, she became very ill with an unidentified fever. As the child grew within her, she became progressively worse. Thomas desperately wished to marry Felice, and as she became more ill and more racked with guilt, he determined to do so.

'He arranged to have banns read on one of the tiny island dependencies of Grenada, and they married in the Catholic church there. However, he also obtained a special license through the offices of a good friend, who managed to keep the transaction a secret. This young man, and one other, volunteered to act as witnesses, and traveled with Thomas and Felice to another remote village, where there lived an eccentric, retired British cleric. This gentleman performed a second, Church of England ceremony, after which the couple went back to Felice's home and delivered the glad news to her father.

'Mr Wharburton was ecstatic to learn that his daughter had become, in the twinkling of an eye, the Viscountess Standing and the future Countess of Falworth, and it was all Thomas could do to prevent his new father-in-law from dashing off a letter full of felicitations to Westerly. Thomas persuaded him to keep the marriage a secret until after the child was born, feeling that the family would take the whole thing better when presented with a child – hopefully an heir. Actually, he confessed in the letter that he was merely trying to put off the inevitable. Poor Father, he was made literally sick at the thought of the consequences of his action. His eyes were not so blinded by love that he could not picture with horrific clarity the reception he would get at Westerly when he appeared home with a bride of the Indies on his arm.

'When Felice died giving birth to her son, she was buried in the village where her mother had been raised, and I was given into the temporary care of one of Felice's maternal relatives. Here, fate took an unexpected, and, I might add, a bizarre hand.

'The night of Felice's funeral was a black and rainy one. Despite advice to the contrary, Mr Wharburton refused to wait until morning before leaving the village to return to his home – he had never got on well with his wife's family. At any rate, he came unseeing upon a washed-out bridge and fell to his death.

'Thomas truly grieved the loss of his Felice, but it seemed as though fate had conspired to grant him a reprieve. Only a very few people in the world knew that he had wed Felice, and none of these persons was likely to spread the word beyond the tiny environment of a small island in the West Indies.

'Thomas told no one of his marriage, and shortly thereafter, he was called back to Westerly. He went to the home of his wife's relatives to make arrangements to insure that his son would be cared for. Something happened to him during that visit. His grief for Felice rose to overwhelm him, as did guilt at the idea of abandoning his son. In a single instant, he made a decision that would change his life – and mine. He decided to bring the boy back to England with him, to be raised at Westerly.'

There was a long silence, as David folded the paper, already creased and rumpled, and returned it to his pocket.

'If you don't mind my saying so,' said Lucius at last, 'it seems to me the real bastard in this story is your father.'

'One could look at it that way, I suppose,' replied David, a faraway look in his eyes. 'I prefer to think that Thomas was a weak man, but not a bad one. Even though he could not bring himself to acknowledge what he had done, it still took a great deal of courage to face down his family, with his supposedly illegitimate son in tow.' His mouth curved in a wry smile. 'What a comment on our society that a man may be forgiven a bastard son sooner than a mésalliance.'

'But,' put in Kate indignantly, 'Uncle Thomas almost didn't write that letter at all. Up until a few days of his death, he intended to let Lawrence accede to the title – and to Westerly. He let Aunt Regina bully him into practically banishing you from the place you loved with all your heart. He sent you off to war knowing you might be killed!'

'And what a burden it must have been to him,' murmured David. 'I wonder if that wasn't what led to his paralytic stroke.'

At this, Lucius rose and made his way to a small table on which rested a brandy decanter and several glasses. Returning with a tray, he smiled.

'I propose a toast. To the Earl of Falworth, and new master of Westerly.'

To Kate's pleasure, David's tired eyes lit as he returned the salute.

The three talked companionably for another hour or so, listening to David's assessment of all he had learned from Mr Smollett.

'Tomorrow, I'll have to have a long talk with our bailiff, for by what Smollett can tell me, things are in very bad skin around here. Well,' he sighed, gesturing at the worn furnishings and shabby hangings surrounding them, 'I didn't need a statement of accounting to tell me that.'

'Yes,' said Kate, her eyes shining, 'but, now that you are here, you will have things set to rights in no time.'

David looked steadily at her, and it seemed to Kate that a shadow fell across his face. He smiled, though, and put out a hand to her. Kate was instantly conscious of his touch, and its warmth crept through her body with a startling immediacy.

'Your faith in me is touching,' he said, 'if somewhat misplaced, my dear. I fear. . . .'

He was interrupted by the sounds of altercation to be heard in the corridor outside the door.

'Le' me 'lone, Smirke!' All present recognized the voice, which was raised to a hysterical pitch. 'I may not own this place, but ish' still my home.'

The door flew open to admit a staggering Lawrence, accompanied by his valet, who was engaged in a futile attempt to restrain his extremely inebriated young master.

Lawrence lurched into the room and, focusing a hazy stare on David, advanced with upraised hand. David rose, but stood composed at his chair.

'You!' Lawrence choked. 'Look what you've done. You've no right, damn you!'

Lucius also rose, and moved to stand at David's side.

'You're drunk, you young fool,' he said dispassionately.

His words served only to inflame Lawrence, and to Kate's dismay, the young man strode to stand, weaving, directly in front of his half brother.

'Why'd you have t'come back?' His words came in a slurred rush. 'Ever'thing would've been all right if you'd never showed your stupid face here!'

He raised his hand again, and this time David grasped his wrist. Kate gasped, and suppressed an urge to go to David's assistance, an act, she very well knew would only serve to exacerbate matters.

Lawrence's face contorted, and he fell back, stumbling into the valet, Smirke. He struggled to right himself, and for a moment looked as though he would lunge into an attack. Then, his eyes met David's, and it was as though he had been penetrated by a silent shaft. He sagged, and his hand lifted to dash away a sudden spate of tears.

' 'S not fair,' he wailed. 'It was to've been all m-mine. Now, I have nothing.' He rubbed his sleeve over his eyes. 'Won' be 'n earl – won' even be a v-viscount.'

David eyed him for a moment, and exchanged a glance with Kate. She relaxed slightly, as she read in his gaze a mixture of pity and exasperation.

He moved to fling an arm around his half brother.

'There, old man. It's all right. You're still a Merritt of Westerly. This is your home, Lawrence, and you still have your family.'

Lawrence merely hiccuped. For an instant, a horrified awareness of what he had said flickered in his red-rimmed eyes. He opened his mouth as though to say more, but uttered only a strangled growl, and allowed himself to be led away by Smirke.

David turned to grin ruefully at Lucius.

'Well, if I've made an enemy, I don't think he's much of a threat.'

'If he were the only one to have his nose put out of joint, I'd say you're right. I shouldn't think the cub will cause you much trouble. The she-wolf, however, may be another story.'

'Regina?' David sighed again. 'You may be right, but I'm simply too tired to consider it all now. I suggest we call it a night, my friends. I have a feeling the morrow will bring its own problems.'

Good nights were said all around, and the three filed from the gold saloon to seek their bedchambers. Kate felt she would not close her eyes all night, but her head had no sooner nestled into her pillow than she fell into a dreamless sleep.

She was jerked into consciousness some hours later. What was it that had awakened her so suddenly? She sat for some moments in the darkness, silence ringing in her ears. Then she heard it again – a cry that seemed to fill the room like a physical presence. Once more, it came. It was a sound of such primal terror that Kate nearly fell to the floor in her haste to find and succor whoever had cried out in such torment.

Chapter Seven

It was not until she reached the corridor that she realized the sound was coming from David's room. As she ran, she observed Lucius, hurrying from the opposite direction, hastily tying a sash about his dressing gown.

She was the first to reach David's door, but Lucius's hand came down on hers as she reached for the handle.

'No! Don't go in, Kate,' he said in a low voice. 'David has these nightmares fairly often, and he comes out of them none the worse for wear. Curle will be with him already.'

'But I must go to him! He's in the most awful agony!'

'He's dreaming only. Please believe me. He would not like you to see him at such a moment.'

At this, Kate paused. She met Lucius's earnest gaze, and dropped her hand.

'How long has this been going on?' she asked in a stricken whisper.

'Since Badajoz.'

'But that's where Philip was killed!'

Lucius shifted uncomfortably.

'Yes, well, as I said, it isn't something he wants to talk about. Now, I'd better nip in and see if Curle needs any help, although it sounds as if David has quieted.'

Indeed, Kate had heard nothing from inside David's room since just after she had left her own. Reluctantly, she stood aside while Lucius slipped through the door. She made her way back down the corridor, the terrible sound of David's cries still ringing in her ears. Once she returned to her bed, she found it impossible to go back to sleep.

She pondered on the inconceivable horrors that David must have undergone. Not just David, of course. How many young men on both sides of the conflict had returned to home and family, wounded beyond repair in body and spirit?

When she descended to the breakfast room in the morning, to her surprise, she found David breakfasting in solitary state, perusing a copy of the *Times*.

'Good morning,' she said, gesturing for him to remain seated. 'I thought you would be in conference with Mr Pettigrew.'

'I have an appointment with him in a couple of hours.' He laughed rather self-consciously. 'I have been sitting here in some bemusement, I must admit. I still cannot take in all that has occurred.' He hesitated for an instant. 'Did you sleep well last night?'

Kate busied herself at the coffee cups on the sideboard.

'Um, why yes, of course, thank you. And you?'

Shooting a surreptitious glance at him, it seemed to Kate that a look of relief flashed in his eyes before he spoke.

'Of course. By the by,' he continued, 'you're looking particularly fetching this morning in that, what is it – some sort of cotton?'

'It's India muslin,' she smiled. 'And in the latest mode, I'll have you know. This ruffled hemline' – she pirouetted so that her skirt swirled becomingly – 'with the open embroidery work appeared in *La Belle Assemblée* only last month.'

'Behold me chastened. I shall freely confess to an abysmal ignorance of anything concerning the world of fashion.'

Kate laughed. 'Perhaps Lawrence can be prevailed upon to give you the benefit of his expertise.'

'Perhaps – if he can be prevailed upon to speak to me ever again.'

'Oh, I'm sure he will come out of his sulks eventually. This has been a hard pill for him to swallow.' Her face lightened. 'As soon as I've finished here, I'm going out to the villa. If you have time before Mr Smollett arrives, would you like . . .' She stopped in embarrassed confusion. 'That is, perhaps you would not enjoy it – the terrain is rough, and. . . .'

'I may not be of much use,' David replied smoothly, 'but I'd like to see more of what you've accomplished.'

Mentally, he cursed himself. Why had he said yes to her invitation? He must practice keeping his distance from her, after all. Soon enough, she would wish to have nothing to do with him.

'But what about Lucius?' Kate was saying. 'You'll want to show him about Westerly, won't you?'

David smiled, and cravenly put down this opportunity to back away. He assured himself that this would be the last time that he would pander to his need for her company.

'If I know Lucius, he won't put in an appearance for at least another three hours. Till then, I'll avail myself of the opportunity to examine your find.'

Kate flushed a little. 'Perhaps you'd like to bring your sketchbook,' she said lightly. 'I remember you rarely stepped outside without it. You know, I kept all the drawings you left.' She smiled at David's disparaging gesture. 'Yes, I know you would never admit to your talent, but I still treasure the portrait you made of Philip when he was sixteen – and, of course, there was that scandalous sketch you made of me bare legged in my shift – when I was five. At any rate,' she continued as David joined in her laughter, 'I would greatly appreciate an accurate rendering of some of the artifacts.'

The two finished their breakfast in companionable conversation, and it was not long before they left the house – Kate garbed in one of her working ensembles and David in leather breeches and boots.

They rode slowly over meadows glowing in the clear light of summer. David took a bittersweet pleasure in the luxury of her companionship.

'Sometimes,' mused David, 'in Spain, when we trudged over endless miles of hot, brown, dusty plains, it seemed the only thing that kept me going was the memory of these perfect green fields.' He gestured over the rolling hills, sloping to the broad plain that bordered the Avon. Beyond, another range of emerald undulations could be seen, softened by the haze of distance.

' "This sceptered isle," ' quoted Kate softly. ' "This throne of kings. . . ." '

' "This England," ' finished David, with a satisfied sigh. Their mounts drew near to one another, and unthinking, his hand lifted to touch Kate's. Recollecting himself, he turned his horse away and hastened his pace.

He pointed to the thinly covered fields he had noticed the day before.

'What happened here? Come harvest, those acres will produce less than half of what they should.'

'They haven't been properly fertilized for over three years,' replied Kate. 'The money for it just isn't there. Or, at least so said Uncle Thomas.'

David grunted.

'Apparently there's no money to fix the tenants' cottages, either, but plenty to keep Lawrence decked out like the princeling of a small country.'

'You're right,' she sighed. 'Things have come to a sad pass. Uncle Thomas kept saying it was only temporary, and with a little luck we would come about.'

'That's what he was saying when I rode away from here six years ago. Even then, matters were getting serious.'

When they reached their destination, David searched until he found a boulder with which he could dismount without help. As he accomplished this maneuver, Kate scrambled from her little mare and climbed along the rocky hillside until she was out of sight. In a few moments he joined her, and they silently tethered their horses.

'It's unfortunate,' Kate said as they picked their way gingerly along the rock outcropping, 'that the owner of the villa chose to back his home up against the side of the hill. It's an extraordinarily beautiful site, of course. See? The lord and lady of the house could sit here – perhaps they even created some sort of terrace – and watch the traffic below on the Via Julia and the river beyond while the children played beside them. Unfortunately, all the hills around here are riddled with tiny springs, and according to my reading, this area was subjected to heavy rains at one point in the history of Roman Britain. There was a lot of flooding, and that's when the house must have been smothered in mud slides.'

'Lord,' responded David, 'I hope everyone got out all right.'

Kate shivered.

'I hope so, too. I think they must have, for I have found no skeletons. Perhaps the slides came gradually, although the inhabitants must have rushed out in rather a hurry to have left things like the boy's head behind.'

They had now reached the entrance to the excavation, and David glanced uneasily at the meager wooden supports wedged into the earth surrounding them. Inside Kate lit the lanterns she kept there, and David glanced about with interest.

Here, at the front of the house, the hill had stopped its advance, and the roof had managed to withstand the mud onslaught. Kate, with Jem's help, had placed reinforcing supports around the room, and by the light of the flickering lantern, it could be seen that they stood in what might have been a dining chamber. The rotted remains of a wooden table lay scattered on the tessellated floor, and in one corner a pair of bronze urns lay askew. There were niches cut into the walls, all empty except for the marble head David had seen before.

'This is absolutely amazing,' David breathed.

'There are two other rooms whose walls still support the roof. I don't know what their functions were. The furniture was evidently made from wood, but what were probably tables and chairs are now little more than piles of mold. There are some artifacts, though. See . . .' She led him to a second chamber. 'In here are a few copper bowls, and a small statue, perhaps of a goddess.'

David joined her, and picked up a small iron hoop.

'A child's toy?' he asked, brows lifted.

'Possibly. Or it may have been part of a tool, or utensil, or even some sort of adornment.'

As he prepared to toss the hoop aside, Kate stayed him with her hand.

'All the items you see here are just as I found them. I know that many so-called devotees of what is coming to be called the science of archaeology see it merely as a means to acquiring pretty objets d'art for their drawing rooms, but I have been reading the work of Samuel Lyson – he has examined remains in many locations – even in Bath, and I agree with him in thinking of archaeology as a pathway to knowledge of the ancient world. I have been trying to make a careful record of everything I find, and note precisely where I find it.'

'I see,' responded David with some amusement. 'I take it, that's where I come in.'

'Yes. Once an object has been sketched in situ, I will remove it to a safe place. Are you managing all right?' she asked as David limped across the chamber to examine an oddly shaped bit of metal.

David opened his mouth to return a cutting rejoinder, as was his habit when offered what might be construed as sympathy, but observing the concern apparent in her hazel eyes, his expression softened.

'Yes, I'm fine. Thank you. Is this the other room you spoke of?' He moved toward an opening in the wall, which apparently led deeper into the house.

'Oh, do be careful! I have constructed no supports in there as yet, and there must be a considerable weight of dirt above it.'

Lifting his lantern high, he peered cautiously into the darkness. The room was a large one, and, smothering an exclamation, he moved into the gloom toward the far end.

'Look! A wall painting! Is this – it's a soldier, isn't it?'

'Yes,' replied Kate eagerly. 'The drawing appears to be a rendering of a battle scene. See? There are more soldiers in the background, with spears and swords. At least, I think so. I've been trying to figure out a way to scrape off some of this mold without ruining the picture.'

David did not reply, but stood before the painting in rapt attention.

'This is incredible, Kate! To think that this has lain here for centuries. . . .'

David found himself almost unable to tear his eyes from the figure before him. The man's features could not be seen clearly behind the helmet that covered not only his head, but part of his face. Dressed in full armor, he brandished a sword, fending off a foe who appeared to be not nearly so well equipped. There was something about the soldier that held David mesmerized.

From the ornate design on his breastplate, he deduced the warrior was an officer. Yes, for surely he was leading the men who could be dimly seen beyond his shoulder. His attitude spoke of determination as well as a certain fury. David almost smiled. He could well remember the ferocity with which he had so many times cloaked himself in battle. A blood rage helped silence the fear that whispered in a man's ear, and anguish at the slaughter around him.

Suddenly, he found the confines of the dark room oppressive. He cast an uneasy glance at the ceiling, some of whose beams already lay in broken fragments on the floor. Turning to leave, he stumbled over a small object on the floor. He picked it up and, mindful of Kate's admonition, did not carry it from the room, but held it up to the lantern light to examine it.

It was small and triangular, and made of stone. He called to Kate, who moved to his side and took it from him delightedly.

'Why, I believe it's what is called an antefix. I have read of them – many have been found at other ruins, but this is the first I've seen. They were used to cap the ends of roof sup-ports. And look, there's a design cut into it. Often they were individually ornamented to relate to the owner of the home.

'It looks like letters – L – E – G, I think, and two XX's. There seems to be some sort of animal carved underneath.'

'The Twentieth Legion! Oh, David, the owner of the villa must have been a soldier! The Twentieth was stationed in Chester. And their symbol was a boar!'

'But, why would he have lived so far from his camp?'

David curled his fingers around Kate's hand, turning it so that he could see the inscription on the small triangle more clearly.

'Perhaps he retired here,' she replied. 'Many Roman officers did, you know. Just as military men often retire near Bath in our own time. It is thought Bath was a popular spa, even in those days. A great many artifacts have been found in and around Bath, you know. Lyson says that beneath the Pump Room and the Hot Baths, there probably lies a great Roman Bath. Oh, David, just imagine it!'

A silence fell, and Kate became conscious of the warmth of David's hand cupped around hers. With a sudden intake of breath, she moved abruptly away from him. She stooped to replace the antefix on the ground, glad of the opportunity to hide her heated cheeks from David's view.

David said nothing, but when Kate again raised her head, he had moved back into the first chamber.

'I think,' he said, in a flat voice, 'I'll sketch the boy first. Then you can take him to a safe place. I shouldn't wonder,' he added, 'if some-day this whole place doesn't crumble about your ears. The structure can't be stable.'

'No, you're quite right.' She emerged to join him. 'But I think this room, at least, is safe enough, and the second one as well, for I'm sure they're adequately supported.'

David's face assumed a skeptical expression, but he said nothing.

'And next week,' she continued, oblivious, 'I have secured Jem's services for three whole days in order to shore up the third room. You have no idea the amount of pleading and wheedling it took to obtain Moody's consent. You'd think the stables would fall into chaos without Jem's constant presence.'

'Well, our stables have always been a busy place,' he said. 'I see that Father still maintained his string.'

'Yes, and all of them eating their heads off, but he wouldn't hear of parting with any of them.'

Kate moved to where her digging tools stood against the wall and selected a small spade.

'I believe I'll work outside. There's an area just beyond the entrance that I've been meaning to look at. The ground has an odd curvature there that I think might indicate a courtyard, or perhaps an anteroom.' She glanced uncertainly at David. 'Do you have enough light to work here? I have more lanterns. Will you be comfortable? Perhaps a stool. . . .'

He lifted a hand in protest.

'I'll be fine. Do you want just a sketch of the head, or do you need the whole room?'

'Oh! I didn't think of that. Well, I suppose a preliminary sketch of the whole room would be best, with a second, detailed drawing of the head.'

'As you wish, madam.'

David waved her from the room and lit two more of the lanterns stored in a corner. Settling himself against a large, stone urn, he set down a few preliminary lines. A small smile curled his lips. How had he let Kate talk him into this? A morning spent in a dark, damp ruin was not high on his list of pleasant recuperative activities. It had been well-nigh impossible, however, to resist the appeal in those great hazel eyes. He thought back a few moments to when her hand had lain in his. He had been conscious of its warmth all the way down to his knees, and when she had moved away so suddenly, he had the oddest sensation that a part of him dropped away to move with her. Strange that her touch affected him so profoundly. He had not realized that her unguarded affection would be so unsettling – perhaps because he knew it to be so badly misplaced. He turned his mind resolutely to the task at hand.

It was not long before he became immersed in his work, returning to reality some time later at the sound of Kate's voice.

'David! We've been here for almost two hours!'

With some difficulty, he hefted himself into an upright position. Limping badly and blinking in the sunlight, he emerged from the entrance to the villa, clutching at a tree for support.

'I feel as though I've been in there for a week,' he complained, flexing his fingers. 'No, no, I'm all right,' he continued impatiently as Kate flew to his side. 'I stiffen up when I stay in one position for very long. Just give me a few minutes to work out the kinks, then we'd better get back, *pronto*. Lucius will have the guard out looking for me. Here, how's this?'

He handed his sketch pad to her and leaned back against the tree, slowly stretching his aching leg muscles.

'Oh, David, they're wonderful!' she cried, examining the two drawings. Before her was displayed, in precise proportions, the room containing the marble head, and a detailed representation of the head itself. 'It's just what I needed. Now I can take the head away with me!'

She hurried into the darkness of the ruined house and returned in a moment with her treasure, wrapped in its scarf.

'I believe I'll keep it in my room for a while,' she continued, 'just to look at, and then I'll lock it away for safe keeping.'

'Where?'

'Well,' she replied slowly. 'I thought I might use one of the rooms in the west wing. Aunt Regina has closed almost all the rooms there, and there are plenty of sturdy cupboards, where no one would think to look.'

'And is it to stay there, locked away, where no one else can look at it, either?'

David's tone was gentle, but Kate flushed. She raised her head to meet his level glance.

'I know it's not right.' There was a long moment before she continued. 'All right. At the end of the summer, I'll announce my find. As for the artifacts, I'll create a place, perhaps in Bath, where people can come to look at them.'

'Good girl! I can just picture you giving learned lectures to a spell-bound audience of bespectacled academics.'

Kate laughed rather self-consciously, and the two moved toward their horses. Here, David paused uncertainly. Kate eyed him in silence.

'I'm going to need help in mounting,' he finally said in a harsh voice.

Kate sensed the effort it had taken to say the words, and she turned carelessly toward him.

'Of course. What can I do?'

'I think I can manage once I clamber onto the boulder, but old Barney will have to stand perfectly still during the operation. Will you hold the reins?'

'Of course,' she repeated in the same casual tone.

Luckily, Barney was of a placid nature, and did not dispute Kate's firm instructions to remain motionless. In an awkward motion, David hoisted himself onto the boulder and attempted to maneuver himself into the saddle. Suddenly, he halted, and gasped with pain.

'What is it?' cried Kate, her own heart wrenched to see him so. 'What can I do?'

'Nothing. Oh God!' The words were torn from him in an involuntary cry as he endeavored to inch his leg out of its crabbed position.

Maintaining her hold on the reins, Kate moved to put her shoulder under his good hip. To her vast relief, this provided the needed leverage, and with a grunt, David slid into place.

His face was white, and his breathing labored. Kate turned away to busy herself with Belle, and by the time she was settled in her own saddle, she was relieved to note that a tinge of color had returned to his thin cheeks.

They turned their horses toward Westerly, and when he could speak in a normal voice, David muttered, 'I appreciate your help. I must have looked ludicrous back there.'

He shot her a sidelong glance and braced himself for the spurious denial and the outpouring of sympathy he was sure would follow. Instead, to his astonishment, Kate chuckled.

'Yes, you did look somewhat odd, but not nearly so silly as the time you fell bottom first into that bramble bush, and had to ride home on your belly. I thought Philip would laugh himself sick at you, clinging to the horse with your toes while your rump bobbed up and down in the air. At least this time, you ended up with your bottom in the saddle, where it belongs.'

Kate held her breath. Would he resent her cavalier treatment of his pain? Please God, don't let him think she was making fun of him. Please let him laugh with her!

She almost shuddered in relief as his rueful chuckle joined hers.

'Next time,' she continued, 'we'll figure out a better way to manage.'

'A ladder, perhaps.'

'Or a scaffold.'

They proceeded a few more paces in silence before David turned to Kate, his eyes warm.

'Thank you.'

'I beg your pardon?'

'For – for not saying all the wrong things.'

Kate found she could not reply, so she merely shook her head, smiling, eyes downcast. In a moment, she lifted her face again to his, her face now serious.

'Is there no possibility of your regaining more mobility? I mean, through exercise, perhaps. . . .'

David lifted a hand in an almost defensive gesture.

'No,' he said sharply. 'This is my permanent condition, and I shall have to learn to live with it. There was one among the quacks who labored over me who suggested that a planned series of exercises might prove therapeutic, but I consider that nothing but painful nonsense. There was another doctor who mentioned the possibility of more surgery in the future, after the tissue had a chance to heal, but after the hours I spent on the table at that time, I have no wish to subject myself to their instruments of torture again.'

Kate shook her head in bewilderment at this statement. It seemed utterly foreign to David's nature to give up so easily. She searched in her mind for a topic with which to change the subject.

But, David was before her, with a matter that had been on his own mind since Regina's announcement that first night over dinner.

'I have been remiss – I forgot to wish you happy.'

Kate stared at him blankly. His face was a mask of cool courtesy, and she could not, for a moment, fathom his meaning.

'Your betrothal to Lawrence,' he prompted, his eyes giving nothing away.

'Oh!' Kate blushed furiously. 'I am *not* betrothed to Lawrence. I don't know what got into Aunt Regina to say such a thing.'

'Don't you? Lawrence said a union between the two of you had been Father's dearest wish.'

Kate fairly gasped in indignation.

'Well, if it was, Uncle Thomas never mentioned it to me! At – at least . . .' She faltered. 'At least, not in so many words.' She stiffened in her saddle. 'I have no intention of marrying Lawrence. And I can assure you that Lawrence's plans do not include marrying me.'

'But, if not Lawrence,' said David, after a moment, 'then, who? Surely, you are not without admirers, even in this backwater. Is there no one,' he continued lightly, 'on whom your maidenly favor has settled?'

Kate could feel the blood rise to heat her cheeks, but she tried to reply in a like vein.

'My maidenly favor has not been offered many options. I don't go out much, even to the Bath assemblies.'

'But, during your Season, you must have—' David paused, his eyes narrowed. 'Surely, you had a London Season?'

'Oh, yes, of course,' she replied hastily. 'But, I'm afraid I did not put myself forward as Aunt would have liked. I was a little over-whelmed by all the glitter and fuss, and never could enter into the festivities with any degree of enjoyment.'

'Still, the young bucks must have flocked around you at the balls and breakfasts, and, of course, Almack's.'

'Well' – Kate smiled – 'actually, there weren't that many balls and breakfasts. Aunt knows very few people in London, you see – since her marriage, she said, she has not kept up with very many of her old friends, thus we were not invited about much. We were offered vouchers for Almack's, but the few times we went, Aunt developed a headache and we left early.'

'I see,' said David, his jaw hard, 'or at least I'm beginning to. Tell me, wasn't there any one young man who swept you off your feet?'

Kate's cheeks reddened again.

'Oh, there was Charles, of course. Lord Stevendon, that is. He seemed to find me – attractive. He came to call several times, and took me for rides in the Park. He did become rather particular in his attentions.'

'And?' David prodded.

'And, nothing. Oh, he was very nice, and I liked him immensely. In fact, for a while, I thought perhaps . . . But, in the end it came to nothing. Aunt and Uncle found him unacceptable, they said. They thought him rather coming – said there was bad blood in the family. At any rate, we left London shortly after that to return to Westerly.'

'I'm not surprised,' said David dryly. 'And did you weep and wring your hands?'

Kate laughed merrily.

'Heavens, no! Oh, I did miss him for a while, but I was quite content to come home. I fear,' she sighed, 'I am not a very social sort of person. I love my rambles here, and reading, and a comfortable coze every now and then with some of my friends in Bath.'

'What a giddy life you do lead, Miss Millbank.'

Kate opened her mouth to frame an indignant retort, but they had by now reached the stable yard, and were met by Josiah Moody. As he assisted David from his saddle, Kate began her descent from her own steed.

When she completed her dismount, David was at her side to catch her as she sprang to the ground. In the instant she was pressed against his body, she absorbed the fact that a great deal. of strength remained in his thin frame. In a far corner of her mind, she acknowledged another fact; the contact was surprisingly pleasurable.

Chapter Eight

In the following days, Kate saw little of David. He spent much of his time in what had formerly been Thomas's study, closeted with Mr Smollett, Richard Pettigrew, the estate bailiff, and William Pennyforce, his agent in chief. Interspersed with visits from these personages, Lucius could be seen slipping into the study at odd hours, at which times Kate was rewarded by the sound of David's laughter.

Lawrence was largely invisible, skulking about the house like a petulant shadow. He had asked David's pardon on the morning following his drunken tirade, but his self-important apology could hardly have been called conciliatory.

'For don't think,' he said, 'I'll just disappear gracefully into the woodwork. May not be the Earl of Falworth, or even Viscount Standing, but still have my position to uphold. I shall present a list to you shortly of my current needs. Trust you'll be able to spare a few minutes from your pressing new responsibilities.'

He glanced at David's desk, barely visible under the mountain of account books, tenant lists, land surveys, and a hundred other pieces of paper, each clamoring for immediate attention. Turning abruptly, Lawrence strode from the room, tossing over his shoulder the information that David should not look for him at dinner, since he would be spending the evening in Bath with a few choice spirits.

David closed his eyes for a moment, then sighed and returned to his mountain.

Of Regina, Kate saw nothing for a full week after the funeral. From Aunt Fred, she learned that a modiste had been commanded to make up a wardrobe of blacks for my lady, and from Cook, she learned that her ladyship had sent down a fistful of special menus, complaining that her appetite was so poor, she could not eat the fare consumed by the rest of the family. She now required such items as plovers eggs coddled in wine and broiled fawn prepared in the Hungarian method.

'I know Aunt Regina's grief is deep and genuine,' sighed Kate, late one afternoon as she sat in Lady Frederica's chambers, assisting her aunt in the winding of one of her innumerable spools of colored wool, 'and the staff is glad to do anything that will comfort her, but it took me almost an hour to soothe Cook's sensibilities today. I hope Aunt Regina will be able to dine with the family soon.'

'Oh, I think she will, in due time,' replied the older woman, sucking judiciously on a morsel of toffee. 'She just wants to keep everyone guessing. After all, what has she got left?'

'Well, she still has the running of the house. I'm sure David will wish to leave that in her hands.'

'Unless, of course, he asks her to leave.'

'Leave!' Kate squeaked. Then, as she considered the idea, her expression turned thoughtful. 'Well, I can see where the two won't rub along very well here. And she has treated him dreadfully, but – she's his stepmama, after all, and she's still the Countess of Falworth. He can hardly boot her out of her home. Besides, David's not like that!'

'Mmph,' replied her aunt. 'More's the pity. I meant merely that he might suggest she remove to the Dower House. At any rate, I heard from her maid that Her Majesty will be gracing the board with her presence this evening. I think Lawrence will be here, too, and Crawford and Cilla. So, we can look forward to a charming evening *en famille*.'

'Major, if you don't sit still, this 'ere cravitt is goin' t'end up tied under yer ear!'

David eyed his former batman balefully in the large mirror before which he was seated. At the insistence of Collier, Westerly's steward, he had moved his things into his father's chambers, and he felt rather like a turtle who has suddenly been transferred into a shell several sizes too big.

'Curle, just what is this – this edifice you're constructing? Are you trying to strangle me?'

'Nossir, that is, yer lordship, I'm tryin' t'make ye look like a swell.'

David grasped one end of the voluminous neck cloth and wrenched it from around his neck.

'You may as well give it up, Curle. I don't know what your idea of a swell is, but I fear I am doomed to failure in trying to measure up to it. I'm still plain David Merritt, and I have no intention of trying to look like anything – or anyone – else! Now, if you please, I've been tying my own neckwear for some years, and I plan to continue doing so.'

He had been wrapping the cloth in neat layers about his neck as he spoke, and tied the bow with a flourish as he finished his sentence. He quirked an eyebrow at Curle.

'What was all this in aid of, anyway?'

'As it happens, me lord, I've been talking to Smirke, Lord Lawrence's man. The feller's a reg'lar gilliflower, prancin' about like a circus pony, but he does know ever'thin' there is t'know about how a swell should dress. Y'know . . .' He perched on the edge of David's dressing table, his reverence for his master's newly acquired status forgotten. '. . . I'd no idear this lordship business was so complicated. Ye'll have to watch whatcher wear from now on, Major, and how ye wear it – and where ye wear it to.'

'Ah,' said David, a glint in his eye, 'you wish to see me togged out like Lawrence, do you?'

Curle, recognizing that devil's light, rose hastily from the edge of the dressing table.

'No, o'course not.' The revulsion in his voice was marked. He paused a moment, then shot a sidelong glance at his master. 'Not that ye hadn't ought to be careful of his precious lordship. He'll do ye a mischief if he gets a chance. And his mama, too. There's a pair that ye don't want to turn yer back on. Anyway,' he continued in a rush, as David raised a protesting hand, 'all I'm sayin' is that ye need some new duds. It won't do anymore fer ye to be walkin' around like a – a. . . .'

'Scarecrow?' finished David. He stood and eyed himself in the mirror, an expression of deep gloom creeping over his face. 'But, you're right. I'll drive into Bath soon and order a few things.'

'Ye'll take the captain with you?'

'Lucius? You don't trust me to buy my own clothes?' responded David stiffly.

'Ye bought them that yer wearin', dincher?'

Silenced, David accepted the handkerchief proffered by his valet, and strode from the room with as much dignity as his limp would permit.

He paused at the head of the stairs. He did not look forward to this evening's meal, with all of the family gathered in the mahogany-paneled dining room. This would be the first time they had all been together since the reading of Father's will, and, he thought, the atmosphere would be tense at best. The last time he had seen Regina, she had been pale and fairly screaming with shock and rage. Would her anger have subsided in the eight or nine days of seclusion she had imposed on herself?

Lawrence should not present an overwhelming problem. His long nose had most definitely been put out of joint, and there was no doubt plenty of threat and bluster left in him, but David was experienced in handling difficult young men. Crawford, too, should be easy to deal with. Regina had not put forth the effort to foster a hostility toward him in her second son. And he would have little to do with Cilla beyond providing a suitable roster of eligible young men for her.

Having run through the family roll, David's thoughts settled on Kate. Thank God for Kate, he breathed. She was the one bright spot on his horizon. A smile began to curve his lips, but it was immediately curtailed. Good God, what was he thinking? The scene in the Roman villa rose up before him, and he again experienced the warmth of Kate's hand. No, he could not allow himself the solace of her company. The less he saw of her, the better. Not that he had much to worry about there. As soon as he told her of his role in Philip's death, her anger and contempt would provide its own barrier. As always, when he thought of the events of that night in Badajoz, a cold knot bunched in his stomach and a wave of such overpowering shame and humiliation swept through him that he thought he would vomit.

He closed his eyes and breathed deeply, forcing his attention to the problems at hand. As he began his descent of the great staircase, Lady Falworth materialized at his elbow. Right on cue, thought David, bestowing a sardonic glance on her. In her weeds, Regina was a figure of almost fairylike fragility. The heavy black fabric of her gown accentuated her pallor, and her widow's cap framed her face appealingly.

'My lord?' The words were spoken in tones of abject submission, and David nearly smiled despite himself. Now what was she up to? He crooked his arm and placed her slender hand on his sleeve.

'My lady,' he replied with what he hoped was an earl-like nod. 'But, please – not "my lord." I have been David to you all my life, I hope you will continue to call me that.'

Regina's returning nod was definitely countess-like, but her smile was unsure.

'I'm so pleased,' continued David in patriarchal tones, 'that you have returned to us. Too much solitude, even in the throes of a grief such as yours, cannot be good for one.'

Regina shot him a surprised glance from under her brows, and the corners of her mouth folded into deep lines.

'Grief is a luxury I cannot permit myself,' she said, her voice little more than a whisper. 'I must attend to my duties, burdensome as they are.'

Her gaze swept up to his again, speculative and measuring.

'To be sure,' David responded smoothly. 'Your touch has been missed in the house. We have all awaited your direction to set things to rights.'

She expelled a breath of what might have been relief. They had by now reached the gold saloon and entered to find the rest of the family assembled. David's gaze went directly to Kate, and as her own glance flicked from his face to Lady Falworth's gloved hand on his arm, her amused grin warmed him.

Kate, too, had found herself looking forward to the evening with considerable dismay. What if Aunt Regina snubbed David? Would Lawrence behave himself, or would he take further opportunity to belittle his half brother? She could not say why she felt so protective of her old friend. Certainly, he was old enough to fight his own battles. Yet, she knew that beneath David's harsh façade, some of the old vulnerability remained, and she could feel the pain of his rejection as if it were her own. She took her chair with some misgiving, wishing Aunt Fred were not absent, dining with friends at a nearby estate. She comforted herself with Lucius's presence. If anyone could be counted on to spring to David's defense, it was this staunch comrade.

As it turned out, dinner was not quite the debacle that it might have been. Regina swept to her usual place at the foot of the table, gesturing graciously to indicate that David might take his place at the head. David admitted to himself a certain satisfaction as he gazed around the room. For how many years had he sat at the long, stately table, bowed under the imagined disapprobation of the painted ancestors who looked down at the cuckoo in their midst? He could not help a feeling of pleasure at the knowledge that he was, after all, truly one of them.

Startled, he observed that the chef had apparently outdone himself in this first meal attended by the new lord of Westerly. David accepted with a dignified nod portions of larded fillets with truffles, buttered lobster, and raised giblet pie, accompanied by prawns in a wax basket, a dish of asparagus with sauce, and an assortment of creams and jellies. When a second course was laid, even more lavish than the first, he found himself itemizing each dish in pence and shillings. He caught Kate's glance on him, and when she threw him a rueful smile, he was certain she must be reading his mind.

Conversation was muted, but reasonably cordial, with only Lawrence glaring sulkily from time to time at the figure seated at the head of the table.

This state of affairs lasted until just before the last covers had been removed. Lawrence, who had scarcely touched his portion of Gateau Mellifleur, tossed back the remainder of his wine and gestured to a waiting footman for a refill. He sipped noisily from his brimming glass, the latest in a long procession of refills, and turned a flushed face to David.

'I say, Davey,' he drawled, placing an insulting emphasis on the last word, 'I ran into Shelford the other day. He agreed to let me buy that gray I've been after for months. Told him I'd ride over this week to pick it up.'

David, who had been conversing with Lucius on his right, nodded abstractedly.

'I'm a little short of the ready this month,' continued Lawrence casually, 'so I'll have to ask you to sport the blunt.'

David's attention was caught in full.

'Oh? How much blunt are we talking about?'

'Really, old man,' replied Lawrence impatiently, 'we don't discuss money at the dinner table, surely.'

'Of course, not, my dear,' Regina chimed in. To David, she spoke gently. 'You must strive to remember you live in a gentleman's home now, David. Lawrence can give you the details of his purchase later.'

'I fear, my lady,' replied David, his voice sharp, 'that circumstances being what they are, money will soon become a commonplace topic in this particular gentleman's home for some time to come.' Without giving her time to respond he swung back to Lawrence.

'What is the price of the horse?'

Fortifying himself with another swallow of wine, Lawrence answered sulkily, 'Two hundred guineas.'

For a moment, David simply stared at him before breaking into a bark of laughter.

'Why not two horses – a matched set? And a curricle or two, and possibly a phaeton to go with them?' His features hardened. 'What do you think you are about, Lawrence? I cannot let you have two hundred shillings, let alone guineas.'

Lawrence gaped in astonishment.

'B-but, it's for a horse! Really, old man, tremendous bargain. Shelford breaking down his string, y'know. Prime cattle, all of 'em.'

'Ho, that's all you know,' interposed Crawford, who had been listening intently to this exchange. 'Shelford's been trying to unload that showy hack of his for months. As for his precious string – bone-setters, every one of 'em.'

'As usual, you little twit, you don't know what you're talking about,' retorted Lawrence. 'If you. . . .'

David interrupted with a weary gesture.

'I don't care if they're direct descendants of winged Pegasus. We have enough nags eating their heads off in the stables as it is. If anything, we'll be decreasing our stock, not adding to it.'

If he had proposed serving up the animals for dinner, Lawrence could not have been more affronted.

'*Decreasing?* Decreasing our . . . You can't be serious!' he gasped.

'I'm perfectly serious. You know, Lawrence,' he continued medita-tively, 'one day very soon you and I will be sitting down for an extensive chat on finances here at Westerly. Or, I should say, the lack of. In the meantime, I advise you to curtail your spending radically. I assume, since you are applying to me, that you have spent your quarterly allowance. Be advised, there will be no further funds forthcoming until next quarter.'

And you will find yourself severely curtailed even then, my lad, thought David. He felt Lawrence had sustained enough of a shock for one evening, however, and forbore to express the words aloud.

He returned calmly to his dessert, but Kate, from her position at the other end of the table, turned immediately toward Lady Falworth. Sure enough, in the deafening silence that followed David's remarks, she cleared her throat softly.

Instantly, all eyes were on her.

'David, I'm afraid you don't understand,' she said in a voice of patient instruction, as though speaking to a dull child. 'I'm aware that you must be in the habit of squeezing your pennies, but now that you are the Earl of Falworth, you must realize that you need not continue in your shabby genteel little economies. We must maintain our standards, after all,' she concluded with a repressive shrug of her shoulders.

'Quite,' added Lawrence, in haughty indignation. 'Must maintain the consequence of a gentleman, you know.'

'I see,' returned David, with deceptive gentleness. 'You must teach me how to go on, Lawrence. Does it add to a gentleman's consequence to spend money he doesn't have?'

Lawrence stiffened, his mouth an ugly slash against the pallor of his face. He opened his mouth to retort, but Regina intervened once more, with a lift of her hand.

'*Pas devant les domestiques!*' She rapped out the words sharply, glancing at the footmen standing about the perimeter of the room. 'We shall discuss this later.'

'There is nothing more to discuss, ma'am,' said David indifferently, once more addressing his plate. 'I shall not give Lawrence two hundred guineas to buy a horse.'

At this, Lawrence leapt to his feet, overturning his wine glass, which had once more been filled to the brim.

'By God, you jumped-up nobody, do you think you can turn

Westerly topsy-turvy?' he raged.

'Why, yes, that is precisely what I think,' was David's mild response. 'However,' he continued, 'it is not my plan to do so. Quite the opposite, in fact.'

Lawrence made no reply, but strode from the room. Regina pushed her chair from the table and rose.

'I, too, believe I shall retire. It has been a fatiguing day.'

In a moment, with a hiss of her skirts, she, too, had departed, hurrying in the direction her son had taken.

Lucius lifted his quizzing glass to follow her with a contemplative gaze and murmured something to David that Kate could not catch. She let out the breath she felt she had been holding for the past several minutes, and turned to address a neutral remark to Cilla, who sat on her left, tittering self-consciously.

Conversation soon returned to a semblance of normalcy, and Kate found her glance returning again to David. He had displayed an aspect she did not know he possessed. How silly of her to think that he needed her protection in dealing with his erstwhile 'betters.' He had faced them down with dignity and authority.

No, David didn't need her as an ally. Did he need her as a friend? When the gentlemen joined the ladies in the drawing room after dinner, she sent a hesitant smile to him as he entered the room. Though it seemed to her that his glance had sought her out, he did not return the smile, but instead looked quickly away.

Kate's heart sank. He could not have rebuffed her more pointedly had he turned his back on her. Miserably, she followed Cilla to the piano to accompany that young lady in a song. Cilla was blessed with a singularly sweet voice, and in a few moments, she was joined by Lucius. The two performed several duets, apparently growing more pleased with one another with each note.

Afterward, a game of piquet was suggested, but Kate had by that time developed a raging headache. Pleading fatigue, she retired to her room before the tea table had made an appearance. David, deep in conversation with Crawford and Lucius, apparently did not notice when she left.

Once in her bedchamber, she did not immediately slide beneath the coverlet. Having undressed and donned her night rail, she dismissed her maid and slumped into a small armchair by the fire and gave herself up to gloomy ruminations.

She had found David changed on his return to Westerly, but she did not doubt that his affection for her remained strong. Now, he had been catapulted into an exalted position, and seemingly had forgotten his childhood playmate.

She scolded herself. She had got along very well without him for the last six years, and there was no reason why she should become glumpish at the prospect of getting along without him for the rest of her life. She was happy for him, of course, for now Westerly would always be his. As for herself, she thought rather forlornly, she must get about the business of her own life. As David had said, she was not a child anymore. Beginning tomorrow, she told herself, she would look about to expand her horizons. Explore possibilities. And see what the world had to offer.

With these admonitions clutched firmly to her breast, she climbed into bed and blew out her bedside candle and waited for the sleep of the just and the sensible to descend upon her.

Instead, it hovered somewhere above her, near the ceiling, refusing to be grasped. After an hour spent in restless kicking of covers and adjusting of pillows, she gave up. Slipping on a robe, she tiptoed out into the corridor and hurried in the direction of the library.

Turning to descend the great staircase, she paused a moment at a sound that reached her from the other end of the corridor. Again it came, and this time Kate recognized it. It was David, beginning one of his dreams, and without thinking, she hurried toward the bedchamber of the master of Westerly. As she ran, she recalled that Lucius now slept far from David's room, and she had no idea where Curle spent his nights.

The sound came again – a low moan of inutterable despair, and without hesitation, she turned the door latch and entered David's room.

Chapter Nine

The chamber was in darkness, illuminated only by slices of moonlight slanting between the draperies. The sound of a muttered groan led Kate to the great bed where David lay, tossing in unconscious anguish.

She sat on the bed and bent to grip his shoulders. His nightshirt was soaked with sweat.

'David!' she called softly, shaking him.

His only response was an unintelligible murmur as he twisted in her grasp.

'David!' she repeated, shaking him again.

He sat upright, his eyes wide and staring.

'My God!' he cried. 'The water! Do you see? Look – he's. . . .'

She raised a hand to smooth the dark hair falling damply over his forehead and tried in vain to control his convulsive shuddering.

'It's all right, David. It's all right. You're safe now.'

'Look!' His voice was a hoarse shout. 'Oh, Jesus! They're falling – they're all falling! Ferris! Halloran!'

He flung an arm out, nearly knocking Kate to the floor.

'Come back! The ladders . . .' And then, again. 'The water! Can't you see? He's drowning. Somebody . . . Lucius!'

With all the strength she possessed, Kate threw her arms around him and flung her body against his in an effort to bear him back against his pillows.

'David!' she gasped, pressing her face against the muscles bunched beneath her. 'It's all right. Wake up. You're safe – at Westerly.'

He uttered a long, shuddering groan and suddenly was still.

For a moment, the only sound in the room was the rasping of his breath. Kate remained silent, holding him close against her, aware of the pounding of his heart against hers. His arms crept slowly about her.

'Kate?' The word came in a whisper. 'Kate.'

Over and over he said her name, burrowing his face in her shoulder. His breath was warm in the hollow at the base of her throat, and without volition she curled her fingers in the softness of his shaggy hair.

Kate did now know for how long they remained thus, locked in a primal giving and taking of comfort. She did not know when she became aware of the heat of his body invading the thin linen of her night rail, or of the feel of his lips on her skin. The need to provide solace was giving way to another need, one she did not understand. She sensed that David had wakened, but he did not pull away from her. Instead, he began a caressing motion along the length of her back that made her arch against him involuntarily. She uttered a sound that was not quite a moan, and David stiffened. His arms dropped and he pulled away from her.

Suddenly cold, she rose from the bed.

'Kate!' He spoke her name quietly, but his intonation was sharp. 'You should not be here.'

She shivered, and, feeling bereft, hugged herself.

'No,' she whispered, 'but you cried out.'

There was a moment's silence before David replied in a barely audible voice.

'Yes, I suppose I did, but – please, just go now.'

Without a sound, she whirled and ran.

Once in her own room, she plunged beneath her coverlet and lay trembling and breathless, as though she had been running for her life.

What had happened in that moonlit chamber?

When she had taken David in her arms, her only intention had been to provide solace for a friend. She had been wholly unprepared for the torrent of emotions that had engulfed her like the first waves of a storm at sea. She relived the feel of him – the roughness of his beard, the strength of his fingers, the shattering rightness of his arms about her. Even the scent of him – the sharp, musky odor of masculine sweat – filled her senses and elicited an unfamiliar, almost frightening response.

Most alarming of all, she hadn't wanted it to stop. Her breasts, pressed against him, had suddenly swelled with longing.

Lord, was she a wanton, then? Granted, her experience with men was limited. Her first kiss, taken hastily by one of Lawrence's friends had been unpleasant. His mouth had been wet and demanding, and she had felt nothing but disgust at his furtive gropings. The shy kiss bestowed on her by her London beau, Charles, Lord Stevendon, in a secluded alcove at her comeout ball was another matter. She had experienced a definite tingle on that occasion. Would she have welcomed a further encroachment on her virtue? Possibly, but being a correctly reared maiden, she did not indicate this to her smitten partner, so none had been forthcoming.

No such reserve had troubled her tonight, however. In the urgency of David's embrace, she had been filled with an aching desire to melt into his very bones.

Forcing herself to abandon this dangerous line of thought, Kate turned her mind to the words David had uttered in his nightmare delirium. His cries undoubtedly had been torn from the heart of a battle somewhere in Spain. Water? Drowning? Most of the captured towns she had read of lay in strategic river positions.

Lucius had said that David had changed after the Battle of Badajoz – where Philip had been killed. Did the nightmares have something to do with her brother's death? Lucius said David did not want to talk about Badajoz, but perhaps talk was what was needed. Surely it could not be good to keep such horror locked inside, festering in the dark corners of his memory. Sighing, she resolved to insert a gentle probe into David's emotional wounds. She wouldn't press, of course, but if she could get him to air his pain, perhaps it would begin to heal in the warmth of a little friendly concern.

Yes, friendly concern. She liked that phrase. It had nothing of a fire in the blood in it, nor the delicious feel of a muscular body pressed against her own. She turned her face into her pillow. David had need of her friendship, she told herself firmly, and tomorrow she would search him out for some quiet, reasonable conversation.

Her quarry, however, proved to be singularly elusive. She made an early appearance in the breakfast parlor the next morning, garbed in the most becoming of her mourning gowns, only to be told that his lordship had taken toast and coffee early, and then disappeared into the library with orders not to be disturbed. Nor did he appear for luncheon, having asked for a tray to be sent in for himself and Mr Pettigrew, the bailiff, with whom he had been closeted for several hours.

Kate did encounter Lady Falworth and her son, however, each of whom were apparently laboring under a strong sense of ill-usage.

'B'God,' muttered Lawrence morosely, crumbling a slice of bread onto his plate. 'He's becoming insufferable, practically ordering us to attend him at a time of his choosing. Does he think I have nothing else to do with my afternoon that I must attend his every whim?'

'It is most annoying,' agreed her ladyship. 'May I have just a little more of that chicken, Carstairs? I was planning an inventory of the linen cupboards with Mrs Seagrave, but of course that means nothing to him.'

'And if he intends to lecture me on my spending habits,' continued Lawrence, his eye kindling, 'I – well, I won't stand for it.'

'Never fear, my dearest, if he starts anything of the sort, he will have me to deal with.' Regina's voice was filled with calm authority. 'In fact, I have a little something to say to him on that matter. I did not at all care for the way he spoke to you last night.'

'Nor I!' Lawrence responded, reaching for a plate of grapes lying within his reach. 'It's not for the likes of him to be telling me how to live my life.'

Kate, who had grown increasingly angry during this exchange, could contain herself no longer.

'What do you mean, the likes of him? Have you already forgotten that his birth has proved to be as noble as your own, Lawrence? Why do you think the servants now address him as Lord Falworth instead of yourself? As for his right to. . . .'

'Please Kate,' reproved Regina gently, 'manners. And I hardly think we can speak of David's, er, background on a level with that of Lawrence, when one considers the low birth of his mother.'

'Only fancy,' added Lawrence angrily, 'Father's first wife wore a grass skirt. What a blot on the family escutcheon.'

Kate opened her mouth to deliver a stinging retort, but was fore-stalled by a voice drawling from the doorway. 'I believe, my dear boy, you're thinking of the natives of the Sandwich Islands.'

She whirled to observe Lucius entering the room.

'Those from the West Indies,' he continued, the mildness of his words belied by the glint of his eye, 'favor brightly colored cloth.'

Kate cast him a grateful smile, and gestured to a chair next to her.

'What difference does it make?' Lawrence asked pettishly, as Kate helped Lucius to fruit and meat and the prime cheese of the region, a sharp Cheddar. 'The fact remains that Father betrayed everything that he should have held sacred by bringing a – a prancing native into the family. People will say that the Earl of Falworth has tainted blood in his veins.'

'Perhaps, my dear . . .' Regina's smooth voice held a warning. 'It would be better to simply acknowledge the fact that David's mother was a resident of the Indies. I cannot see that anything would be gained by advertising to the outside world David's, er, plebeian origins.'

'Closing ranks, my lady?' Lucius queried, idly twirling his quizzing glass on the end of its silk ribbon. 'Just as the third earl's family did when it put it about that the infant he had brought to Westerly was the son of a mythical friend?'

Regina leveled a steely glance at him.

'You go too far, Mr Pelham. You have intruded on a discussion of private matters, and since you obviously have no concept of the behavior expected in polite society, I shall take leave to tell you that your remarks are singularly inappropriate.'

Lawrence thumped the table with his wineglass in agreement.

'Anyway,' he said, 'why are you still here? Thought you didn't plan to stay above two or three days.'

'But isn't it obvious, my dear?' interposed Regina with a malicious smile. 'He has just discovered that his old comrade-in-arms is a peer. How foolish it would be for a farmer's son not to take advantage of such a relationship.'

'Aunt Regina!' cried Kate, her hazel eyes flashing like new-minted pennies. Crawford uttered an inarticulate sound, and Cilla breathed an agitated, 'Oh, Mama!'

Regina fluttered her hands.

'Perhaps I was a little blunt, but with persons of a certain order, sometimes one has to make oneself plain. For example . . .' She turned again to Lucius. 'I believe you have overstayed your welcome, Mr Pelham. I'm sure you must have more pressing demands on your time in, er, Kent. I shall inform the servants that you will be taking your leave no later than tomorrow morning.'

'It is David who invited Lucius to remain,' cried Kate hotly. 'And he may remain here for the rest of his life if he'd like.'

'God forbid,' murmured Lucius.

As though she had not heard, Regina replied complacently, 'I believe my wishes still hold some weight in this house. When I inform David that his so-called friend has made himself unwelcome here, I am sure he will be the first to insist on your departure.'

Lucius, unscathed, sat back in his chair and smiled with great sweetness.

'For all that you had a lifetime to become acquainted with his lord-ship' – he placed a deliberate emphasis on the words – 'it astonishes me that you know him so little.'

Regina did not reply, but rose swiftly, forestalling any further discussion on the subject.

'Come, my dear.' She laid a hand on her son's shoulder. 'It is nearly the time appointed for our interview with our new master.'

Lawrence remained slouched in his chair.

'Let him wait. I have not yet finished my wine.'

Regina's fingers tightened.

'I would prefer to go now. As I said, I have other matters requiring my attention this afternoon.'

She turned and glided from the room, and Lawrence, after sullenly tipping his wine down his throat, rose to follow her.

There was a moment of silence in the faded elegance of the dining room, and portraits of Merritts in periwigs and ruffs and doublets gazed down in startled disapproval.

'Whew!' breathed Crawford in awed tones. 'A complete rout! You should have stayed in the army, Mr Pelham. You'd probably be a general by now.'

Kate laughed aloud and rose from her chair to bestow an impetuous hug on David's friend. Cilla said nothing, but her eyes rested on the young man from Kent for a long time.

David stood at one of the long windows in his study, staring blindly at the scene outside. The vista was a pleasant one, of a broad sweep of lawn sloping to an ornamental lake, but David saw only a shadowed face hovering above his and a tumble of red curls turned to black in the darkness of his bedchamber.

Dear Lord, had he dreamed the whole thing? Usually his dreams were not so pleasant. But no, the soft whisper of her voice, the curving, pliant warmth of her body pressed against his had been real to the point of agony, and the sweet lavender scent of her seemed still with him.

She had come to ease his distress, but thank God she had left at his command. For if she hadn't, he surely would not have been able to deny the almost overpowering urge that had swept through him to seek her mouth with his own and to push aside the fragile linen that presented such an insubstantial guard to her virtue.

It must not happen again. She was under his protection for God's sake! He had already become aware that he was growing much too fond of his erstwhile playmate, and last night's interlude proved the danger of any further intimacy between them.

He permitted himself a bitter smile. How fortunate that the means of ending their friendship completely lay so easily at hand, for when he spoke to her of Philip, and how her brother had died, he knew with painful certainty that she would not wish to be in the same drawing room with him, let alone a moonlit bedchamber.

His reverie was interrupted by a diffident knock at the door as Fleming announced the imminent arrival at his study of his stepmother and half brother. He rose to greet them at the door; this was not an interview to which he looked forward with any degree of pleasure, and he wished to get things started in as cordial a manner as possible.

He gestured them to chairs by the fire, and took another for himself.

'I have spent a number of days going over the estate accounts,' he began quietly. 'And it is clear that matters have come to a desperate pass. We are all of us going to have to rein in sharply or we'll be in the suds.'

He had tried to put as light a face on it as he could, and now, glancing at Lawrence's impatient expression, saw that he had erred in doing so.

'What I mean is,' he continued hastily before either Lawrence or his mama could interrupt, 'the estate has become so unproductive that it is bringing in very little income, and the same can be said of Seldon Hall, in Buckinghamshire and the place near Cambridge. Our expenses, on the other hand, have maintained a steady increase over the years, until the point has been reached where our extravagant lifestyle has outstripped our ability to pay for it.'

'I think you're making a great deal of fuss over nothing,' said Regina. 'We've had bad years before from time to time, but we always come around again. You'll see, my dear.'

David's face hardened.

'I don't think you understand, my lady. It is not just low water with us, it is near ruin.'

To his astonishment, Regina only laughed.

'You've been listening too much to Smollett,' she said with a dismissive wave. 'And Pettigrew. Every time those doomsayers put their gloomy noses in the door, they preach of economy and other tiresome things – always putting Thomas in a fury. He usually ended up showing them out of the house within an hour after they'd arrived.'

Gripping his temper and his patience with both hands, David said shortly, 'Perhaps he would have done better to spend more time listening to the doomsayers and less in his club at the faro table.'

At that, Lawrence stiffened.

'Are you proposing to teach your betters how to spend their time?' he snarled.

His words were returned with a level stare, and after a moment, Lawrence dropped his eyes to begin a minute study of his boots.

'Let's get one thing straight, brother,' David said in a tone no one at Westerly had ever heard him use. 'I have never perceived anyone living under this roof to be my better. And, no, I do not propose to instruct anyone on the use of his time. What I am saying is, very simply, that everyone in this family has been living beyond the means of the estate, and it must stop.'

David watched as Regina's eyes narrowed to slits and her nose pinched unbecomingly. He said nothing more, but simply waited, smothering the thought that this little chat was proving to be every bit as painful as he had envisioned.

'I am not,' her ladyship began portentously, 'considered to be an extravagant woman. And I will *not* be dictated to according to your shabby-genteel notions of household management. Would you have us sit down to boiled mutton at dinner? Do you intend to make us the laughing stock of the county by dressing us in homespun?'

It was quite evident that she did not expect an answer, and David did not attempt one.

'You have spent over a week,' she continued, 'absorbing, apparently without question, the petty complaints of persons who have no concept of life in a noble home. Now, let me make something clear to you. One can only decry the circumstances that contrived to make you Falworth of Westerly, but as such, you have a position to uphold. My son, though he has been denied the title that should have been his, is still Lord Lawrence Merritt of Westerly, and his position is one that must also be maintained properly.

'Since,' she concluded, and David could only marvel inwardly that she scarcely found it necessary to draw a deep breath, 'you have not the smallest notion of the standards that have always been observed in this house, you will do much better to leave things in more capable hands than yours.'

She rose, abruptly, like a monarch signaling the end of an audience, then turned to deliver an apparent afterthought. 'By the way, I have instructed the servants that Mr Pelham will be leaving us first thing in the morning. He has been a disruptive influence here, and was most unpleasant at lunch. I trust, David, we will not be receiving any more visits from your unsavory companions.'

She gathered her skirts preparatory to making a stately departure, and Lawrence, with a triumphant glance at his half brother, made as though to follow her. They were both brought up short by the sound of David's voice.

'Sit down, both of you.'

Again, he spoke quietly, but there was that in his tone that caused Regina to look over her shoulder at him in astonishment. Lawrence, still crouched above his chair, sank back, openmouthed. After a moment's hesitation, his mother followed suit.

'As you say, ma'am, I am Falworth of Westerly, and however distasteful the situation may be to you, it is my word that will be obeyed here.' He ignored Regina's outraged gasp and continued composedly. 'I have outlined some specific areas in which our expenditures may be decreased.' He limped awkwardly to the desk and selected a paper from among those littering its surface. 'If you would, please, confer with the staff as to their implementation.'

He held the paper out to her, but Regina remained where she sat, tree-trunk stiff, her hands folded in her lap. David rubbed a hand tiredly over his eyes, and spoke again, in a softer voice.

'Really, ma'am, we must contrive to rub along better than this. I will see these measures taken with or without your assistance, and unless you wish to be on the losing end of a very bad situation, you will choose the former. Please believe me, I do not want to create chaos here. I don't like boiled mutton, nor do I propose to see you swathed in homespun, but I cannot emphasize too strongly the need for stringent measures. Surely,' he finished, with a lifted eyebrow, 'it is as much to your advantage – and Lawrence's – to see Westerly restored to solvency as it is to mine.'

For an instant, hard blue eyes locked with flinty black ones, and it was the blue that gave way. Regina accepted the paper with a great show of condescension, and David was pleased to note a flash of respect in her glance before she bent her head to examine it.

He permitted himself an inward sigh of relief as he turned to his half brother. 'I'm afraid, Lawrence, I have found it necessary to cut your allowance.'

'*What?*' The young man fairly paled in outrage. 'B-but,' he sputtered, 'I am just getting by now!'

'No, you are not getting by. You have continually applied for additional funds far beyond your stipend, and that will cease.' David fixed him with an icy stare. 'Do you understand me, Lawrence? From now on, there will nothing forthcoming once you have spent your allowance. I will pay no debts, and I shall certainly not sport the blunt for sweet-goers or any of your other extravagances.'

Regina had been staring at David during this last, an odd, unreadable expression on her face, and when he was through, she cut into Lawrence's agonized babble of protest.

'Never mind that, now, my dear. I must have a word in private with David. Please leave us.'

Lawrence was unprepared to cease his lamentations, but after one glance from his mother, he fell silent immediately, and left the room without further argument.

David gazed watchfully at Regina as she took a turn about the room, pausing to riffle her fingers through the documents that lay in untidy heaps on the desk.

'Well, my lady?'

She turned and gave him a measuring stare.

'I was merely wondering, if, in all these plans and schemes of yours, you have made provisions for Lawrence's marriage to Kate?'

Chapter Ten

David stared in bemusement at Regina.

'Marriage?' he echoed stupidly.

'Well, of course it's early days to be making any plans.' Regina's laugh was soft and agreeable. 'We shall have to wait a year, although here in the country, we might see it done a little earlier.'

Why was he having such difficulty in absorbing her words? Perhaps because the idea of Kate and Lawrence together was ludicrous – as though one were discussing a bad play or something else equally outside the bounds of reality.

'I was unaware of a betrothal between them,' he replied coldly.

'But surely you have not forgotten.' Her eyes were wide and ingenious. 'We spoke of it at dinner the evening you came home – the understanding that has stood for some years.'

'But, ma'am, I have seen no evidence of such an understanding. Indeed, Kate has given me to believe that she does not wish for such a marriage.'

Regina chuckled amusedly.

'Kate is such a dear. I believe sometimes she does not know her own heart, but she and Lawrence have grown very close since you and Philip left.'

'An affection that can at best be called sisterly hardly seems a basis for marriage.' David fought an urge to take Regina by the shoulders and shake that complacent expression from her face. As if reading his thoughts, she smiled confidently.

'It has been many years since Kate thought of herself as Lawrence's sister. The signs have been obvious for some time. For example, when we were in London for Kate's Season, her favorite partner was always Lawrence, and she compared every would-be suitor to him – generally to the disadvantage of the suitor.'

'Odd,' mused David, 'I have seen no sign of such lover-like behavior since I've been home – on the part of either of them.'

Regina shot him a brief glance from beneath her carefully darkened eyelashes, and brushed her fingertips once again over the papers on the desk.

'I've noticed that, too,' she replied off-handedly. 'I believe they had a tiff some weeks ago, and now they're behaving like tiresome children. Kate never misses an opportunity to put her claws out at him, and Lawrence simply sulks at her.'

David raised a skeptical eyebrow. He was well aware of Regina's dilemma. She was no longer the wife of the Earl of Falworth, and the continuing control she had always assumed would be hers through her son had slipped from her grasp. Thomas had had virtually nothing to bequeath to her, and she was now all but penniless. The idea of applying to her hated stepson for every farthing of her existence would no doubt be galling beyond endurance, hence her urgent desire to get Kate's inheritance under her fingers. Her ladyship, he knew, would not stop at bending the truth in the matter of their supposed 'understanding.' Still – could there be a grain of truth in her explanation of Kate's seeming indifference to Lawrence?

Observing the glimmer of concern in David's gaze, Regina prudently chose to drop the subject. She turned as though to leave. David watched her through narrowed eyes, and suddenly called out to her.

'One moment, my lady.' He moved to overtake her at the door. 'Regarding Lucius, please be advised that he will not be leaving in the morning or at any time soon. I have invited him to remain at Westerly for as long as he chooses.'

Regina's features hardened.

'But, have I not told you of his behavior?'

'I regret that his presence discommodes you, ma'am, but he will stay.'

An unbecoming flush spread over her cheeks as she drew a sharp breath.

'Really, David, to make such a fuss over a farmer's son. . . .'

'It is you who is making the fuss, my lady, and as for Lucius being a farmer's son . . .' A glint of amusement sprang into his dark eyes. 'You have been uncharacteristically obtuse in your judgment. Lucius's father does indeed call his home a farm, but in actuality it is an enormous and luxurious estate. Have you never heard of Horace Pelham, ma'am? He is one of the wealthiest men in the country.'

Regina's eyes widened in disbelief, then quickly became thoughtful.

'Horace Pelham. Yes, I believe I have heard his name. He's a mill owner, is he not? From Leeds or Manchester or one of those places.'

'He was born in Manchester. He owns several mills, but he has his fingers in many other pies. Foundries and other manufacturing, shipping, and investments in a variety of extremely profitable industries.'

'And your friend is his son?' The words were spoken in some wonderment.

'His only son. And heir.'

'But why did he spin me that faradiddle about his being a farmer?' Regina asked in some indignation.

'Possibly because you were so anxious to believe the worst of him. Did you not think it odd,' he continued, his eyes still laughing at her, 'that a son of the soil would appear dressed in the first stare of fashion?'

'Y-yes, but I thought he must have found a wealthy patron, or – or spent his entire army severance pay on his back.'

'And did you think he also purchased his Eton-educated speech?'

Regina chose to ignore that thrust. 'Well!' was her only response.

David inclined his head. 'Indeed,' he said with an ironic smile, but he spoke to the empty air, for his stepmother had already swept into the corridor.

David turned back into his study, but instead of seating himself again at his desk, he moved on impulse to the double doors at the other end of the room that gave out onto a broad terrace. Opening them, he breathed in the warm breeze that ruffled his hair, and turned his face to the sun. Lord, he'd been indoors for a week! He felt like a bear emerging from a winter's enforced sleep.

He strolled onto the lawn from the terrace, noting its unkempt condition, and turned to survey the manor house behind him. The whiteness of the Bath stone was almost blinding in the early afternoon sunlight, and David gazed appreciatively at the classic lines of the building. That was one thing, at least, he needn't worry about. It had originally been built in an Elizabethan square, and subsequent additions had been well conceived and executed. The structure remained sound. The roof, he sighed, was something else again. And the interior – well, there wasn't a room that did not need new plaster on the walls and new hangings, carpeting and lighting fixtures. The chimneys were on the verge of collapse, and the cellars were a disaster. He shook his head. He wouldn't think about that now. The list of projects on his desk was already long enough. The needs of the estate must be met first, time then to consider the manor house.

He rounded a shaggy hedge, and caught a flash of color at the other end of the formal garden he had just entered. The next moment, Kate appeared in full view, a basket of roses over one arm. David hesitated a moment, ready to turn to the house. Then, squaring his shoulders, he flung up an arm in greeting.

From the other end of the garden, Kate, too, knew an urge to flee. How could she face David after last night's encounter? On the other hand, she could not avoid him forever – nor did she want to. There was, after all, that quiet conversation she had promised herself. She raised her own hand and continued on her path toward him..

Neither spoke until they were a few feet from one another, close enough for Kate to note the wary expression on David's face. Their good afternoons said, an awkward silence fell between them, expanding to envelop them like the spell of a malicious fairy.

'About last night. . . .' Kate began tentatively.

'I'm sorry you were disturbed,' David interrupted, his dark brows drawn together. 'I'm afraid I – dream fairly frequently. Curle is usually nearby, but he has not yet made the move from his old quarters to the ones adjacent to Fa – my chambers. He will do so today. I appreciate your – the concern you displayed last night, however inappropriate, but as you can see, your intervention will be unnecessary from now on.'

110

All this was uttered in a tone of such aloof disapproval that Kate could feel her cheeks begin to burn. She *had* shown herself to be a wanton! What must he think of her? She struggled to maintain her composure. Her feelings, she reminded herself, were not important right now.

'But what causes your dreams, David?' she asked. 'Have you ever tried to. . . .'

'I know what causes the dreams, and I do not wish to discuss the matter.'

His eyes glittered darkly against the sudden pallor of his cheeks, and it seemed to Kate that he had closed himself against her with a finality that was as irrevocable as it was hurtful.

'Then there remains no more to be said,' she replied in as calm a voice as she could muster, determined that he would not perceive her dismay.

She turned to leave, but David, ashamed at his abruptness, laid his hand on her arm.

'How goes the digging?' he asked.

Her expression lightened. 'I was just going indoors to change into my working garb. Would you like to come to the villa with me?'

'No, I have promised the rest of the day to Pettigrew. We're going to ride out over the estate on an inspection tour. Lucius is going to accompany us and, I think, Crawford as well.' He hesitated, then smiled uncertainly. 'Would you like to come, too?'

It was not long before the little group set out from the stable yard in high good humor. Crawford appeared to be on his best behavior and kept the company entertained with bits of gossip about the inhabitants of the estates surrounding Westerly. Lucius then took over, relating anecdotes from his and David's tour in Spain. As they rode under the July sun, a soaring happiness suddenly took possession of Kate. Westerly belonged to David now! The land he loved so was his to possess and to cherish for the rest of his life. She tried to ignore the shadow cast on her joy by the knowledge that she, herself, would eventually be obliged to leave Westerly. She was not, after all, a member of David's immediate family, and when she came into her inheritance she would be off to Bath, or maybe even London, to set up her own establishment. That she might marry did not occur to her.

As though these disquieting thoughts were contagious, a certain grayness began to settle over the entire group. John Pettigrew led his new master over ill-tended fields and through unkempt woodlands. Tenants flocked from houses badly in need of repair, eager to catch a glimpse of the young lord. David spoke with them and tried to address their concerns, but he felt like a charlatan promising miracles to children.

As the party moved farther afield, the signs of neglect and misman-agement increased, and David's countenance, too, seemed to acquire an ashen hue.

Some hours later, after much too long in the saddle, David's wound had become once again a throbbing entity and he clenched his teeth against the pain.

Watching him, Kate's heart sank, and when they finally clattered wearily back onto the cobblestones of the stable yard, she instinctively moved to his side.

'It's bad, but it's fixable,' she whispered.

'Oh, without a doubt,' David agreed in a sardonic tone. 'If one had the gold of Ind at hand, all could be set to rights in a twinkling.'

'It's fixable,' Kate repeated. 'Even without the gold of whatever. It will take attention and care and a severe retrenching, but you can make it work, David. I know you can.'

David gazed into the clear eyes, shining with faith and the love of a friendship too strong for words, and knew a moment of terrible grief. Out of sheer cowardice, he had rebuffed her effort to talk to him about what had happened in Spain, but he could not postpone the telling for much longer. He dreaded the soon-approaching moment when the glowing affection in her gaze would turn to contempt, the warmth of her smile to chill disdain. The appalling thought skittered through his mind that, having found the star in the darkness that was Kate, how was he going to find his way again with-out her?

A young groom approached to assist David out of the saddle, only to be shouldered out of the way by Josiah Moody. 'Careful now, Mr Da – me lord, that is.'

With a gentleness and dexterity surprising in one of his rugged appearance, Moody bore David's weight as he eased himself from his horse's back. The young man straightened and turned to thank the head groom, but his attention was suddenly caught by a small group rounding the far end of the stables.

At its head strode Lawrence, looking back over his shoulder to issue a stream of instructions to the three men following him, one of which led a showy gray hack.

David stiffened and moved awkwardly to intercept his half brother. Lucius, observing the sudden tension in David's attitude, hurried to walk by his side. Kate dismounted hastily and ran after them, with Crawford bringing up the rear.

Upon catching sight of David, Lawrence halted abruptly and made as though to turn back. Then, with a defensive shrug of his shoulders, he continued on the path which brought him directly in front of David.

'H'lo, brother,' he drawled, a belligerent spark in his eye.

David merely nodded. He looked past Lawrence at the gray, then back again. 'Am I right in assuming that this is the animal we were discussing last night?' he asked tightly.

'Yes.' Lawrence's voice was casual, but Kate could sense his uneasiness. 'Shelford's man just delivered him.'

'And why did he do that, Lawrence? Surely you told him that you were no longer interested.'

The younger man's face reddened.

'No, I didn't,' he said pugnaciously. 'Good God, David, I told you – I gave him to believe we had a deal!'

'And I told you to tell him there was no deal. Now, you will have to put Shelford's man to the trouble of taking the horse back.'

'B-but, I can't do that.' Lawrence's pale eyes went wide. 'We shook hands on it last night. I promised him he should have his money by the end of the week.'

'Last night!' David's voice was a harsh rasp. 'You said nothing of this in our discussion this morning.'

'Knew you'd cut up stiff,' Lawrence muttered sullenly, dropping his eyes to where clods of mud bespattered his glossy top boots.

For a moment, David said nothing, but eyed the younger man assessingly. When he spoke, his voice had lost none of its anger.

'Yes, Lawrence, I am going to cut up very stiff. You have forced my hand, and while I will pay the two hundred guineas, I will not tolerate such behavior in the future. The money will be subtracted from your next quarterly allowance, as will any other expenses you incur between now and then.'

Lawrence's head jerked up to stare at his half brother in outraged astonishment.

'That's three months from now! Do you expect me to live like a hermit until then?'

'You may become an anchorite for all I care, but you will not add to our already staggering financial burden.'

He pivoted on his good leg and prepared to limp away, but Lawrence sprang at him, clutching at his sleeve. The move caught David off balance, and he struggled to right himself as Lawrence tightened his grip and began shaking the arm he held.

'You can't treat me this way, David! You may have choused me out of my inheritance, but you can't make me live like a veritable pauper.'

'Choused you out of your inheritance?' David whitened at the words and flung Lawrence's arm from his sleeve.

Ready tears had sprung to Lawrence's eyes, and his own face had become as flushed as David's was pale.

'If you hadn't come back – sucking up to Father like you always did – I'd be the Earl of Falworth now, not you. It isn't fair!' he gulped, echoing the phrase he had hurled at the walls of Westerly many times over the past days.

At this, David's rage suddenly evaporated, to be replaced by an appalling urge to burst out laughing. How could he have allowed his temper to have been roused by this spoiled infant?

His expressive eyes betrayed his thoughts, and Lawrence, uttering an inarticulate howl of rage, lunged at him. In an instant, Lucius had interposed himself between them, and Crawford moved quickly to grip his brother's shoulder.

Their efforts proved unnecessary, as Lawrence halted abruptly, his contorted features suddenly curving into an ugly sneer.

'Oh, don't worry,' he grated, 'I shan't assault our cherished lordship. I never hit cripples.'

David went rigid, and the expression on his face made Kate want to cry out. She knew an urge to fly at Lawrence, fingers curved into rakes, but Lucius was before her. In a surprisingly swift motion, his fist connected with Lawrence's nose, and the next moment, the young man lay flung on the stable yard cobblestones, blood streaming from between the fingers he pressed to the offended protuberance.

Kate's attention was wholly taken with David, who remained frozen where he stood, despair and humiliation written in every line in his cheeks and in the hopeless slump of his shoulders. Out of the corner of her eye, she saw Lucius turn toward him. Moody, too, had swung about to give him assistance.

No! she thought wildly. He must have time to gather his emotions back into their tight little ball. He must not have to bear their sympathy. She whirled around and dropped to her knees beside Lawrence, who still lay sobbing.

'He is bleeding!' she cried. 'How could you, Lucius? Give me your handkerchief at once.' She issued swift orders to Pettigrew and Crawford to assist Lawrence to his feet, and sped Moody on his way with the gray, who was prancing agitatedly at all the commotion.

It was some moments before Lawrence was brought to his feet, still lamenting and mopping ostentatiously at his face with Lucius's handkerchief. Kate darted a glance at David, and was relieved to see that he had regained his composure and stood watching the proceedings with aloof disinterest.

Lawrence was given into the care of a footman who had come running from the house, and after hurling one or two largely unintelligible threats at David, was led into the house.

'My Lord Falworth,' said Lucius in an awful tone. 'I am likely to do serious damage to that puppy one of these days.'

'But, my dear fellow,' replied David plaintively, 'he is my heir, after all. I cannot have you bloodying up my relatives.'

'Umph!' was Lucius's only response as the group returned to the house.

The rest of the day passed uneventfully. Lawrence took to his room and was served dinner there, and Regina, too, chose to absent herself from the table. Thus, the conversation was considerably lighter and more convivial than it might have been. Afterward, a lively game of whist took place in the drawing room, and such was David's good humored participation that Kate could almost believe the ugly incident in the stable yard had not taken place. She noted, however, that David's sociable smiles never quite reached his eyes.

As the group finally dispersed to seek their bedchambers, Kate bade everyone good night and left the room on Aunt Fred's arm. David left the room directly behind her.

'Kate, before you go upstairs, may I have a word with you?'

She swung around at the sound of his voice, but merely smiled her acquiescence and nodded to Aunt Fred, who continued on her way with a warbled good night.

Back in the drawing room, Kate reseated herself on the confidante she had just vacated, and watched in puzzlement as David paced the floor before the fireplace, frowning in abstraction. After a moment, he looked straight at her.

'You never did get to your digging.'

'No,' replied Kate, 'but I shall probably go first thing in the morning. Would you like. . . ?'

'I am pleased that you have found something in which you can take so great an interest. Such an opportunity is not given to many of us.'

'No, I suppose not.' Kate felt as though she were feeling her way across a midnight landscape full of pitfalls. 'However,' she continued cautiously, 'you, too, now have a challenging occupation.'

He smiled at that.

'Yes, I guess challenging is the word for it.'

'It's too bad, in a way, that in all those years in Spain, you did not know that you had this to look forward to.'

David stilled. After a moment, he sighed heavily and sank slowly into a small chair opposite Kate's confidante.

'About those years in Spain. . . .' He trailed off as though uncertain of how to continue.

'Oh, David – I've never been to war, so I suppose I can't comprehend the awfulness of it, but I can imagine. I don't know how one could survive whole in heart and mind, let alone body. I grieved, and still do, at Philip's death, but watching him die must have been unbearable. I wish I could help you get through this. I wish I could heal you. If only. . . .'

David made a chopping motion with his hand as though to destroy the flow of her words before it could reach him.

'You may spare your sympathy, Kate,' said David in a voice so void of expression that she barely recognized it. 'For, you see, it was I who killed Philip.'

Chapter Eleven

She must not have heard him right, Kate thought. But she knew she had.

'W-what?' she stammered, staring at him.

'I did not kill him, precisely, but I was just as responsible for his death as though it were I who sent that ball crashing into his spine.'

She continued to stare, unable to grasp the words he uttered, for they made no sense. Had she gone mad? Or was it David, saying something unspeakable in that conversational tone, who had become deranged? Then, she looked in his eyes, and it was as though she gazed at death.

'I don't understand,' she whispered.

David closed his eyes for a moment, and then rose to stand before the fireplace. He turned away from her, staring into the flames.

'Badajoz lies on the border of Spain and Portugal. It is a fortified city, and squats on the bluff overlooking the Guadiana and Revillas rivers like a great, malevolent toad. The surrounding walls are huge – over twenty feet high and several feet thick. Nine bastions are set into them at intervals and these are some thirty feet high. The French inside the town believed the place to be impregnable, and with good reason. They used to range themselves on the parapet and call down to us, jeering and inviting us to do our worst.

'The Guadiana flows to the north of the town, and the Revillas, really a small feeder stream, follows the line of the walls to the east.

'We arrived at Badajoz on March 17, St Patrick's Day, a fact that our many Irish troopers believed boded good luck. Their trust could hardly have been more misplaced. From that day on, it rained for a solid week. The sappers dug the parallels, working hip-deep in mud. The plain between the Revillas and the wall became flooded, and it was from there, of course, that the powers-that-be decided we must launch our attack.

'Philip, as usual, had volunteered for the Forlorn Hope. That's a. . . .'

'Oh, dear God,' Kate half sobbed. 'Lucius explained to me about the Forlorn Hope. Why did Philip want to be a part of – of what must virtually have been a suicide squad?'

David's mouth twisted in a sad smile.

'Because he wanted to win a promotion. He could have purchased one, but he was determined to earn it on his own merit. The Forlorn Hope was the quickest route to that goal. When I heard of his plan, I sought him out and tried to dissuade him. I was his superior officer, and, while I could not forbid his going out, I laid out every ounce of authority I possessed to change his mind.

'Those tactics might have worked with any other young officer in the force, but it pulled no weight with Philip. `Don't be such an old woman, Davey – Major Davey, that is,' he laughed in that cajoling way of his. He said he would think over what I had said, but refused to promise anything.

'We finally attacked on the night of April sixth. It was dry and cloudy, but the Revillas was still swollen, and the land surrounding it was a sea of mud. We marched to our position at the southeast of the fortress, where we were to smash through a breach that had been made between two of the bastions.'

'And Philip was not with you then?' Kate's voice was choked, for it seemed she had not breathed since David had begun his monologue.

'No. I could not expect to see him, of course. Remember, though Philip and I were in the same division, we were in different regiments. We were to begin the attack at ten, and ahead of us crept the Forlorn Hope. I strained my eyes to see if Philip was among their number, but of course I could make out nothing in the darkness.

'We waited in position for the attack to begin, while the night settled about us like a physical presence. All was silent, except for the voices of the French sentries atop the ramparts, calling to each other. Then, fifteen minutes before we were to march, while the Forlorn

Hope was still making its way up the glacis, the sky was lit suddenly by a flaming barrage of artillery fire. We learned later that Picton's troops – the Third Division – had been spotted as they prepared for their attack farther along the wall, near the castle.

'The Forlorn Hope was mercilessly exposed in the light, and their only course was to begin the attack early. They jumped up from their positions, carrying their scaling ladders and the grass bags they used for cushions, and ran for the ditches that had been created at the foot of the walls between the palisades. These ditches were too wide to be leaped, so the stormers had to descended into them by means of their ladders.

'The rest of us came plummeting after them, and when we reached the ditches, we were met by as horrible a scene of fire and destruction as any of us had ever encountered. The whole area was alight with the blaze of artillery and musket fire, for the French were lined above us, pouring everything at their command down upon us. The ditches themselves were flooded, and were deeper than we had anticipated. On the surface floated the drowned bodies of the Forlorn Hope, and the engineers who had led them. Underneath the water were impediments strewn there by the enemy – broken tools, overturned wheelbarrows, discarded boats – all of which had been sharpened to knife-edge.'

David paused for a moment, and the silence was broken only by the crackle of the flames in the fireplace and the sound of Kate's soft sobbing. His own eyes were dry and lifeless as he gazed at her. *Save your tears, little one, for the worst is yet to come.*

'I stood for a moment, at the brink of the ditch, trying to assimilate the horror spread out before me. It seemed to me that it was no good trying to cross there. We did not know the depth of the water, and it was all too apparent that it served simply as a death trap. I have tried to tell myself that my decision to turn south and east, to where the Light Bobs were assaulting another section of the breach, was sound military thinking. There, the ditches were still dry. But, Sweet Jesus, Kate, I was more afraid of entering that patch of water, red with blood and reflected flames, and with God knew what lurking under the surface, than of anything I've ever faced in my life. As I turned to gather my men, I heard my name called out in a hoarse shout.

120

Following the sound, I saw – oh, God . . .' David's voice failed him, and it was some minutes before he could continue. 'Philip was in the water, his head just above the surface.'

' "I've caught one, Davey," he cried, his voice barely audible above the din of the firing and the screams. "Can't move. . . ."'

'Lucius was at my side, and I called to him to take the men toward the Santa Maria bastion. Then I started for Philip. I could see him clearly as I plunged into the water, for the exploding barrels of gunpowder and the flaming shells lit the whole bloody scene like a landscape from hell. I splashed toward him. Then. . . .'

He broke off.

'Yes? Then?' prompted Kate, her voice a tortured whisper.

'I don't remember,' he replied abruptly, passing a hand over his eyes. 'The next thing I knew, it was morning. I was lying on the edge of the ditch, and almost the first thing that met my eyes was his – Philip's body, floating facedown among all the other poor sods who'd given their lives in the assault.'

Kate uttered an involuntary groan. David lifted a hand toward her, then dropped it immediately to his side.

'He had a number of wounds – one ball was lodged in his spine. But that wasn't what killed him, Kate. He drowned. I was not three feet from him, and I let him drown. All I had to do was reach out, and he would have been saved. But I didn't, and that's why Philip never came home to you.'

He moved stiffly to stand in front of her. With a terrible effort, he forced himself to look into her eyes. They mirrored his own anguish, and his hands clenched with the effort it took not to take her in his arms to comfort her. He knew that such a gesture would be met only with outrage and contempt.

'I know there's nothing I can say,' he said. 'The words I'm sorry are so inadequate as to be ludicrous. I – I didn't want to tell you, but I couldn't let you go on thinking of me as a cherished friend.'

Kate said nothing, but continued to stare at him in shocked silence. He continued awkwardly. 'I don't know what you want to do now. If you feel you can't live under the same roof with me anymore – if you wish to leave Westerly' – he almost gasped at the pain the words caused him – 'I will make some sort of arrangements. . . .'

Kate interrupted. 'You can remember nothing?' she asked softly. 'You don't know how you came to be lying at the edge of the ditch? Were you hurt?'

'No. I wish I had been – I would be glad of an excuse for my ineptitude – or cowardice. But there wasn't a mark on me.'

Kate rose and moved to stand before him, her hands reaching to grasp his.

'Oh, David, how terrible for you! To know that Philip died only a few feet from you. To have to see. . . .'

David stared unbelievingly down at her.

'Did you not hear what I said?' He spoke in a harsh growl. 'Philip didn't just die – I let him die!'

To his utter astonishment, Kate simply shook her head.

'I don't believe that. I know you, David. I cannot believe that you would stand idly by while your best friend sank into that – that cesspool.'

David could only gape at her, willing the spark of hope that had sprung up at her words to expire before it could fan itself into a false warmth.

'You don't understand,' he rasped. 'I told you, I was deathly afraid of that ditch. The only explanation for my not going into it to save Philip is pure funk.'

'No, David, not you,' said Kate with calm insistence.

David fought the bile that rose in his throat, and his features hardened.

'You are very sure of yourself, Little Miss Sunshine.' He watched in bitter satisfaction as Kate's startled gaze lifted to his. 'How pleasant it would be if you had the slightest idea of what you are talking about.'

An expression of anguished confusion crept into Kate's eyes, and she lifted a hand as though in protest. Ignoring his own rising agony, David continued in a harsh tone. 'You say you know me so well?' He barked in a parody of laughter. 'You do not. My God, what do you know of fear? Tucked safely away in this little green paradise, and swathed in your impenetrable innocence.'

'David!' Kate's voice was choked with pain. 'I. . . .'

'Fear is not something that can be overcome by nobility of soul. I have seen good men wet their britches at the first sounds of battle, and cry out for their mothers at the first sight of blood. I had thought I was above all that, but in the final analysis, I proved as craven as the most lily-livered recruit. No, never mind,' he grated, as Kate opened her mouth to cry out in protest. 'Spare your sympathy. It is wasted on me. Cry for your brother, if you will – not for your brother's murderer.'

But, Kate did not cry. She stood before him, white-faced and silent, a blind expression in her eyes. Goaded, David continued, expending with an effort the last of his will to alienate the young woman who stood before him. 'Just go, now, goddamn it. We have no more to say to each other.'

Kate hesitated, her eyes wide with misery. For a moment David thought she meant to respond to the unforgivable things he had just said. She lifted a hand to him, but then turned, and with great precision, made her way from the room.

David sank into a chair and buried his face in his hands. He sat thus for several minutes before himself exiting the room. On entering his chambers, he found Curle waiting for him. The valet hurried to him.

'Yer late t'bed this evenin', Ma – my lord. Will ye. . . ?' he stopped short. 'What is it? Are ye hurtin' then? Here, let me. . . .'

David silenced his man with an angry gesture.

'Yes, I hurt, and I wish to be left alone.'

'Now, now, then my lord, let old Curle help ye, and we'll have ye right and tight as soon as the cat can lick her ear.'

The gaze David bent on the valet was murderous.

'Loyal to the core, eh Curle?' he snarled. 'The more fool you.' He turned away from the bewildered surprise in Curle's face. 'Just – leave me.'

As Curle moved to the door, David tossed over his shoulder, 'Send up a bottle of brandy.'

Sighing heavily, Curle closed the door behind him.

When the brandy arrived some minutes later, David uncorked it, leaving the delicate crystal glass that accompanied it behind on the tray, and sank into a shabby, velvet-covered chair by the fire. Then, for the second time in his life, he proceeded to drink himself into insensibility.

*

In her own bedchamber, Kate dismissed her maid and stood in the center of the room, staring blindly before her. Dear Lord, she thought in desolation, what hell David must have gone through. The words he had just hurled at her had scarcely penetrated her mind, for she knew they had been prompted by the need to turn her against him, thus providing even more punishment for his supposed transgressions.

To watch his best friend die before his eyes was bad enough, but to suffer the exquisite torture of believing himself responsible for that death must be almost unbearable. No wonder David had nightmares. And she, in sublime insensibility had thought herself competent to probe his emotional wounds!

She lifted her head as a sudden thought struck her. Was it guilt that had driven David to volunteer for the Forlorn Hope himself? Lucius had mentioned the mad risks that he had begun to take. Had he felt compelled to offer his own life in propitiation for the life he had failed to save? She felt sick at the thought.

And was it guilt, she wondered, that had made him give up on his injury? Perhaps he felt he deserved the pain and immobility that would curse him for the rest of his life. She sank onto the bed and rubbed her eyes with a shaking hand. She would give anything she possessed to help David climb out of the pit of shame and remorse he had dug for himself, but she didn't know how. She raged silently at her own inadequacy.

As she slid beneath the coverlet, another thought occurred to her. She had, without thinking, repudiated David's guilt in Philip's death. Her first thought had not been of Philip at all, but rather of the alleviation of David's torment. Why had she been so ready to believe in his innocence? His explanation certainly held more logic than her frantic, exculpatory theories. What if his assessment were correct? Had he turned coward when his friend's life was on the line? Her fists curled into balls at her sides. No! To be sure, the David who had whispered his tale of horror tonight was not the David she had grown up with. He was changed – tragically so, but – *no* – she would have sensed such a cataclysmic reversal of character. Something had happened to David in that river of fire, something so dreadful his mind would not allow him to comprehend it.

She raised her eyes sightlessly to the ceiling. 'Please, God,' she whispered. 'Please.' She turned to bury her face in her pillow, unable to put her prayer into words.

Chapter Twelve

'Good heavens, Kate,' Regina spoke sharply. 'Can you not come out of the sullens for just a few moments? One would think you were on the way to the guillotine instead of on a pleasant outing. What on earth is the matter with you this morning?'

Kate withdrew her gaze from the landscape that flowed past the carriage window.

'I'm sorry, Aunt, I was woolgathering.' She glanced at Cilla, who sat by her side. 'Do you plan to buy anything in Bath?'

In contrast to Kate, that young lady seemed in excellent spirits.

'I don't know,' she replied, smiling. 'We shall be in our blacks for sometime to come, of course, so I shan't want to be decking myself out, but I had thought to purchase some ribbon, perhaps, and a length of lace.'

' "Ribbons and laces for pretty girls' faces," ' hummed Lady Fred from her seat next to Regina.

'And you, Aunt?' Kate turned once more to Regina.

'No, I, too, have all I require for the present. In any event, I should now fear to purchase so much as a reticule for fear of my lord earl's displeasure.'

She shot a malevolent glance out the window, where David, in company with Lawrence, Crawford, and Lucius rode on horseback beside the carriage.

'No,' she continued, 'I shall probably make a few calls, but my purpose in traveling to town is to assure that David makes the proper choice in clothing for himself. It took the combined efforts of Lawrence and myself as well as Mr Pelham, and, I understand his own

126

valet, to talk him into this trip.'

Kate, too, watched David as he cantered in remote silence. She had not spoken to him for two days. Indeed, it was only too apparent that he was avoiding her, for on meeting her in the corridor outside the library the evening before, he had dropped his eyes and merely murmured something unintelligible before continuing hurriedly on his way.

When Regina had suggested in a bright tone of voice at breakfast this morning, that it was high time for David to make his promised foray into the tailoring establishment in Bath favored by the family, Kate's hopes had risen. For, her ladyship insisted, since the day was fine, they should make a family expedition of the outing. 'The servants can open the town house for our use during the day. And,' she added for emphasis, 'there will be a full moon tonight, so we shan't have to worry about getting home by dark.'

David, however, had maintained his detachment from her, agreeing to the journey, but making it plain that it was no wish of his that the ladies of the house be included in the journey. This, of course, held no weight with her ladyship, thus a full complement of Merritts, and their guest, jangled along the road to Bath.

'Have you any errands in town, Aunt Fred?' asked Kate.

'As a matter of fact,' the old lady replied, smoothing her silken skirts, 'I would like to stop in at Godwin's to purchase some writing paper, and I must go to that place in Stall Street for some of their lovely green wool.'

'Kate,' interjected Cilla, 'we must go up to Mrs Vivier's confectionery shop. It's in Brock Street – number thirty-two, I think, and she sells the most scrumptious meringues. When I was at Miss Sedgewick's seminary, we used to scamper up Gay Street and positively gallop across the Circus to buy them.' She shot a glance at her mother. 'That was, of course, before I grew to be a young lady.'

Regina smiled and tapped her daughter's hand. 'I'm not sure I should allow you to jaunter about the town without your maid, but since there will be the two of you – and since we are, after all, in Bath, I suppose it will be unexceptionable. Be sure to return to Falworth House in time for luncheon, however. Afterward, perhaps, you might like to show Mr Pelham around the town a little – the Pump Room, of course, and the Abbey, with Lawrence and Kate to keep you company.'

'Oh,' replied Kate quickly, 'but perhaps Aunt Fred will require some assistance. Milsom Street is quite steep, after all.' She shot the plump little woman an anguished glance.

'Nonsense.' Regina's voice was calm and authoritative. 'I shall accompany her, of course, and we shall hire a chair. Will that be all right with you, my dear?' Her question was directed at Aunt Fred, who opened her mouth as though in dispute. The countess continued quickly. 'We shall have a footman with us to carry any parcels we may accumulate.'

Aunt Fred shrugged apologetically at Kate, then settled back in her seat and popped a morsel of toffee into her mouth.

'But, Aunt Regina,' continued Kate in some desperation. 'Won't Lawrence be busy? I mean, he seems particularly anxious to assist in the selection of David's attire.'

'Nonsense,' repeated her ladyship. 'David has informed me that he does not intend to 'rig himself out,' as he puts it. As I understand it, he merely wishes to dress as modestly as possible while still maintaining his new station in life. They will have assuredly made all their purchases by lunchtime. If not, I'm sure Mr Pelham's advice can be trusted.'

Cilla's brown gaze traveled outside the carriage to Lucius's impeccable form. 'Oh, yes,' she breathed. 'Mr Pelham dresses exquisitely.'

Regina smiled fondly at her daughter.

'Yes, his good taste is always evident,' she said.

Kate caught Aunt Fred's eye, and turned her head to hide her own smile. It was amazing how Lucius had risen in her ladyship's estimation since she had discovered the existence of a wealthy father in his background.

The Avon could be seen now, flowing in its ancient course beside the old Roman road, and it was not long before the carriage pulled up before the front door of the Falworth town house in Henrietta Street.

Disembarkation was accomplished, and after fortifying cups of tea for the ladies and tankards of ale for the gentlemen, the group dispersed, each to their own pursuits.

Kate watched David disappear in the company of his half brothers and Lucius, noting with disappointment that, though he had bade farewell to Aunt Regina and Aunt Fred – even Cilla coming in for a nod, he had not so much as looked her way before setting off.

A flicker of anger began to stir within her. Why was he treating her this way? She had done nothing but offer her sympathy, and he had lashed out at her like a wounded beast. She was not responsible for his pain, yet it was she who was being punished for it. Why would he not let her help him?

The next moment she chastised herself for being childishly insensitive. A human being in pain was just as likely to lash out as was a wounded animal, and could no more be held responsible. Her own hurt feelings faded to insignificance beside David's anguish. She would help him, she vowed, but she must be patient.

With a sigh, she turned to Cilla, who was burbling in her delight at being away from the dismal confines of a home in mourning.

'Come *on*, Kate,' she cried. 'Don't be such a slowcoach. Let's go first to Mrs Vivier's!'

The girl waved to her mother and Lady Fred, who were being deposited in their sedan chairs with utmost tenderness by the footmen who had accompanied the carriage on its short journey from Westerly to Bath. Then, she grasped Kate's hand and drew her away toward Gay Street.

Kate resolutely turned her thoughts away from David, determined to enjoy her rare outing, and it was not long before she found herself strolling along George Street at Cilla's side, nibbling one of the coveted meringues.

'Good heavens, look at that bonnet,' said Cilla, indicating a shop window with one sticky finger. 'Who would be seen in such a creation?'

'Yes,' agreed Kate judiciously, 'so very deedy, isn't it? But look at the one next to it. Quite lovely, don't you think?'

'Mmm, yes, I suppose. I don't at all care for the color of the ribbons, although I understand that peach blossom is all the rage now.'

The two young ladies walked in silence for another few moments before Cilla spoke in a hesitant voice. 'Tell me, Kate, what do you think of Lucius Pelham?'

Kate glanced at the girl in some surprise. Though only two years apart in age, she and Cilla had never been close. In fact, Kate could not recall ever having been the recipient of a confidence from her young cousin.

'Um, well, he seems like a nice young man,' she replied cautiously.

'I only ask because the two of you seem to be on such friendly terms.' Cilla's gaze dropped to the pavement. 'That is, you and David have always been close, and Mr Pelham is David's best friend.'

'Yes, I suppose that's true.' Now what is all this in aid of, she wondered.

'Has he ever mentioned being – well, involved with anyone?'

'You mean, as in affianced?' asked Kate in some amusement.

'Well, yes – or perhaps an – understanding with a lady?'

'I don't recall his ever mentioning anything like that, but I have really not had that much conversation with him.'

'Oh. Well, I only wondered.' Cilla's expression was casual. 'I mean, I'm surprised that he isn't married, or betrothed, or – something.' She trailed off uncertainly.

'That hardly seems surprising. He's been out of the country for several years.' Kate laughed. 'Or did you picture him scooped up by some Spanish belle?'

'It would not be surprising if he had,' returned Cilla seriously. 'I'm sure he could have had his pick of any of them. He's very handsome, don't you think?'

'Indeed, he's very well-looking. And charming, too.' And so plump in the pocket, thought Kate, though that particular attribute was no doubt of more interest to Cilla's mama than to Cilla.

The two ladies turned into Milsom Street and entered a fashionable draper's establishment, where they soon became engrossed in the selection of ribbons and laces that might be thought proper for the embellishment of mourning blacks.

David, too, was in the throes of choice. He stood among a welter of fabric swatches and pattern cards, feeling very much like a somewhat inferior horse set up for auction. Lucius and Lawrence perused the cards in absorbed silence, while Crawford sat some distance away in bored attention.

'This morning coat, I think,' said Lucius finally, 'in the Bath suiting.'

'Mmp,' sniffed Lawrence. 'Seems a bit drab, but perhaps with a waistcoat of that primrose figured satin. . . .'

'Oh, my God,' replied Lucius, wincing. 'No. Figured, perhaps, but of a gray or white silk. We'll save the satin for evening wear.'

Lawrence huffed protestingly. 'Lord, you'll have him looking like a parson.'

'Better a parson than a Bond Street beau. Now, for afternoon wear – for you will eventually have to receive callers, you know, David, this superfine will be adequate. One or two in mulberry, the rest in shades of dark blue.'

'Oh, but can't you see?' jibed Crawford. 'Poor Lawrence has already set his heart on that yaller stuff over there.'

'Fustian!' snorted Lawrence.

'My dear boy!' replied Lucius, deliberately misunderstanding. 'Fustian is unthinkable.'

Crawford snickered.

'But . . .' cried Lawrence, incensed. Lucius, however, had turned his attention to another set of drawings. 'You won't be attending many evening functions out here in the wilderness, David, and I shouldn't think the family will be giving any large dinner parties in the near future, so for now, I should think three or four evening suits will do.'

Here, David felt it necessary to intervene. 'Lucius, I appreciate your efforts, but I am trying to practice a little economy here. I do not require a cupboard full of morning and afternoon coats. I certainly don't need more than one evening rig, and I already have that.'

'You mean that set you bought in Canterbury right after you got out of the hospital? You can't be serious! You look like an underprivileged footman in that outfit. Besides, it probably doesn't fit anymore. You've filled out some in the last couple of weeks.'

David sighed in defeat and watched gloomily as his friend and his half brother wrangled over breeches, pantaloons, shirts, handkerchiefs, and cravats.

In a few moments, his thoughts, as they had for the past two days, shifted back to his verbal attack on Kate. He should be pleased with himself, he thought grimly. He had accomplished his goal of setting Kate apart from him permanently. Oh, she had disputed his confession, but her demeanor when she hastened from the room had indicated her deep disturbance at his revelations. A little reflection on her part, he was sure, would serve to disabuse her of any remnants of her affection.

But, God, how he missed her already. Without her laughter and their shared confidences, the day was just so many hours to get through before he could lose himself again in the oblivion of sleep. How was he to get through the rest of his life? To be sure, she would not live at Westerly indefinitely. She would marry – probably within a year or two, once she achieved her majority and moved into her own establishment in London. Then, surely, he would be free of his desire for her.

He looked up suddenly, and with coating material draped across his shoulders, and a tailor busy at him with chalk and pins, David realized that he would never be free of Kate Millbank because he was hopelessly, irretrievably, and permanently in love with her.

For a moment, he simply stood in appalled silence, oblivious to the murmuring of the tailor, and the increasingly fractious stream of advice issuing from his two counselors. How could he have been so stupid as to let this happen? How could he have been such a fool that he did not realize the inevitability of loving her? During all the years of his absence from Westerly, he had thought of Kate as a little sister. He had blindly assumed that he would continue doing so. Though, he should have known the moment he felt his heart catch as she descended the stairs that first evening, dressed in that clinging silk gown, her hair a glorious blaze in the candlelight.

He contemplated the emptiness of the years ahead of him. Years of mouthing friendly commonplaces to her. Years of longing to put his lips against the brightness of that hair and on the curved softness of her lips. A wayward notion flickered in his brain for an instant. Was there a chance that in time Kate might cease to think of him as friend and confidante – that she might come to think of him as. . . ? You fool, he thought savagely, and the idea died aborning.

Why should Kate, who undoubtedly could have any man who brightened her eye, choose him, an impecunious peer with a debt-ridden estate? More importantly, how could she possibly think of an alliance with the man responsible for her brother's death?

There was also the all-too-real possibility that she had already given her heart to Lawrence. He could feel his insides curl at the idea. She had assured him she had no interest in his half brother, yet look at the way she had hurled herself in a protective frenzy over Lawrence's prostrate body the other day after that painful confrontation in the stable yard. He winced at the memory of the hurt her seemingly instinctive gesture had contributed to the anguish inflicted by Lawrence's jibes.

Added to these stark ruminations was the underlying conviction that Kate was bound to interpret any lover-like behavior on his part as the act of the veriest fortune hunter. Their relationship had been long and close, but it had never been comprised of more than strong friendship. Now, suddenly, he had a pressing need for cash. Would Kate not see his abrupt about-face to ardent suitor as more than coincidence? His lips curled in self-disgust.

'But, really, David. Nothing out of the way here.'

With a start, David turned his attention to Lucius. 'What?' he asked blankly.

'The handkerchiefs. Nothing to disapprove of here, old man. The linen is quite fine, and very reasonable. I have ordered your crest embroidered in the corner. That is, of course de rigueur.'

David waved his hand impatiently and began divesting himself of the length of superfine being pinned into place, to the agitated squeakings of Mr Dilson, the tailor.

Lucius, incorrectly inferring from David's expression that his leg must be paining him, indicated to the tailor that the session was at an end.

'No, never mind,' he said. 'We have pretty much concluded our business. Anyway,' he added, taking his watch from his pocket, 'we must be on our way. It's time to join the ladies for lunch.'

Lawrence, after a last, wistful gaze at the primrose satin, picked up hat, cane, and gloves preparatory to leaving the tailor's shop. Crawford lounged behind him, and with a sigh, David followed.

Ah, yes, he thought, the ladies.

Chapter Thirteen

The group gathered around the luncheon table, with two exceptions, chatted amiably of the morning's accomplishments. While Cilla burbled happily to Crawford of her purchases, and Aunt Fred exclaimed in satisfaction over her acquisition of several skeins of the most exquisitely colored wools, Kate surreptitiously watched David push cold beef and salad around his plate in silent, endless circles.

'And what,' Regina exclaimed brightly, 'have you children in mind for the rest of the day?'

At this, David looked up. 'I thought we would be returning to Westerly,' he said. 'I have much to do there.'

'But no!' cried her ladyship prettily. 'Since we have made the trip into town, it would be a shame not to make the most of it.' She turned to Lucius. 'Would you not like to see more of the sights of Bath, now that we are here?'

'Yes, indeed, I would,' exclaimed Lucius stoutly, ignoring David's minatory stare. 'I don't suppose the place has changed all that much since I was a boy, but still, I barely remember it.'

'Splendid!' Regina beamed. 'Then a tour is definitely in order. Cilla, would you be amenable to acting as guide? Kate will go with you, of course, and I know Lawrence will be delighted to accompany you.'

Lawrence's face did not indicate delight or anything close to it. He had resumed his familiar expression of sulky boredom, and he opened his mouth to protest his mother's dictum. As usual, it took only one steely glance to silence him.

'Well,' said David grudgingly. 'I suppose I could look in on Smollett, while you're all busy. If he's in his office, I have some matters to discuss with him.'

'*Au contraire*, my lad.' Lucius spoke in a voice not to be brooked. 'Today has been officially declared a holiday by your stepmama, and it would be rude to gainsay her.'

Staring at him, Regina nodded in wary acknowledgment, and Lucius continued. 'So, we shall all make the tour. May we start at the Pump Room? I daresay you will find the waters of benefit, David – to your disposition if nothing else.'

David flushed, but said nothing more, and shortly the entire party, minus Aunt Fred who had announced her intention of immersing herself in the library book she had procured at Godwin's along with her writing paper, sallied forth in the direction of Great Pulteney Bridge and the town center.

It was not long before David realized he was actually enjoying himself. He took a nostalgic pleasure in strolling about the Pump Room, relaxing in the muted chatter that surrounded him and noting that the valetudinarians who raised cups of the steaming mineral water in shaking hands, were apparently the same as those he had encountered on his last visit, over six years ago. Unthinking, he shot an amused glance at Kate and surprised an answering twinkle in her eyes. Hastily, he turned his attention to his own cup.

The Cross Bath and the Hot Bath were next on the agenda, along with the nearby Colonnades. A few streets away, Kate pointed out a recently discovered Roman site that had come to light during the construction of new buildings. The group then made their way to the Guildhall, where Lucius exclaimed in suitably awed accents at the Banqueting Hall. The Abbey, Regina had saved for last, determined that in its cloistered shadows, Cilla should at last have the eligible Mr Pelham to herself. So busy was she in her machinations that she neglected to instruct Lawrence as to a like strategy with Kate. When she looked around, both her sons had disappeared no doubt into some low ale shop, she raged inwardly. And where were Kate and David? She peered into the dimly lit depths of the cathedral, but they, too had vanished. Muttering a distinctly unladylike epithet under her breath, she began to search for them.

In another part of the church, Kate slipped into a small chapel near the sanctuary. Noting gratefully that it was empty, she sank into one

135

of the pews, closed her eyes, and gave herself up to reflection. So unpleasant were her ruminations, however, that she was almost relieved when she heard footsteps approaching. Suddenly, she knew, even before she opened her eyes, who had come to interrupt her solitude.

David, entering the little chapel, was immediately aware that he was not alone there. He started, peering at the figure who sat in the shadows.

'I beg your pardon,' he began, as he moved to retreat. Then . . . 'Kate?'

Kate rose from her seat. 'Yes, it is I, David. No, I'll leave. You have expended enough effort in avoiding me.'

'Kate!' David repeated, this time in a voice ragged with anguish. He stood squarely in the entrance to the chapel, and Kate waited, eyes downcast, for him to move aside. He did not do so, but remained like a sinner frozen in stained glass, gazing at a vision of Heaven denied.

Kate, her own voice catching, laughed softly. 'I've always loved the name of this chapel – The Prior Birde Chantry. A place for singing named after a prior called Birde.'

There was no answering smile in David's eyes, but, taking her hand, he led her back to where she had been seated.

'You're right, my dear, I have been avoiding you. Foolish of me, I know, but after our – conversation the other night, I simply don't know what to say to you.'

'Perhaps you think it is I who should be avoiding you?'

'Well – yes. Knowing what you know about me, now. . . .'

'And what is it I know about you?' Kate held her breath.

David's answer came in a rush of bitterness. 'Do you wish to punish me further by making me repeat it all? Knowing that my cowardice killed your brother, of course.'

Kate took another deep breath and uttered a silent prayer before speaking in a steady voice. 'Yes, I do believe you have acted the coward.'

David whitened, but before he could respond she spoke again. 'Not on the night Philip was killed, but since then. I believe that deep down you know you would not have acted so, but you are afraid to trust in yourself. You have heaped punishment and abuse upon your head until now you have begun to wallow in it.'

Kate watched as David, gazing at her with eyes like stones, tensed as though ready to turn away. She grasped his sleeve.

'Please, David. I do not say these things to wound you. Nor did I express my belief in you the other night in order to excuse you. Good God, did you think I was just spouting sympathetic nonsense? Philip was my brother! I loved him more than anyone else in the world. If I thought that you were in any way responsible, I would never have anything to do with you again.'

David held her gaze, but said nothing, and Kate continued softly. 'I only want to help, my dearest friend.'

At this, he stiffened and pulled away from her.

'You have no right,' he growled.

As soon as he uttered the words, David would have given all he possessed to have them back. Stricken, Kate took a step backward, and he knew he could have said nothing that would have given her more pain. Unconsciously, he raised a hand toward her.

A rush of footsteps suddenly bore down on them.

'Here you are, you naughty children!' Regina's lips were smiling, but her eyes spit fire. 'Why ever have you hidden yourselves away here? It is growing quite late. Lawrence and Crawford are outside, and Cilla and Mr Pelham await us as well. Come now, we mustn't keep everyone standing about.'

As she spoke, she interposed herself between Kate and David, and began urging them out of the little chapel. David cast one last desperate glance at Kate, but she had averted her eyes and turned to walk down the church aisle behind Regina.

It seemed to Kate that the ride home from Bath lasted an eternity. At David's urging, the gentlemen rode ahead of the carriage, and he was nowhere to be seen when the ladies arrived at Westerly. Pleading a headache, Kate fled to the sanctuary of her room, where she sank into her favorite faded armchair. She curled into a ball of misery and, as the room faded into darkness, she pondered mournfully on the day's events.

'*You have no right.*'

The words reverberated in her heart, slashing and splintering, until she felt as though she must be bleeding inside. Why had he spoken so to her? Despite the changes his long absence from Westerly had wrought in him, she had believed him to be her friend. She could have sworn that their relationship was more than that of distant cousins – that his affection for her, and hers for him, had warmed him and helped him through the last few difficult weeks. But, he could not have more clearly indicated that she had no real place in his life.

What was she to do now? To be sure, Westerly was large enough so that its inhabitants, with only a small effort, could avoid meeting each other in its multitude of wings and passages. Thus, she and David could coexist for years, she supposed, without any meaningful contact.

No. She couldn't bear that. For so long she had yearned for his return to Westerly. Now that he was here, she knew she would find it impossible to share his home on such a basis. She would reach her majority in less than a year, and she would be mistress of her own destiny. She would flee Westerly and move to London where she would do nothing but go to parties and balls. Or perhaps she would set up an establishment in Brighton. She had always loved the sea, and Brighton was so very fashionable. She would lead a life gay to dissipation. She would never think of David Merritt again. He could wallow in his guilt for the rest of his life; it didn't matter one whit to her.

A light tap at the door interrupted this wholly unsuccessful attempt to bring herself out of the dismals. It was followed by the entrance of Aunt Fred and a footman bearing a tray.

'I thought I'd find you here,' said the old woman. She directed the footman to place the food-laden tray on a small table near the fireplace and pulled up a chair to seat herself.

When the servant had departed, she gestured impatiently to Kate, who had risen at her entrance. 'Sit down, child. It's quite late, and you must be famished. I know I am.' So saying, she began arranging plates, cutlery, and glassware.

'Aunt Fred, this is very good of you. . . .' began Kate.

'But you're really not hungry. Is that what you're going to tell me? It's no wonder, with you sitting here in the dark in a fit of the mopes. Now sit, and tell me about this quarrel you've had with David.'

'How did you kn. . . ? That is, what makes you think. . . ?'

'Oh, for heaven's sake, Kate. Anyone with two eyes in his head could tell, what with you silent as a bed post all the way back from Bath, and David galloping off as though he were being chased by Satan and all his minions.'

Kate expelled a shuddering sigh. 'It is of no importance, really. Simply put, David has made it clear to me that our friendship means nothing to him, and . . .' Tears sprang to her eyes, and her voice broke. 'And, he wishes me to stop interfering in his life.'

Angry with herself for revealing so much of her inner turmoil, she sat down and poured herself a glass of lemonade. She fixed a bright smile on her face. 'Tell me, Aunt Fred, how would you feel about moving to Brighton with me next year?'

Lady Frederica's hand paused briefly as she ladled out a portion of soup and handed it to Kate. She served herself as well before she replied in a calm voice. 'No, I think not. I'm quite happy here, and Brighton is always as full as it can hold with the Regent's set. Ramshackle bunch, I've always thought. I don't think you'd like it there, either. You love Westerly, almost as much as David does.'

Kate choked. 'Yes, well that's neither here nor there. I must leave Westerly some time, and it might as well be sooner than later.'

'I see. Did David tell you that he wants you to leave?'

'No – that is, not precisely, but he made it perfectly clear. . . .'

'Yes, you already said that. Tell me, my dear, what did he say – precisely?'

After a moment's hesitation, Kate said slowly, 'I'm afraid I can't tell you, Aunt Fred. It would mean revealing a part of David's life that I don't think he wishes anyone else to know about right now.'

Lady Frederica eyed her speculatively. 'Yet he told you. Would it have anything to do with his dreadful nightmares?'

Kate's eyes widened. 'How could you know about those? But, of course, I might have known nothing could go on in this house without your knowledge. Yes,' she finished painfully. 'He suffered a – horrible experience in Spain that still haunts him.'

'And you would leave him to deal with the problem himself.'

'That's just the point. I tried to help him, and he shut me out.' She gulped at her lemonade in order to forestall the tears that threatened again.

'David is a proud man, Kate. I think it is hard for him to accept help.'

'But, I am his friend!' cried Kate. 'Or, at least I thought I was. Besides, he seems to feel he's beyond help.'

The old woman sighed. 'That is very bad, indeed. But you must not give up, child. The relationship between you and David' – she paused to glance sharply at Kate – 'is very special. You must remain his friend, for he does need one, whether he will admit it or not. And,' she finished with a comforting smile, 'I would wager my second best cap that he didn't mean it when he told you to bugger off.'

'Aunt!' gasped Kate. 'Where do you *learn* these things. Surely the footmen don't speak so around you!'

Lady Frederica chuckled delightedly. 'The stable hands like toffee, too. In addition to my other failings, my dear, I fear I have an affinity for low company. Don't worry, I don't speak so in Polite Society – present company excepted, of course. Although, it might be worth my complete ostracism to watch Regina's face just once, if I. . . .'

'Please, Aunt,' Kate begged. 'Don't.'

The two broke into laughter then, and Kate suddenly found that she was hungry after all.

Yet, when she retired some hours later, her sleep was troubled. Angry black eyes haunted her dreams, and a harsh voice cried endlessly, 'You have no right! . . . no right . . . no right!'

She woke early, unrefreshed, and knowing she would not return to sleep, she slid from her bed. She could not face anyone this morning. Though light had barely broken through the window hangings, she slipped on her work clothes and made her way through silent corridors to the stables. There, she saddled her little mare and set off at a hurried pace toward the villa.

To her astonishment, when she arrived at the outcropping, she found Barney, the bay used by David, tethered there, and heard the sound of digging coming from behind the trees that hid the entrance to the remains. For a moment, she knew an urge to flee but instead, dismounted and tied her horse next to Barney.

She had no sooner begun to make her way toward the villa, when David himself emerged. He moved slowly along the slope, his eyes fastened on hers.

He, too, had passed an uncomfortable night. Over and over he had berated himself for the reprehensible way he had behaved toward Kate. Reprehensible and stupid. He had denied himself the opportunity to seek her love. Why had he effectively cut himself off from her friendship as well? Was he buffleheaded enough to think it would assuage his pain if she never spoke to him again?

He anxiously scanned her face, and what he saw there was not encouraging. She was pale, and her gaze, though not actively hostile, was not welcoming. When he reached her, he stood for a moment, then put out his hand.

'It seems that once more I must apologize for my ill temper.' The smile that accompanied these words was tight and painful, and it drew no answering lightening of her face. He continued doggedly.

'Will you talk with me?'

Still she did not answer, but looked back at him gravely before seating herself on a nearby boulder.

'I have been doing a lot of thinking since our, er, conversation yesterday. In fact, the reason I am out here at such an ungodly hour is that I couldn't stand my bed anymore and felt this would be a good place to escape my thoughts.'

Kate swallowed a smile, for this had been her own purpose in her flight into the dawn. Encouraged, David continued. 'I had no right to speak to you as I did,' he said slowly. 'And I did not mean what I said – about your having no right to say the things you did. You have every right to say anything you see fit to me.'

Kate's throat tightened. 'Then why did you. . . ?'

'Because I cannot bear that you should continue under a gross misapprehension in your perception of me. You persist in thinking kindly about me, and' – he drew a deep breath – 'that is the worst punishment you could deal me.'

Kate opened her mouth to speak, but then closed her lips firmly.

'Nothing,' he continued soberly, 'can excuse what I did – or, rather, what I failed to do. That is something I will have to learn to live with.' His mouth twisted in a rigid smile. 'I suppose I should be grateful that you have not cast me into outer darkness.' He rose, and grasping Kate's hands, pulled her to her feet. 'Your – friendship means a great deal to me, Kate.'

141

Kate felt suddenly breathless at his nearness. His eyes as they reached into hers brimmed with warmth, and it seemed to her that something besides friendship lay hidden in their black depths. The pounding of her heart was astonishingly loud in her ears.

Abruptly, David released her and turned away toward the entrance to the villa. 'See what I have found,' he called. 'I decided to do a little more shoring up in the front rooms, and in one corner, behind a fallen beam there is hidden a small painting.'

Kate scrambled up the path behind him, and accepted the lantern David handed her at the entrance. She followed him into the shadowy recesses of the ruined villa, and stopped when he raised his light.

Her eyes widened. She was staring into the face of a young man. His hair curled darkly over a broad brow and eyes of deepest ebony. Of his clothing, only the top of a light-colored tunic could be seen, and the beginnings of what looked like a leather corselet.

Without turning her head, she whispered in astonishment, 'But, David. It – it's a portrait of you!'

Chapter Fourteen

David looked blankly at Kate, then back at the portrait. 'I see no resemblance,' he said, puzzled.

Kate examined the drawing more carefully. Did the young man portrayed really look like David? Or was it merely the coincidence of hair and eye color? Her gaze traveled along the painted features. This man's face was a trifle fuller, and he lacked David's angular bone structure. Yet, there was something . . . She stiffened. It was his eyes! They were hard and haunted, their gaze anguished. She might have been exchanging glances with the flesh and blood man beside her!

'Perhaps I was mistaken,' she said carefully. 'It is something in his – attitude, perhaps. Yes, that's it.' She turned to David. 'I believe he was a soldier. Oh, David! Do you think he was the owner of the villa?'

David held the lantern higher, frowning.

'I suppose it is possible.' Carefully, he brushed dust and mold from the portrait. 'The painting is pretty faded, and – oh, my God!'

Kate, too, had drawn her breath in quickly, for across the soldier's cheek lay an ugly scar, carving a path from temple to chin.

'Dear heaven,' she breathed. 'He must have received that in battle – and look, if he had turned his face a little the other way when posing, the scar could hardly have been seen, but he chose to tilt his head so that the viewer cannot escape it. Why would he wish to display his pain so boldly, I wonder?'

'Why, indeed,' murmured David. He remained staring at the picture for some moments. Then, shaking his head, he gestured toward the lower part of the painting.

'Look here,' he said in a voice that was little more than a whisper. 'In the corner! It looks like a signature.'

Kate strained to see. 'Yes! Yes, it must be, although it's so faded and moldy it's hard to be sure. Is the first letter an *L*?'

'I think so, but that's all I can make out. Leonidas, perhaps?'

'Or, Longinus?'

David reached for his sketch pad and began to trace the lines of the face before him, but Kate turned her gaze toward the villa entrance. 'It's such a lovely day,' she said. 'Would you like to sketch outside? The last time I was here, I uncovered what I think is part of a stone wall. I found no artifacts, so it's not very exciting, but I believe a record should be made of it.'

'Very well,' responded David. 'I'm a little tired of all this ancient gloom, anyway.'

The two made their way into the sunlight, where they spent a companionable hour with spade and pencil. At last, David rose stiffly to his feet and held out his hand to Kate.

'I must be getting back,' he said, easing limbs stiff from sitting. 'Are you ready to return as well, or did you plan to spend the morning here?'

Kate, too, straightened and began to move toward the villa entrance, tools in hand. 'No, I promised Aunt Fred to help sort the wool she purchased yesterday, and after that I have to get some things together for my visit to the tenants at Northedge.'

David swung around in surprise. 'Northedge! That's almost an hour's ride. How often do you do that? Do you visit the other tenants as well?'

'Oh yes,' she replied casually. 'I take one day a week for my visits. It seems someone is always ailing or in need of an extra bit of food. I take medicines and things like soups and stews for the older folks who are unable to work anymore, and I generally bring toys and books for the youngsters.'

'Books? Can the children read?'

'Well' – Kate laughed ruefully – 'not terribly well. I've encouraged the parents – those who can read themselves – to teach them their letters, and I read to them from time to time to show them the pleasures of the written word. It is my hope that perhaps someday we can have a real school here for them.'

'Pettigrew told me,' said David slowly, 'that you have taken an interest in the estate, but I had no idea that you were so involved in its workings.'

Kate blushed until her cheeks matched the fire of her hair. How soon she had forgotten her vow to leave Westerly at the earliest possible moment! What must he think of her presumption? She had always known she had no business playing lady of the manor, but she had never analyzed her need to do so. Perhaps it was because Westerly seemed a paradise to her, and the inhabitants of paradise, of course, must all be happy and healthy.

'I know it's not my place. . . .' she stammered, but David took her hands in his.

'Of course it's your place,' he said roughly. 'You're an integral part of this family, and I can only be grateful that at least one of its members is more interested in trying to improve things here than in spending our profits as fast as they come in.'

Kate blushed even more furiously, then berated herself for turning into a quivering jelly at a compliment from an old friend. She turned from him, and continued on her path toward the villa. In her haste, she stumbled and, though she managed to right herself, David sprang forward to gather her in his arms.

Kate stilled, suddenly aware of the pounding of his heart against her cheek. Her own pulses raced, and her arms moved without volition to clasp him in return. At that moment, David stepped back so abruptly that she nearly lost her balance.

She looked at him questioningly, but he bent to pick up his pad and pencils. Then he limped around the outcropping, leaving Kate to return her tools in silence. Silently, she berated herself. It had happened again! Why did the feel of David's arms around her arouse in her the appalling desire to curl into him like a bird settling into its nest? She stood for a moment in the coolness of the villa's interior before going out to join him.

David had already managed to mount himself on Barney, and Kate knew a moment of relief that she would not be required to go to his assistance. She could bear no more of his closeness. She flicked a glance at David, but he was busy with bridle and reins.

'Tell me more about your plans for the school,' he said as they cantered toward the house.

'The. . . ? Oh. Yes. Well, I have no plans, exactly.' She laughed shakily. 'Just a few ideas. Due to the distances involved, we would need two sites, and that, of course, would mean two sets of books and other supplies, and, of course, two teachers.'

She had by now recovered her equilibrium, and went on to speak at some length of her hopes for the tenant children.

'Do you think the money for such a project might be forthcoming?' she asked, finally.

'Not in the near future, I'm afraid.' David sighed heavily. 'I am just beginning to set my priorities, and it looks as though new farming equipment is on the top of the list. We can repair some of it, such as plows and scythes, but much must be purchased. There have been no improvements here for a generation, and new methods – which involve seed drills and drainage machinery, for example, will require the outlay of substantial sums of money.'

'And repairs to the tenants' cottages?'

'That's next.'

'Well, harvest time is almost upon us,' said Kate tentatively. 'It won't be as bountiful as it should, but, with the curtailment in expenses that you've made, perhaps there will be money for some of those things.'

David sighed again, his expression bleak. 'That might be so, if we weren't so heavily in debt. It's going to take time and more luck than we have any right to expect before we can feel our heads are safely above water.'

'But that time will come, David. You know it will.' David's lips curled into a tentative smile.

'I hope you're right. But, speaking of curtailments . . .' he was shaken by unexpected laughter. 'I think I may even have swung Lawrence onto the path of thrift and economy.'

In answer to her expression of astonishment, he continued. 'We talked at some length on the way to Bath yesterday. That is, he talked a great deal of his plans for my purchases, and I listened until I could-n't take it anymore. Finally, with a dismal lack of finesse, I told him again that we are teetering on the edge of poverty and to stop talking nonsense about mother-of-pearl quizzing glasses and emerald stick-pins. Oh yes,' he snorted. 'Lawrence has taken it into his head that I should adopt the emerald as my "signature stone." Goes well with my "black mop," as he put it. He couldn't understand why I did not make it my immediate priority when we arrived in town to order a couple of rings and several encrusted snuffboxes, besides, of course, two or three stickpins.'

'And you replied?' queried Kate in mirthful fascination.

'I did what I should have done several days ago. I quoted him our debt and our expected income for the year. To my surprise, he was completely shaken. Said he couldn't understand why he'd never been told. I forbore to say that perhaps it was because he'd never asked. At any rate, he rode in silence for some minutes and then said in a subdued voice, "Just as soon not sell anything I've already got, old man, but I'll try to do my part in the future." '

'No!' cried Kate, a chuckle bubbling from her lips, but impressed in spite of herself.

'Yes, indeed,' answered David. Then, unable to suppress his own laughter, he continued. 'He did somewhat mar the effect a few minutes later when he added, "You will tell me when the hard times are over, won't you? Don't know how long I can stand being poor, after all." '

At this, Kate dissolved into wails of laughter. David glanced at her quizzically. Her reaction implied that she, too, found Lawrence ridiculous. He knew little of the ways of a woman in love, but could Kate have given her heart to a man she thought ludicrous?

'I suppose I should not speak so,' he said tentatively, 'of one you hold in such esteem.'

'What?' Kate's expression was almost comically blank.

'You flew to his defense like an avenging fury the other day. I must feel myself fortunate that you're not reaching for the nearest blunt object now.'

'Oh. Well, yes.' Discomfited at the memory of her blind need to shield David from humiliation, she glanced at him from under her lashes. 'I do, of course, feel a great deal of – of affection for Lawrence. It was – painful to see him so abused. Tell me,' she continued hastily, 'have you any plans for the Far Acreage?' She waved her arm in distraction to indicate a field that lay some distance away.

'No,' replied David hollowly. This was not the answer he had hoped to hear. Indeed, he felt as though he had caught a load of grapeshot in his stomach. He nearly grunted with the effort it took to regroup his emotions. 'At least, not at the present,' he continued. 'Later, perhaps, when. . . .' His voice trailed off into a chill silence unnoticed by Kate, who was preoccupied with her own thoughts.

'. . . And he hardly had two more words to say for the rest of the time until we got back home,' Kate related to Aunt Fred an hour or so later as she sat in that lady's chambers, up to her knees in green wool. 'Honestly, he can be so moody sometimes. But the main thing is' – she lifted her head in relieved laughter – 'he's speaking to me again. Although,' she added in some irritation, 'I fail to see why I spend so much of my time waiting around like an anxious puppy for a pat on the head.'

'Because you love him – like a brother,' replied Lady Frederica placidly, herself virtually swathed in strands ranging from the color of spring grass to that of a deep forest. 'But I wonder if slogging around in that damp cave of yours can do him any good. Oh! Perhaps he could consult Dr Craven tonight.'

'Tonight?' questioned Kate.

'Yes, didn't you know? Regina has invited a group of our neighbors for dinner tonight.'

'But, we're in mourning.'

'Oh, I don't think it's anything in the way of a party. "Just a small gathering of friends" is the way she put it. What I think,' said Aunt Fred judiciously, 'is that she's trying to ease David into the county gentry without causing too much fuss. Squire Davenport will be here, as well as Sir Peter Bantram and Lady B., and I don't know who else.'

'Does David know of this?' He so far had shown no inclination to become part of the county social scene, nor could she foresee him doing so in the immediate future. She wondered how he would feel about Regina's plans.

'Absolutely not, madam,' David was saying to Regina, who confronted him nearly nose to nose in the manor's great dining parlor. He had wandered in to find her in consultation with the butler and housekeeper regarding arrangements for the evening. 'If you choose to give a party, you are welcome to do so,' he continued firmly. 'But I fear I shall have to decline to appear.'

'It is not a party, David,' replied Regina in the voice of controlled calm that she was beginning to use in all her conversations with the new earl. 'It is merely a small gathering of friends, and I have invited these people solely for your benefit.'

David's mobile brows flew upward.

'Yes,' continued Regina smoothly. 'Because of the, er, unusual aspect of your accession to the title, it behooves us to behave with great circumspection. I'm sure the Merritt family is already the subject of much unpleasant gossip in the neighborhood. If you hide away in your study like a beast in his lair, you will never be accepted.'

'Madam, the opinion of a parcel of gabble-mongers. . . .'

'If you do not care for yourself, my boy,' continued Regina, still in that tone of sweet reason that made David's fingers twitch to be around her throat, 'think of the family. Cilla has just made her come out. Surely, you will not wish to inhibit her chances of a successful *parti* by a display of boorish behavior on your part.'

David was brought up short. Regina was insufferable, but she was right. He could just imagine the rumors swirling through the drawing rooms of London of a half-breed islander installed as the Earl of Falworth, to say nothing of the sanctity of Almack's. Not only would Cilla's marriage prospects be ruined, but so would Kate's. The thought of her marriage to another man was almost more than he could bear, but he could not jeopardize her happiness.

'All right,' he agreed shortly. 'I shall be there.'

He turned on his heel and strode from the room, leaving Regina to smile after him.

The gathering proved to be not so small after all, for along with the full complement of family members, and Lucius, ten other persons lined the huge dining table. From his vantage point at its head, David looked about him in wonderment. Regina had outdone herself, he thought amusedly. The furniture had been polished until it glowed like old jewelry. Chandelier lusters sparkled in the candlelight, and snowy napery provided a background for gleaming silver.

Regina had removed the formal centerpiece from the table, with its huge candelabra and epergnes, replacing it with a low arrangement of flowers, thus providing a casual atmosphere in which cross-table conversation would be permitted. He glanced down the length of the board, noting that Cilla had been placed next to Lucius, and Kate next to Lawrence. At David's right was ensconced Lady Bantram, her small eyes greedily absorbing every nuance of his behavior. For a moment, he knew an insane urge to pick up his soup bowl and down its contents in one, noisy gulp. Involuntarily, his glance swung to Kate, and, as though she had been reading his thoughts, her returning gaze held an expression of mischievous admonition.

He turned hastily to Hector Davenport, seated on his left. This gentleman, balding, portly, and russet-faced, was the embodiment of the hearty English squire, and he expounded to David his theories on the proper management of an acceptable pack of hunting hounds.

'Breeding is everything, of course,' he barked genially. 'I've got sixteen couple of the finest hounds you'll find in the country. Now, you take my little bitch, Sally. To look at her – eh, what?'

'I said, perhaps his lordship is not interested in hunting at this point in his life, Davenport.'

The words came from a spare gentleman seated halfway down the table. David smiled gratefully. He had known Dr Craven for some years, and had always appreciated his wry good sense.

'It's not so much a lack of interest,' he replied good-humoredly. 'Rather a lack of time, and the inability to ride at a pace faster than a sedate walk.'

The squire flushed. Like many others of his type, he was uncomfortable with physical deformity. 'Ah. Well, then,' he began. 'Didn't mean. . . .'

'You seem to be getting about all right, though,' interrupted the doctor once more. 'Had some surgery, did you?'

'Some surgery!' contributed Lucius. 'He spent more time under the knife than a Christmas goose.'

'And the results were very little better, I'm afraid,' David added with a rueful smile.

'Well, at the time, perhaps they felt the removal of necrotic tissue was all they should attempt. I've heard some of the chaps over in the Peninsula are recommending exercise as a method of strengthening weakened muscle and tissue. Have you tried any such? The swelling will probably have gone down, so perhaps more surgery is called for.'

David felt a stirring of unexplained anger, and his lips tightened.

'I think not, Doctor. I have no intention of contorting my frame into the ridiculous positions the sawbones in Spain suggested. Nor do I intend to permit any more whittling away at my bones.'

The doctor raised his brows, but replied placidly, 'Well, perhaps when you've had a little more time to recuperate. I'll be glad to help in any way I can, of course.'

Ashamed of his churlish behavior, David smiled and nodded.

At the squire's left, his daughter Lucinda simpered worshipfully. She was an attractive young miss of some eighteen summers, and was obviously bosom bows with Cilla. The two had giggled together at some length in the drawing room before dinner. Now, her glance slid continually in David's direction. She laughed in almost fevered appreciation at his pleasantries, and fluttered her lashes in abandoned beguilement when he so much as looked in her direction. David could only laugh inwardly, wondering if she would display such eagerness if he were still David Merritt, bastard son of the Earl of Falworth. He shrugged, knowing the answer full well.

From her seat on the other side of the table, Kate watched the antics of Miss Davenport in growing irritation. Good heavens, had the chit no sense of decorum? Just look at her, wriggling her shoulders in that brazen manner. And how could her mother let her out of the house in that tastelessly revealing neckline. If she leaned any farther toward David, her plump little bosom would surely fall into the dish of tenderones of beef before her.

Up to this point in the meal, in an effort to avoid conversation with Lawrence, Kate had confined most of her conversation to Crawford, who sat on her left. Now, however, she resolutely turned away from the charming scene of flirtation and devoted her attention to Crawford's older brother.

At the foot of the table, Regina watched and smiled. She swung her gaze to observe Lucius in oblivious conversation with Cilla, and the smile broadened.

David, too, watched Kate's animated chatter with Lawrence, and the sight of that bright head turned so studiously away from his effectively turned his own dinner to ashes.

It seemed hours later when the gentlemen joined the ladies in the music room after brandy and port. The countess confided in her guests that her famous African acidanthera appeared to be on the point of blooming, and the ladies present commented in suitably admiring phrases, begging her ladyship to send word as soon as the blossoms might be viewed. Those present were then treated in turn to Cilla on the harp, Miss Davenport on the pianoforte, and Kate in what David could only consider an insipid duet with Lawrence. Lucinda continued in her determined flirtation with the earl, and Lucinda's mama watched her progress with complacency. Kate spent most of the rest of the evening in conversation with Aunt Fred, while David's mood grew more and more bleak. It was only after Lucius had been prevailed upon to join with Cilla in a duet that the guests at long last began to take their departure.

David's last memory of that evening of unmitigated tedium and annoyance was the voice of Lady Davenport as she wafted from the room on Regina's arm.

'Really, my dear? I had heard nothing of it. Kate and Lawrence? But when is the joyous event to take place?'

Chapter Fifteen

Kate hummed to herself as she descended to the breakfast parlor the next morning. In the hope of meeting David there, she had arranged her hair in a becoming swirl of curls and had donned a white lace collar to soften the severity of her mourning attire. She was therefore all the more disappointed to discover that the room's only occupant was Lawrence, moodily picking at a plate of eggs and York ham.

'Morning, Coz,' he said indifferently as she entered. Then, as though he had suddenly bethought himself of something, he rose in some haste to pull out a chair for her.

She nodded her thanks, and prepared to seat herself, but Lawrence put out a hand to stay her.

'Looking deuced pretty this morning, m'dear.' Kate's brows rose in surprise, and he continued in a rush. 'Of course, you always look pretty. You're – ah – a dashed pretty girl, come to that.'

Kate sank into her chair with a murmured, 'Why, thank you Lawrence.' She watched in some bemusement as the young man bustled to the buffet and, brushing aside the offer of assistance from a nearby footman, poured coffee and cream into a cup and presented it to her with the air of one bestowing largesse.

'Thank you, Lawrence,' she repeated, her bewilderment total.

Having accomplished this feat, he seemed at a loss as to how to proceed. He returned to his own chair, and dropped into it with a somewhat fevered smile.

'Nice day, what?' he asked, in what Kate could only consider a desperate tone of voice.

'Very nice,' she agreed calmly, sipping her coffee. She eyed him with some misgiving. 'Lawrence, what is all this – this cordiality?'

He donned an ingratiating smile. 'Just trying to be agreeable, Coz. Came to me we rarely talk, you and I.'

'That's true,' said Kate, declining to add that this was much the way she preferred it.

'So,' continued Lawrence, oblivious, 'I thought we'd just have a little – you know, chat.'

Having delivered himself of this sentiment, he apparently could think of nothing more to say, and for some moments, silence reigned in the breakfast parlor.

'I'm pleased to see you in such a good mood.' Kate chose her words carefully. 'You have been rather – difficult lately.'

'Well, who wouldn't be? I mean, it makes a fellow a little testy to be choused out of his inheritance.'

'Lawrence! You weren't choused out of anything. David has acceded to his rightful title. Surely, you don't think he plotted to take your place?'

He slumped in his chair. 'That's easy for you to say,' he mumbled. 'What if you were, say, the Queen of England, and one day you discovered you'd been demoted to scullery maid?'

At this, she burst into giggles. 'Oh, Lawrence, you are so ridiculous! Such a case would not be at all similar to your own.'

'P'raps not, but it's extremely lowering all the same.'

'I'm sure it is,' responded Kate, schooling her expression to one of sympathy. 'But I know you will rise to the situation. It would be most unbecoming in you to sulk, after all.'

'Sulk?' His voice rose to an indignant squeak. 'I never sulk. Anyway,' he hurried on, 'I don't want to talk about that. What do you say to a ride to the river after breakfast?'

Kate twisted in her chair to gaze at him in astonishment. This was the first time in her memory that Lawrence had ever requested her company for so much as a hand of cards, let alone a morning's outing.

'Why, I'd like that very much, Lawrence, only I – I have an – appointment in just a little while, with David.'

Lawrence's mouth turned down in a schoolboy pout. 'Might have known. Seems to me you and his lordship are mighty thick these days.'

'No thicker than we ever were. I've always enjoyed David's company.'

'Yes' – Lawrence sniffed – 'even when you were a grubby brat. Don't mean you have to sit in his pocket.'

At this, Kate set her cup down with a clatter and started up from her chair. The sparks emanating from her flaming curls and her burnished-metal eyes were almost visible to the naked eye.

'How dare you?' she cried. 'I am merely being a friend to David, at a time when he desperately needs one. No other member of the family seems to care about what he's been through, or the burden he has undertaken.'

She ran from the room, and after a moment, a stupefied Lawrence followed her. He found her in a small service room just down the corridor, brushing angry tears from her eyes. Approaching her in some agitation, he placed a diffident hand on her shoulder.

'Sorry to have offended you, Cousin,' he said placatingly. 'Didn't mean to imply you're setting your cap at David. Just meant that – well. . . .' He trailed off unhappily.

Kate sighed. Really, there was no point in flying off the handle at Lawrence. After all, he couldn't help being such a – a twiddlepoop. She had picked up that word from Aunt Fred, and it seemed particularly apropos at the moment. She lifted her head to smile patiently.

'I'm sorry, too, Lawrence. I shouldn't have snapped at you.' She turned to leave the little room, but to her surprise, Lawrence blocked her path. He had whisked his handkerchief from his pocket, and now proceeded to apply it to her eyes.

'There.' He dabbed at the last of her tears. 'Glad you ain't mad at me. Hate to have you mad at me, y'know, for I like you.'

To her vast surprise, he planted a kiss on her forehead, and then stepped back, apparently gauging her reaction to this untoward sign of affection. Kate's eyes widened, but she said nothing, and Lawrence, encouraged, placed his arm about her and bestowed another kiss, this time on her cheek.

My goodness, thought Kate in astonishment, is he up to what I think he's up to? She drew back, but before she could free herself, he planted his mouth on hers with awkward enthusiasm.

'Really, Lawrence!' Kate jerked her head away from him. 'What do

155

you think you're – oh!' She whirled toward the open door. 'What was that? Oh, dear, I think someone just passed. For heaven's sake, what will the servants think to see us—'

But Lawrence was not listening. Bending himself once more to the matter at hand, he recaptured his quarry and began to fairly rain kisses upon her. His breathing had thickened, and his hands began to move on her in a way Kate did not at all care for. She twisted out of his grasp.

'Lawrence, stop! Let me go this instant. Lawrence!' With a shiver of disgust, she thrust herself away from him. 'That will be quite enough of that.'

Lawrence gaped at her a moment, panting, his eyes glazed. 'What d'you mean, enough? We're practically betrothed, you know. We can do this anytime we wish.'

'I think you must be mad!' Kate gasped. 'We are nowhere near betrothed, and never shall be.'

'But Mama said – I mean, you just let me kiss you.' As though that settled the matter, he reached for her again.

'I very much wish I hadn't,' snapped Kate, 'and I certainly never shall again. Now, let me pass.'

Instead, Lawrence lunged at her, capturing one arm, and pulling her toward him. 'I was right, wasn't I?' he cried, his voice a blend of injured pride and thwarted manhood. 'It's David. You *have* set your cap at him, hoping he'll make you the Countess of Falworth. You've always wanted to be mistress here!'

Kate exploded. She delivered a sharp kick to his shin and a well-placed slap across his mouth. Then, ignoring his startled yelps of anguish, she swept out of the room.

A few feet down the corridor, in the opposite direction from the one taken by Kate, David stood watching her until she disappeared into the entrance hall, then he swung about and walked slowly toward his study.

He felt as though a grenade had just exploded beneath his feet. He could not believe what he'd just seen as he strode past the little service closet. Regina was right, there *was* something between Kate and Lawrence! The image of fiery tresses nestled against a flowered waistcoat seemed to burn on his eyelids. A sour taste rose in his mouth.

How could Kate have allowed herself to be manhandled by that whining fop?

He had it within his power to prevent their marrying, of course, but if Kate truly loved Lawrence . . . He could barely force himself to form the words in his mind. If Kate truly loved Lawrence, what right did he have to stand in their way? Besides, he thought wearily, he would have to see her married someday – to someone. Did it really make a difference to whom? Except, of course, that as her legal guardian, it was his duty to see her wed to advantage. Which concept by no means included his ne'er-do-well half brother.

As he headed for his rooms to change for his outing with Kate, his hands remained clenched.

Now what was the matter? Kate thought dismally. She and David had been riding for almost an hour and were approaching the ruins. David had barely said two words to her the whole time. Instead, he sat in the saddle like a bony thundercloud, responding to her every attempt at conversation with clipped monosyllables.

If he is so displeased with my company, thought Kate petulantly, why did he come? She tossed her head and spurred her horse in order to canter ahead of him. It was at this moment, of course, that David chose to clear his throat portentously. Kate reined in and turned to look at him, her glance conveying a question, as well as a certain annoyance.

David, intercepting the look, flushed slightly and said in a flat monotone, 'Have you given any thought at all to your future?'

Kate simply stared at him. What in the world possessed him to ask such a question so abruptly – and during a casual outing?

'Of course, I have. At least, well – that is, not precisely. Surely,' she finished in a rush, 'I have plenty of time to consider that question.'

'You are of marriageable age.'

Really, thought Kate, if his voice became any more colorless, it would be hard to distinguish it from the breeze that sighed around them.

'And, as far as I can see,' continued David, 'nothing has been set in motion to secure a husband for you.'

An unpleasant quiver made itself felt in the pit of Kate's stomach, but she forced herself to remain rigid in her saddle.

'I have always thought,' she said, her voice sharp and precise, 'that if and when I decide I should like to be married, the choice of my life's partner would be mine.'

'And when do you think you will make that decision? You are not getting any y. . . .'

Furious, Kate swung to face him. 'Are you going to remind me of my advanced years – my lord?' she snapped. 'I realize that at twenty I must be considered practically on the shelf, but I do believe I am not quite at my last prayers.'

'I am not going to remind you of anything,' he retorted, sitting very straight astride his mount despite the ache that was already beginning to spread through his frame, 'except that you apparently have chosen to avail yourself of some of the privileges of marriage without first observing the proprieties of a ceremony.'

This was not at all what he had meant to say, and even to his own ears, his words sounded incredibly pompous, thus he was not surprised at Kate's furious reaction.

'What the devil are you talking about?' she cried, her eyes sparking dangerously.

In despair, he listened to himself dig his own pit. 'I'm talking about your disgraceful behavior with Lawrence this morning.'

The quiver in Kate's stomach had now begun to resemble an earthquake. Oh, dear Lord, it had been David who had passed the service room when Lawrence had . . . She could feel the blood burning in her cheeks, and her heart thudded as she observed what she interpreted as contempt in David's eyes. A spark of anger at his accusation flared within her, and she allowed it to blaze into a conflagration of self-righteous wrath.

'You've been spying on me! How dare you sneak around – you have no right. . . !'

'I was not sneaking around,' returned David, coldly defensive. 'In any case, sneaking around was not necessary, since you were so lost to propriety as to fling yourself into his arms in broad daylight – out in the open, where anyone and his dog might witness your disgraceful behavior.'

By now, each of the combatants was in a royal rage, and each experienced a fleeting and quickly squelched awareness of the danger they faced in this venting of pent-up, undefined emotion.

'Disgraceful behavior!' Kate fairly spat the words. 'What about your behavior last night – ogling the luscious Lucinda as though she'd just been served up to you on a pastry plate!'

'I was not ogling,' replied David frigidly. 'I was merely. . . .'

'And what makes you think,' Kate stormed on, 'that you can pass judgment on what I do? How quickly your exalted status has gone to your head.'

Kate could have bitten her tongue the instant the words were out of her mouth. In a tiny corner of her mind, a voice cried out to mind her wretched temper, but David's next words shattered her compunction.

'It is precisely my exalted status,' he said in a voice like splintered granite, 'that gives me the right to pass judgment on what you do. In case you have forgotten, I am now your guardian. It is my duty to see you properly situated, which will become extremely difficult if you insist on comporting yourself like a – a lightskirt.'

If Kate had not been facing him on horseback, she would have struck him. 'If you think,' she began, barely able to form the words for her rage, 'that I will allow my actions to be dictated by your mean-minded sense of duty, allow me to disillusion you. I am perfectly capable of managing my own affairs, and I shall be happy to remove myself – and my regrettable tendency to behave like a lightskirt – from W-Westerly and your – your insufferable m-meddling!'

Kate knew that in a moment the hot tears that had been welling in her throat would spill over and, determined that David would not see how she had been hurt, she whirled about and spurred her mare into a gallop. In a very few minutes, she reached the rocky plateau. Dismounting, she ran for the shelter of the ruins and lit her lanterns with shaking fingers.

She was well into a good, comforting cry, when she heard David's footsteps approaching the villa. Stifling her sobs, she busied herself in a corner of the first room with her back to the entrance, but when David's shadow fell across her work, she spun around and cried, 'Why are you here? I really believe I have had a surfeit of your company, my lord earl. Why don't you just turn around and go back home?'

159

David paused a moment before answering her, allowing his anger to swell and envelop him.

'I am here because you badgered me into coming,' he said shortly. 'I promised I would sketch these ruins, and that's what I'm going to do.' He turned and limped to the other side of the room and faced the painted soldier. Positioning the sketch pad he had brought with him, he began to draw, apparently oblivious to her presence.

With a ragged, indrawn breath, Kate picked up shovel and spade and stalked from the room into the unexplored regions farther back in the villa, shored up recently by Jem during the three days she had wheedled from Josiah Moody. Soon the only sound to be heard was a furious chinking as Kate bored her way further into the concealing dirt.

David looked down at the jagged strokes he had completed and, with an oath, tore the paper from the pad and crumpled it into a tight wad before tossing it to the ground.

Damn! Why had he let himself be drawn into what was really no better than a nursery room brangle? He listened to the infuriated clatter emanating from the dark interior of the villa and was forced to smile. He could just picture Kate working off her temper in an assault on the earth. Her hair must be flying. She'd hardly needed to take a lantern; by the time she had flounced off, her flaming mop looked as though it had reached combustion point.

His smile faded. He knew she hadn't really meant the incensed remarks she had hurled at him. Surely she didn't believe that he had become toplofty since attaining his title. Did she? And, of course, she knew better than to think him mean-minded. Didn't she? Worst of all, she had not denied her quiescence in the passionate scene he had witnessed earlier.

A pall of gloom settled over him as he forced his attention to the task at hand. He began with the face of the man with the scar. He glanced at the battle-scene mural across the room. Was the man he sketched here the same officer who led his men in an attack? Attack on what, he wondered. The object of the assault could not be seen. His men certainly seemed to think highly of him. At least, none of them had taken their eyes from his form as he beckoned them forward. Or, David chuckled, perhaps it was the officer himself who was the artist. His hand paused for a moment, arrested at the thought. Could it be possible? he wondered. He looked around for the marble head before remembering that Kate had taken it to the house. He agreed with her that the boy was more than likely a member of the family who had lived in the villa, and it seemed probable that it had been created by someone who knew the boy personally, perhaps someone who loved him – his father?

David stepped back to look again at the face of the Roman officer. How odd to think that a soldier with a talent for art had lived in this place almost two thousand years ago, leaving his work to be appreciated by another soldier with the same knack.

His ruminations were cut short by a loud, jarring, rumbling noise, followed by Kate's scream. As he whirled toward the sound, the villa was filled with the cracking of splintered wood and the thunder of falling earth.

David leaped for the entrance to the interior room, and peered frantically into the dust-filled blackness.

'Kate? Kate! Are you all right?'

He blundered into a beam of wood leaning crookedly across in his path, and, lifting his lantern, made out others scattered on the floor. He saw what appeared to be a gaping hole in one corner of the room, but of Kate, there was no sign.

Chapter Sixteen

'Kate!' David called again, choking in the dust that enveloped him. 'Are you all right? Can you hear me?'

He moved toward the hole that had opened in the dirt floor in the far corner of the room, calling as he went and tripping over fallen beams in his haste.

'Kate!'

'Yes, I'm here.' David went weak with relief at the sound of the muffled voice issuing from the hole. 'I'm all right – I think.'

By now, David had made his way across the room, and he bent over the cavity, lantern lifted high. For a moment, he could see nothing in the clouded blackness, but then he discerned movement. He flung himself onto his stomach and held the light over the area. To his horror, he beheld Kate – or rather her head and shoulders – trapped beneath several beams of wood. The pit in which she lay appeared to be some five feet deep. One large beam lay across the top, so that both ends rested on the main level of the floor. It had apparently borne the brunt of much of the cave-in, composed of more wood, roof tiles, and the other assorted debris, which had showered down on Kate.

David looked above him and was not reassured to note that those beams which remained upright, evidently part of Kate's reinforcement efforts, stood askew and looked ready to join those already fallen.

'No! Don't do that!' he cried, as he saw Kate begin to twist her body in an effort to release herself from her wooden prison. 'You'll bring the whole place down on our ears. Are you sure you're all right?'

'Yes,' panted Kate. 'I don't think anything is broken, but – I can't move.'

'That's just as well right now.'

He set the lantern down and made a quick survey of the room. Part of the roof, which had managed to sustain itself for over a thousand years, had caved in at last, allowing a few rays of natural light to penetrate the blackness within. Only three remaining supports still stood above the hole. Two were slender, twisted bits of timber, which had been set up by Kate and Jem. The third was one of the original supports, a huge, ancient beam, now disastrously cracked. This was all, thought David in horror, that stood between Kate and certain death from further cave-in.

'Look, Kate. Before I can begin to try to get you out of there, I must figure out a way to strengthen the remaining structure in here. Can you remain very still?'

'Yes,' Kate whispered. 'But, David, you cannot!' she continued as she saw what he was about. 'You cannot lift those – you must go back to the house for help – you will ruin yourself!'

'There's no time. This whole place may crumble at any moment.'

Looking about, he discovered two sturdy beams that lay on the floor, untouched by any of the other timbers. Slowly, and with infinite care, he raised one in his arms and pushed it into a position of support beside one of the remaining, damaged timbers. Once he had it set into position, he gave a final, sudden shove to ram it into place. The faulty beam shuddered and gave way, crashing to the floor near David. Kate gave a little scream.

'No, it's all right,' called David hastily. 'The new beam is holding.'

He turned and lifted the second timber from the floor, and again he raised it and eased it into position.

Kate gasped in fright, for the second, damaged support stood almost directly above the pit in which she lay. If it were to fall in the wrong direction, she or David would surely be crushed. She closed her eyes as David prepared to push the new beam into place, and flung her one free arm over her head.

As he had before, David put his shoulder to the support and shoved it into its new position. And as before, the motion caused the damaged support to collapse. It crumpled noisily to the earth in three pieces. Kate's eyes flew open, and to her shuddering relief, she saw that it had missed David. He had already moved to the large timber that lay across the top of the pit and begun dragging it away. He was soon breathless with exertion, and as he gave a desperate lunge, his weak leg collapsed under him and he cried out involuntarily.

'David!' Kate cried in anguish. 'Surely, I am safe now. The ceiling is supported. Please do not try to do any more yourself. You must be in great pain – please, David!'

'I'm fine,' he replied, his breath coming in gasps. 'And you are not safe yet. I believe the other beam' – here he pointed to the ancient beam still standing above them – 'is ready to collapse at any moment.'

In truth, such had been his preoccupation with removing Kate from her entombment with all possible speed, that he had been oblivious to his own discomfort. He was only dimly aware of the pain that lay on the fringes of his consciousness, like an assailant lying in wait. He struggled to his feet, and with one more push slid the beam into a position where it was no longer an impediment.

He tumbled into the pit and, pausing for only a moment to assure himself that Kate was unharmed, began peeling away the layers of rubble that covered her. She was soon able to assist him, but it seemed another eternity before she was free.

David surveyed her with some misgiving, and his mouth lifted in a weary smile.

'You look like something swept out of the ironmonger's shop, if you don't mind my saying so.' Tenderly, he reached to brush a clot of dirt and what appeared to be a broken nail from her hair. 'You must feel like it, too.'

Kate laughed shakily.

'Well, nothing's broken, but I fear I'm going to present a splendid assortment of bruises once I get cleaned up.'

Above them, the ground shifted suddenly, and the remaining beam shuddered with a terrifying creak.

'Come on, Kate, let's get you out of here. Now.'

David scrambled awkwardly out of the pit, and stretched out on his stomach once more. He held out his arms to Kate, and she fairly leapt into them. As he lifted her clear, the ancient beam chose that moment to give away. David grasped Kate tightly in his arms and rolled away from the lip of the hole, as, with a thunderous crack, the timber crashed to the floor, completely obliterating the spot where Kate had been imprisoned.

Safe in David's embrace, Kate lay shuddering convulsively. She could feel the pounding of his heart against her cheek. For a moment, they remained thus, then David whispered urgently, 'We must leave this place. I don't know how long the timbers I set up will hold.' Rising, he scooped Kate into his arms and ran through the front rooms of the villa and out into the blinding brightness of daylight.

Once free of the ruined dwelling, David set Kate on her feet, but he did not release her. She made no move to step beyond the shelter of his embrace, but allowed herself the luxury of resting her head on his chest. There she remained until, very gently, he lifted her head. She was intensely aware of the length of him pressed against her and as she met his gaze, it seemed as though something hot and compelling in his eyes reached out to touch the center of her being.

He lifted his hand to push a bright tendril of hair away from her face. He stroked her cheek, and continued to gaze at her with a hunger that made her catch her breath.

'Dear God, Kate,' he whispered. 'I was afraid I was going to lose you – so afraid. . . .'

Now the pounding of her own heart thudded in her ears, and her arms involuntarily tightened around him.

'David,' she whispered. Then again, so softly that he was not sure he heard her aright. 'David, my dearest.'

He laid his cheek on her hair, and it took only the slightest motion to bring his lips to her temple, where he could feel the throbbing of her pulse, then to her cheek, soft and smelling of lavender and dirt. She lifted her face to him, so that it was the most natural thing in the world that his lips should next encounter hers. They were warm and pliant and achingly desirable.

At the first touch of his mouth, Kate felt herself responding with an eagerness that both startled and delighted her. She felt adrift in sensation and in mindless wonder at the shattering rightness of his kiss. Her lips parted in welcome as her fingers clasped the dark hair curling on the nape of his neck. Her body arched against him, and as his hands began to move on her back, she shivered with pleasure and a longing for more, although she wasn't at all sure what 'more' might be. She only knew she wanted this moment to last forever – the kissing that grew increasingly urgent, and the stroking that gradually encompassed more and more of her body, and. . . .

When David pulled away from her abruptly, she almost lost her balance. For a moment, she stared blindly at him, her eyes large and bereft.

God, he berated himself, what was he thinking of?

'I – I'm sorry, Kate. I didn't mean – I was so concerned, I. . . .'

Kate, suddenly cold, interrupted.

'I quite understand. I, too, became – flustered, I fear. After such an incident – one's emotions become – that is. . . .'

'Quite,' said David in a barely recognizable voice.

Kate turned swiftly and hurried toward the spot where they had tethered the horses. David moved to follow her, but was brought up short by a stab of white hot pain in his hip. He cried out involuntarily, and, ashen-faced, clutched at a nearby tree for support.

'David!' Kate was at his side in an instant. 'Dear Lord, you *have* ruined yourself.' She tried to ease him to the ground, but he waved her away.

'No,' he gasped. 'If I don't keep standing, I won't be able to move.' He swallowed convulsively in an effort to control the waves of nausea that threatened to overcome him as the pain, so long held at bay, washed over him.

It was some moments before he was able to speak. 'If you'll give me your arm,' he said in a shaking voice, 'I believe I can walk.' Kate drew a sharp breath in protest, but again, he gestured in denial. 'That always seems to be the most helpful thing I can do.'

Kate hesitated, then placed David's arm around her shoulder, and slipped hers around his waist. He took a tentative step forward, and then another. He tried not to let all his weight fall on Kate's slender shoulders, but was unable to stop himself from doing so. She remained steady at his side, unflinching, accommodating her steps to his halting stride.

He expelled a breath that was not quite a groan, and Kate stiffened.

'David, this is madness. You must rest here while I go back to the house for help. I know it will be a long wait, but. . . .'

'I am not going to wait here to be rescued like a maiden chained to a rock,' he grunted through clenched teeth. 'It's getting a little better already, so if you'll just be patient, I'll be all right.'

His white face belied his words, but Kate said no more, merely shifting her position to give him more support. Indeed, his movements seemed a little more free now, and by the time they had reached the horses, he was able to walk under his own power. He even managed to mount his horse with a minimum of assistance from her, and they proceeded at a moderate pace along the faint track that led back to Westerly.

They spoke only of commonplaces along the way, each carefully avoiding the subject uppermost in their minds. David's kiss still burned on Kate's lips, and she thought its effects must be visible. She reviewed her limited experience with this pleasant activity, but it was as though she were comparing bells to boulders when she thought of David's annihilating embrace and the exchanges she had accepted from Charles and the one that had been forced on her by Lawrence. It was as though she had given up a piece of her soul to him through that searing contact. She shot him a sidelong glance. His face was closed and hard, the film of perspiration covering his features an indication of his present physical agony.

Dear God, if only she could do something for him. She ached for the unspeakable suffering he must be going through.

He rode silently, each step taken by Barney a source of exquisite torment. By a supreme effort of will, he found he was able to direct his thoughts in another channel. He grimaced. This new avenue was hardly guaranteed to ease his suffering, since it led him directly to that which he preferred not to contemplate.

What was he going to do about Kate? It had become apparent that he was unable to keep himself under control when she was around. True, he had been in the midst of an exceptionally emotional upheaval when he had clasped her to him. Under normal circumstances, he would have been able to suppress the overpowering need to feel her mouth under his. Surely he would not be called upon to rescue her from life-threatening hazards on a regular basis. Still, he could not place any dependence on his ability to keep a rein on his feelings if he found himself, say, seated next to her on a garden bench in a scented, moonlit garden. He shook himself, which action effectively banished from his mind everything but the relentless ferocity of the pain that radiated to every corner of his being.

He groped frantically for another subject to divert his mind.

'What do you suppose that thing was doing there?' His voice, as he blurted the words, was jagged.

'What?'

'That hole. Why would anyone have a pit under the drawing room floor? Or wherever.'

'Oh.' With an effort, Kate pulled her mind away from its fruitless writhings. 'I don't know. I was digging rather furiously.' She flushed as she recalled what now seemed her perfectly infantile rage at him earlier. To her horror, tears began to spill over her cheeks.

'Kate – don't. . . .' David's face twisted in a hurt that was completely unrelated to his wound.

'I'm sorry,' Kate mumbled. She dabbed at her eyes with one hand, succeeding only in creating smeared circles of mud. 'Perhaps it was a storage pit just think what artifacts we might have found there, and now we'll never see any of them. All that work' – she gulped – 'ruined. Now, I'll never be able to reveal the whole house.'

The tears made rivulets in the mud, but she knew they were not for the hopes that lay crushed in the ruined villa. She cried for her ruined dreams, realizing that the kiss that had made her spirit soar into heretofore undreamed of realms of bliss, had obviously been not at all wondrous for David. He had turned away from her in distraction, seeming almost angry at what had happened.

Observing her tears, David reached for her hand, but they had at last reached the stable yard, and Kate's call for assistance was swiftly answered by Josiah Moody. In an astonishingly short time, Curle appeared on the scene, then Lucius, and David was lifted from the saddle. In another few seconds, he had been borne indoors, and Kate was left to stand forlornly in the center of the yard, staring after them.

Chapter Seventeen

Through long practice, Kate managed to arrive at her chambers undetected by Regina or any of the servants. Once there, however, she sank into a small armchair in her sitting room and gave herself up to gloomy reflection.

For how many years, she wondered, had she loved David. She could clearly remember the day she had arrived at Westerly, a bewildered, desperately weary four-year-old orphan. Philip, at six, was only slightly more comprehending of their bereavement, and, pale and silent, had entered the great front door ahead of her.

The stranger who was Uncle Thomas had made the trip from India with them, lightening the terrifying strangeness of the journey with tales of Westerly and its inhabitants. Thus, she knew immediately that the rather plump little boy with a pouting, sullen air who waited in the hall for them was Lawrence. Urged by his mother, a tall, remote lady in a starchy gown, he had thrust out a hand to Philip and murmured an indistinguishable greeting to her. But where, Kate had wondered, was the black-eyed one of whom Uncle Thomas had spoken with such warmth?

It was not until much later that she had encountered him in the stable yard, wholly occupied with the training of a yearling colt. She had wandered out by herself, and now stood stock still, gaping in wonderment at the sight of the sturdy youngster standing nose to nose with an animal that seemed several sizes too large for his new master.

Curious at the silent communion between boy and beast, she had stepped closer, and the suddenness of her movement caused the mettlesome young horse to rear.

One of the watching grooms ran forward, but the boy waved him away. He clung to the leading rein, and, despite the animal's best efforts, soon brought him to a standstill. It was only then that the boy handed the rein to one of the grooms, and strode to where Kate stood, eyes wide with apprehension.

'You, there – girl! What do you mean by it?'

Kate had merely stared blankly at him.

'Have you no more sense,' he continued, his black gaze blazing into hers, 'than to barge into a training session? What a ninnyhammer you are – and I never saw a girl with hair like carrots before.'

At this, her temper had blazed as bright as her hair. She walked up to her tormentor, and, swinging one tiny fist, caught him squarely on the jaw. Instantly, she fell back, horror-struck at what she had done, and awaited retribution.

Instead, the boy had rocked back on his heels, and, after an astonished moment, burst into laughter. 'A wisty castor!' he cried. 'But if you mean to do that ever again, you must learn to tuck your thumb in – and turn your hand so that your knuckles make contact. Here, let me show you.'

He had then proceeded to instruct her in the proper method of drawing an opponent's cork. Philip joined them some moments later, and after a brief period of wariness, the two became instant friends. He was, he told them, David Merritt, and he was eight years old. Uncle Thomas was his father, but as he explained that Aunt Regina was not precisely his mother, a shadow crossed his young face. For an instant he looked vulnerable and lost, and in that moment, Kate knew she had given him her heart.

Now, she rose from her chair with a sigh, and having rung for a tub of hot water, began to remove the tattered, filthy remnants of her clothing. When Phoebe came to attend her mistress, she found her standing in the center of her bedroom, half undressed, staring out the window at nothing in particular. With a horrified clicking of her tongue, the little maid began divesting Kate of her begrimed muslin gown.

A few moments later, settled into a steaming bath, Kate allowed her thoughts to drift back to the morning's occurrences. How odd, she mused. All these years, she had thought of David as a surrogate brother – someone she could turn to for solace in her bad times and for sharing in the good. Even when he had returned from the war so badly scarred inside and out, she had believed that she wanted only his friendship.

Absently, she slapped the washcloth against the surface of the scented water. His friendship, indeed. Well, yes, she wanted that, in addition to so much more. She wanted not only to share his problems and triumphs at Westerly, but to share his bed as well. Her love was no longer that of a child for a beloved playmate, but that of a woman for the man who meant everything to her – the man to whom she wanted to promise her heart and her life in a church blazing with candles, and whose children she wanted to bear.

No wonder she had been so infuriated last night when pretty little Lucinda Davenport had plied him with her not inconsiderable charms. She had been plainly and simply green-eyed with jealousy. David had smiled at Miss Davenport and conversed pleasantly with Miss Davenport. Would he eventually marry Miss. . . ?

Her heart, already positioned several notches below despair, sank even further. He very well might wed that simpering little chit, for he certainly had no interest in marrying the commonplace girl he had known forever. It was obvious he considered her to have changed little from the tiresome child who had tagged so relentlessly after Philip and him so many years ago. The kiss? Merely a delayed reaction to a nerve-shattering crisis, one from which he'd recovered in short order.

He had told her he needed her friendship. She was more than willing to give it to him, that and anything else he might wish of her, at least until he married. She really could not bear the thought of living here with the Earl of Falworth and his new countess, whomever she might be. By the time David installed a bride at Westerly, she would have packed her belongings and found a place of her own in which to spend the remainder of what looked at this point to be a perfectly dreary life.

Her thoughts continued along this bitter path until the cooling of the water brought her back to her surroundings. Resolutely she soaped herself and washed her hair with great vigor, as though by such an action she could slough away her treacherous longings.

Phoebe had just finished tucking her into yet another dismal mourning ensemble, when she was surprised by a sharp rap on her door, immediately followed by the entrance of Aunt Fred. The old lady strode into the room and grasped Kate by the wrist.

'I want you to come to the conservatory with me,' she announced baldly.

'To the conservatory?' queried Kate. 'Whatever for?'

'I have a sudden yearning to smell the flowers. Now.'

With this, Lady Frederica spun about and hurried from the room, casting a single glance over her shoulder to make sure her instructions were being followed.

Kate followed in bewilderment, but not another word would Aunt Fred say until they had entered the cool moistness of the conservatory. Darting her gaze about the room, Aunt Fred exclaimed in a satisfied tone, 'Good, we're in time.'

Then, clutching Kate's hand once more, she led her to a corner of the room sheltered from view by an assortment of exotic trees.

'Aunt Fred, what in the world is going on?' exclaimed Kate in increasingly baffled tones.

'I told you, I had a sudden wish to walk amidst the blooming what-ever-they-are,' she replied, waving vaguely at a flowering plant.

'Now look here, Aunt. If you don't. . . .'

'Ssst!' – Aunt Fred gripped Kate's arm – 'Here they are. Now for heaven's sake, be quiet!'

Kate peered from behind the ornamental shrubbery to observe that Cilla and Lucius had entered the conservatory. Cilla was erupting in high, girlish giggles.

'Now, don't say you weren't happy to escape from Mama and her positively excruciatingly boring guests. Just because David decided to feign an indisposition, I don't see why we should have to sit and listen to them prose on forever.' She drew him further into the room. 'See? Here is what I wanted to show you. It's Mama's acidanthera – very rare, you know, and it doesn't bloom very often. Isn't it lovely? Don't the blossoms remind you of butterflies?'

Lucius eyed Cilla with a noticeable lack of enthusiasm as he removed her hand from his arm and attempted to back toward the door.

'Yes, very pretty,' he said quietly, 'but I think we'd best be getting back to the others. Your mother will wonder where we have got to.'

'Nonsense,' trilled Cilla, reattaching herself to his sleeve in a playful manner. 'She knows I am in your company, after all. Do look at the lovely flower.' Still retaining the wary Lucius in her grip, she bent for a closer look. Suddenly, she straightened, uttering a squeal of horror.

'Ooh, look! Oh, Mr Pelham – it's a big, nasty bug. Do drive it away!'

Lucius peered at the flower, then at Cilla.

'I don't see anything.'

'Oooh!' Cilla repeated, uttering an even louder screech. 'It's flying. Can't you see it? It's – oh! Oh – oh—oh!' She pressed against Lucius, wriggling frantically. 'It flew down my dress!'

'I beg your pardon?'

'Down my dress – the back of my dress! Ooh!' She flung her arms about Lucius's neck. 'Get it out! Get it out!'

'My dear Lady Cilla!' Lucius's voice had become suddenly cold. 'I shall fetch your mother. She will know what to do.'

'No, no, no!' gasped Cilla. 'Just put your hand on my back. Perhaps you can crush the wretched thing. Oh, please. It's oh – ugh – it's wiggling!'

Lucius merely set about removing Cilla's arms from about his neck.

All through this fascinating scene, Kate had watched as though turned to stone. What in the world had come over Cilla to behave in this appalling manner? She was startled to feel Aunt Fred's hand once more on her arm as the old lady strode forward, a bright smile on her lips.

'Poor dear. A bug, you say? But how unfortunate. Here, let Aunt Fred help you.'

Cilla suddenly ceased her gyrations. Her mouth dropped open and her eyes blinked several times in rapid succession, after which she immediately began to cry.

'B-but,' she wailed, 'we're supposed to be. . . .'

At this moment, the door to the conservatory swung open and a group of elegantly gowned ladies entered, led by Lady Falworth, who spoke to them over her shoulder.

'I'm so pleased,' she was saying, 'to be able to show you – why what is it?' she finished, apparently in response to the questioning expressions on the faces of her guests. She swung about, but the incipient smile that had begun to spread across her features died aborning.

'Wha – what?' were the only words she was able to form. Her gaze as she swung in consternation to Kate and Lady Frederica, was almost ludicrous in its expression of thwarted expectation, and for a moment she simply gabbled. Then, with obvious effort, she gathered the remnants of her dignity about her and spoke to Cilla. 'We – we wondered where you had got to, my dear. How does it happen that – that there is such a large gathering here?'

'Ah, Regina,' warbled Lady Frederica. 'It's so terribly droll. Apparently all of us were struck at the same time with a desire to see your famous acid ant flower. We were engrossed in its beauty, when dear Cilla was apparently, er, molested by some species of beetle – a flying beetle, it appears. I was just about to aid her.' She turned to Cilla and began a vigorous pummeling at the back of her neck. 'So distressing, all that wriggling. The beetle, that is. Perhaps this will dislodge it.'

Cilla jerked away from her. 'Never mind, Aunt,' she said with a look that could have penetrated a tree trunk, 'it's gone now.'

'Well, then,' cried Aunt Fred merrily. 'All's well that ends, don't you think? Come, dear,' this to Kate. 'All this excitement has me very nearly expiring for a cup of tea.

With Kate in her wake, her ladyship swept past Regina, who contented herself with a glare of such malevolence that Kate could feel its effects long after they had made their way down the corridor and out into the Hall. Lucius, however, bestowed upon them a look of abject gratitude.

'Aunt Fred,' breathed Kate in awe. 'How did you know?'

Lady Frederica loosed a peal of her young girl's laughter. 'One of the upstairs maids came to me. She overheard Regina giving Cilla her orders not an hour ago. Really, the woman could put Wellington to shame. Celeste – the maid – had just performed some service for Regina and was still in the room, but you know Regina. The servants are just so many pieces of equipment to her, and might as well not have eyes and ears at all.'

174

'I thought she was going to explode with rage' – Kate laughed – 'when she walked in to find her only daughter, not in a forbidden tête-à-tête with a deliciously eligible young man, as she was most certainly expecting, but in an unexceptionable huddle with the young man and a pair of female relatives.'

'Poor Regina,' Aunt Fred said, chuckling. 'What a disappointment to find that dear little Cilla was not ruined after all, and the gentleman obliged to offer for her. All that lovely money gone a glimmering.'

They had by now reached Lady Frederica's chambers, and the old lady ushered Kate into the room, requesting her to ring for tea.

Over the cups, Aunt Fred eyed her young relative meditatively. 'Why are you wearing long sleeves, my dear, on such a warm day? To cover a succession of bruises, perhaps?' she added when Kate did not reply.

Kate sighed. 'Nothing escapes you, does it? I suppose you recently sustained a visit from Phoebe. Yes, I did run into a little difficulty this morning.' She pushed up her sleeves as far as she was able, to display a burgeoning assortment of dark purple swellings.

'Good heavens, girl! Have you been indulging in fisticuffs?'

Kate ruefully detailed the morning's events, with certain, careful omissions.

'And now,' she concluded, 'I don't know if I'll ever go back to my ruins. I must admit to a certain reluctance in entering the two rooms where the roof is still whole, although I'm sure they're perfectly safe, and I don't think there's much of interest in the area in front of the dwelling. And I feel so awful about what I put David through. He insisted he has suffered no permanent damage, and I hope that's true, but he was in terrible pain. No, I think I'll just let the past lie in the past from now on.'

'Nonsense,' retorted Aunt Fred briskly. 'You must get David to put some real supports in the existing villa, and with a crew of diggers, you can simply start carving at the place from the top. It may take some years, but—'

'I shall not be here, Aunt.'

'Oh?' The old lady eyed her sharply. 'And where would you be besides Westerly?'

'Westerly is not my home, Aunt Fred. It has provided a haven for me, but it is not my home. That I must make for myself.'

'I see.' Lady Frederica's brows lifted, and when she spoke again, the brusqueness that was characteristic of her was gone from her voice. 'What else happened this morning, my dear?'

'Goodness, Aunt,' responded Kate brightly. 'Wasn't that enough? You should see the bruises on the more unmentionable parts of my anatomy!' When Aunt Fred made no reply, Kate lifted her eyes, then dropped them swiftly. At last, she continued in a colorless voice, 'I discovered that David thinks of me as nothing more than a dear friend.'

'But, I thought that was what you wanted.'

'So did I, until . . .' She straightened. 'Please, Aunt Fred, I'd rather not talk about it.' She made as if to rise from her chair, but Lady Frederica stilled her with a gesture.

'Then don't talk, just listen. You and David have known each other for a very long time, my dear. Your relationship had become a comfortable nest for both of you. You each had your little niche in the heart of the other. Now you are grown, and it is inevitable, perhaps, that you must carve new places.' She smiled tenderly. 'I'm sure the operation must be as painful as it sounds. Worst of all, it takes time to accomplish.'

'You are very wise, Aunt Fred, and you're right, I suppose. The trouble is, my heart seems to have cracked in the process. As for David, he obviously prefers the old niche. I shall grow to accept that, perhaps, but not from such close range. So' – she brushed away the film of tears that had gathered in her eyes – 'how would you like to live in Brighton with me – or how about oh, say, Canterbury. Not too far from London, but. . . .'

'You're talking nonsense, girl,' Lady Frederica interrupted. 'But I shan't plague you anymore. You'd best go downstairs and search out young Pelham. He is probably still rooted to the spot in the conservatory, quivering like a jelly. Tell him he'd best get his bags packed and flee this place before Regina gets any more bright ideas.'

As it happened, Lucius was not quivering like a jelly in the conservatory. He was doing so in the gold saloon, putting himself outside a glass of brandy with all possible speed. He raised his head with a jerk at the opening of the door to the saloon, and a hunted expression filled his eyes. When he saw who had come to join him, however, he heaved a ragged sigh of relief and lowered himself into a nearby chair. With a shaking nod, he gestured to another, nearby.

'A narrow escape, that, eh, my lad?' Kate grinned. She and Lucius had rapidly established a friendly, informal rapport, and she felt no hesitation in chafing him on his *affaires de coeur*.

'My God,' breathed Lucius. 'Do you realize that this afternoon I came within Ames ace of acquiring that dreadful woman as my mama-in-law? I shall be leaving in a few days – I received a note from Papa in this morning's post requesting my return home. Now, I want your solemn promise, Kate, that you will not let me out of your sight until my carriage toils its way past the gates of Westerly and is nothing but a distant point on the horizon.'

'Ah,' said Kate wickedly. 'But then you run the risk of being coerced into marrying me. I am looking, you see, for my own transportation away from Westerly.'

Lucius lifted his brows.

'I rather thought you a permanent fixture here. Are you planning to leave?'

'Not until I have reached my majority, but that will not be many months from now.'

'Does David know of this?'

Kate shrugged. 'I have not told him in so many words, but I'm sure he does not expect me to live out my days here, turning into a maiden aunt for his children. He will no doubt marry in the not-too-distant future, and I hardly think his countess will want to share her home with one of her husband's leftover relatives.'

Lucius opened his mouth as though to say something, but then shut it abruptly.

'How is David, anyway?' asked Kate hurriedly, moving to a subject that had not left her mind all day. 'He looked dreadful when he was being carried into the house. Do you know how he fares now?'

'The last I saw of him, he lay abed, the center of a considerable controversy between Curle and Moody. Curle took it upon himself to prepare a hot tub laced with Epsom salts, which, he informed us grandly, he has found to be most helpful in the past to aid 'the major' when he was in particularly bad straits. Moody, on the other hand, insisted that cold compresses and fomentations were what was needed now. That, of course, is his sovereign remedy for a horse with joint problems. If it's good enough for his lordship's mount, it's apparently good enough for his lordship.'

'Oh, dear,' said Kate, unwilling to let Lucius draw her into laughter. 'He must be in terrible pain. I will go up to him.'

'No – no, you mustn't, Kate.' Lucius grasped her sleeve. 'He won't want you to see him like that.'

Kate looked at him straightly. 'You said that to me once before,' she said in a quiet voice.

'I was right then, too,' he replied in an equally serious tone. She sent him a rueful smile. 'You are a good friend, Lucius.'

'To both of you, I hope.'

When Kate made no reply, Lucius lifted his hand with a smile, but as he prepared to leave the room, he was barred by the entrance of a breathless Curle.

'Captain!' he panted. 'Miss. It's 'is lordship – we've 'ad to send for the doctor!'

Chapter Eighteen

Kate's face whitened. For an instant, it seemed that the room and all its furnishings had dropped away, leaving her frozen in a void of anguished disbelief.

'But you said he was all right!' she threw over her shoulder at Lucius who followed her as she ran down the corridor and up the great stairs. When she hurtled into David's bedchamber, however, she was brought up short. There, standing at his bedside, was Lady Falworth, engaged in a verbal brangle with David, who lay atop the covers, fully clothed, and looking to be very far from death's door.

The two turned their heads at the entrance of Kate and Lucius.

'Kate!' said Regina in a tone of extreme exasperation. 'Perhaps you can talk some sense into him – and you as well, Mr Pelham.'

'But, what is it, David?' Kate's voice trembled with the effort it took not to shriek her question. 'Why has the doctor been sent for?'

'Because,' he answered tiredly, as Regina opened her mouth once more, 'I am tired of fighting the pain. And I am tired of being so damned fragile and useless.'

'Useless!' squeaked Kate. 'You saved my life this morning, and. . . .'

David struggled to a sitting position and gestured to the others in the room.

'Please, all of you. May I ask you to leave for a moment? I must have a few words with Kate – alone.'

Regina stiffened.

'Certainly not!' she said, incensed. 'It would be most improper. Whatever you have to say to her can be. . . .' She stopped as Lucius moved to take her arm.

'Whatever villainous intentions he may have, your ladyship,' he said smoothly, 'I hardly think he's in any position to carry them out.' With these words, he towed her from the room as she still gasped in outrage. Curle, who had entered the room behind Lucius, followed.

David leaned forward with some effort, and grasped Kate's hands in his own.

'I've been thinking all day about what happened in the villa – and I've been thinking about what you said to me in the Abbey.'

'David, I had no business. . . .'

'But you were right. Not about my responsibility for Philip's death – I still hold myself to blame for that. I would give all I possess to have that night back, but it's not possible. So, I shall have to learn to deal with it – at least better than I have done so far.' He drew a deep breath. 'Ever since Badajoz, I have sunk further and further into a swamp of self-pity. That may have been all right, as long as I had only myself to consider, but things are different now. I have a responsibility to Westerly and all those who live here. In short, my dear' – his grasp on her hands tightened – 'I have decided to take off my hair shirt and get on with my life.'

Kate returned the pressure of his fingers. 'Oh, David, I am so glad,' she whispered. 'But what is this about the doctor? I was told you had suffered no real damage.'

David abruptly released her, and when he spoke, his voice was brisk and purposeful. 'Step One in the David Merritt Improvement Program is to rejoin the world of the useful. As you so perceptively pointed out, I was rather taking comfort in my helplessness, but after this morning – and, yes, I do recall that I saved your lovely hide – I have become quite inflated in my own estimation. Despite my general decrepitude, I performed in a manner that quite astonished me.'

Kate was forced to laughter.

'David, you are being quite ridiculous. It did not astonish me in the slightest, for I know you would give everything that's in you to save a friend.' This last was delivered with careful emphasis.

'Which,' he continued, as though she had not spoken, 'leads me to the belief that I am not quite as helpless as I thought. This being the case, it behooves me to get off my admittedly scrawny backside and do something about it.'

'Oh, not nearly as scrawny as it was,' interposed Kate, her eyes twinkling. 'There is nothing like country air and good food to flesh out one's, er, anatomy.'

'How very gratifying. Anyway, I have decided to follow Dr Craven's advice and let him remove the ball from my hip.'

'What!?' The amusement fled from Kate's face. 'Oh, no – oh, you can't David. Surely, it's much too dangerous.'

'There is some danger, yes. The ball lies very near the nerve. But,' he continued gazing directly into her eyes. 'It is a risk I must take. I trust Craven – he's an excellent surgeon. He has gained some experience in this sort of wound, having first traveled to London for instruction before performing similar operations on Peninsula veterans living around here.'

'But, David, I don't think. . . .'

His hand reached to stroke a few tendrils of bright hair curving along her cheek.

'Don't you see, Kate? I must do this – I cannot continue any longer as a worthless cripple, unable to ride at more than a sedate walk – powerless to clamber through my own fields and woodlots. Lord, I can't even climb into a hayloft – and here's harvest coming soon.'

Kate sat silent for several moments before lifting her eyes to David's.

'If that's what you want to do,' she said slowly and with painful effort. 'I'll help in any way I can.'

David uttered a pent-up sigh.

'Good girl. Perhaps you could start by relieving me of Regina's motherly solicitude. On the other hand, perhaps that won't be necessary. I'm sure she is against my little project merely because it's something I want to do.'

His laugh was cut short by a knock on the door, followed by the appearance of Curle.

'The doctor's 'ere, me lord,' he announced austerely.

Two hours later, Kate sat in a chair in the corner of David's bedchamber, utterly drained. She watched the figure on the bed, motionless beneath the bedcovers, and listened to the stentorous breathing of his laudanum-induced sleep. Dear Lord, had they done the right thing?

To her horror, David had announced on Dr Craven's arrival his intention of having the surgery performed immediately. The doctor must have surmised the reason for David's summons, for he had brought everything with him necessary for the operation. He had begun bustling Kate and Regina out of the room, stating that he had need of Curle and Lucius to hold his patient down.

Sickened as she was by these words, she had refused to leave, and in the end Dr Craven, who had worked with her before on setting bones and stitching the cuts of estate workers, allowed her to stay. It would be her job to hand him his instruments.

As they readied David, he lay quiet, only his eyes alive and dark in the pallor of his face. He did not look at Kate, but his fingers wound tightly around hers until the laudanum began its work. It was not long before his eyelids drooped and his hand loosed its grip.

Kate's breathing quickened at the first incision, but she had, after all, seen blood before. It was only when the flesh was peeled back to reveal the throbbing tissue beneath it that she was forced to bite her lip to fight off the dizziness that threatened to overpower her. Dear God, this was David to whom Dr Craven was doing unspeakable things! Curle and Lucius were not obliged to hold him down, after all. Kate sensed that he was aware of the outrage being perpetrated on him, but the blessed laudanum kept most of the pain at bay.

As the surgery progressed, she was able to focus her mind and energies on her duties. She mopped blood and fluid when ordered, and passed over the shining instruments, trying not to think of their purpose. Finally, the doctor pulled from David's bleeding body, a small metal pellet. Kate stared at it. So seemingly blameless – how could it have caused such suffering?

At last, a weary Doctor Craven sewed the incision closed, so that it resembled the others that lay near the web of former surgery scars to form an obscene tapestry.

Now, they had all gone. She had had a difficult time overcoming the objections of Lucius and Curle, but she had finally prevailed upon them to go down to dinner. She would take first watch, she said, and would send down when David awoke. Why it meant so much to be alone with him when he opened his eyes, she was unwilling to contemplate, but after calling for candles to be lit against the deepening twilight, she had drawn her chair close to the huge bed to watch in fascination the slow rise and fall of the chest of the man who lay there.

She reached to smooth the lock of hair that had fallen across his forehead like a smear of ink. In sleep, the deep lines in his face had been smoothed and an awaiting innocence lay on his features.

Unthinking, she rose from her chair and seated herself on the bed. Her hand seemed to lift of its own volition to trace the roughly chiseled planes of his face. She searched for traces of his island ancestry, but aside from the crow's-wing black of his hair, she could find none.

How often, she mused, had she pictured his face during the years he had been gone? Every line, every curve formed an achingly familiar landscape for her mind to explore and her heart to dream over.

Her fingers drifted over his lips, and it seemed to her that a faint smile lifted them. On an impulse she bent to press her mouth lightly against his and for one shocking instant, allowed the tip of her tongue to caress those firm contours. The next moment, she sat bolt upright as an abrupt change in David's breathing pattern indicated his imminent return to consciousness.

As she watched, his eyes opened and his gaze swiveled to hers in an unfocused stare. Almost immediately, recognition and awareness grew in them.

'Kate?' He smiled muzzily at her.

'Yes, my dear.' Her hand went back to his cheek, and she returned his smile with a shaky one of her own. 'The surgery has been completed; the ball is gone. How do you feel?'

David blinked and began a mental examination of the left side of his body. It hurt like hell, but the discomfort did not seem to emanate from his very bones as it had before. He wriggled tentatively, and was rewarded with a sharp twinge in his hip. But the grinding, stabbing pain was gone! God, was it possible? Was he free of it?

He raised his head and, grasping Kate's hand, struggled to lift himself to a sitting position. A wave of dizziness forced him back into the pillows, and he pulled Kate down beside him.

'Um – nice,' he whispered into her curls, his voice blurred.

'David!' She pulled away from him with a little gasp. 'This isn't at all. . . .'

But he drew her toward him once more, and placing his arm about her shoulders, settled her against him. 'Jus' for a li'l while,' he murmured. 'So nice – jus' right.'

His eyes closed again, and his breathing deepened. Yes, it did feel just right, she admitted to herself, and ignoring the guilt that tugged at her conscience, she snuggled into the hollow of his shoulder and luxuriated in the feel of him against her, and in the slow, strong beat of his heart against her breast as he slept.

She must have dozed herself, for when she again noticed a change in his breathing, it was as though she had just returned from a long way off. She opened her eyes to find her face close to David's, and he was gazing down at her with an expression that made her breathless. She jumped to her feet.

This time David's efforts to right himself were successful. Having heaved himself to a sitting position, he made as though to fling his covers back, but at Kate's sudden intake of breath, he followed the direction of her gaze to discover that, except for the bandage that covered his hip, he was stark naked. His eyes narrowed in sudden memory of silken curls splayed across his chest, and the feel of warm breath on his skin.

'Nightshirt,' he barked. 'Second drawer in that cupboard.'

Kate whirled to follow the direction of his pointing finger, and when he had slipped the garment over his head, he pointed again. 'If you'll look in the large wardrobe, I think you'll find a pair of crutches stashed way in the back. They're leftovers from Spain – kept them on Lucius's advice.'

This time she stopped short and turned to face him. 'David, you're not thinking of getting up!'

'Yes, I am. I'm wide-awake and I do not feel it necessary to stay in bed like a pampered invalid. Will you help me?'

'But you *are* an invalid, David!' Kate cried, appalled. 'You just underwent major surgery.'

'Well, I don't plan on doing somersaults or handstands. I'll be very careful, and I'll start with just a tour around the room.'

'I will not be a part of this,' she said firmly. 'I shall call Lucius. And Curle. Then we'll see how you lark about.'

'I told you – there will be no larking about. Will you help? You always used to be a willing partner in crime. Remember the time we stole into Father's bedcham – into this room – and took all his quizzing glasses to build a telescope?'

'David, this is not a childish prank. You could do yourself irreparable damage – oh, no!'

She hurried around the bedside just as he swung his legs over the side and grasped the bedpost in preparation for lifting himself to a standing position.

'All right, you win. Wait. Just don't move.' She scurried to the indicated wardrobe and burrowed in its depths, surfacing a few moments later with the crutches. Returning to the bedside, she put her shoulder under David's, and he clutched at her with one hand, while drawing one of the crutches to him with the other.

His face whitened, and he gave an involuntary groan, but when Kate would have lowered him back to the bed, he shifted impatiently. 'No,' he growled, 'let's get on with it.' Slowly, with Kate's help, he stood, and when he was fully upright, took his arm from about her and thrust both crutches into position. With Kate close beside him, arms outstretched, he took a cautious step forward, swinging his left leg free of the floor. After a few careful paces in this fashion, he allowed more and more weight to fall on his injured hip, and by the time he had circled the chamber once, he was putting almost his full weight on it.

He moved back to the bed in this fashion and paused there, letting the crutches slide to the floor. He turned to face Kate, and his face, though drenched with perspiration, wore such an expression of blinding joy that her breath caught in her throat.

'Kate,' he cried weakly, 'he's done the job! It hurts like hell, but I can tell – it's not the same. Oh God, Kate, I'm free of it!'

He gathered her into his arms in a crushing embrace, which she returned with all the strength that was in her, laughing and crying at once. Neither of them heard the brisk knock at the door, and sprang apart only at the sound of a high shrill voice.

'Kate! David! What is going on? Whatever can you be thinking of?'

'Aunt Regina!' Kate gasped, as David collapsed into an awkward heap on the bed.

185

Chapter Nineteen

'Really, Kate, I don't know why you're making such a fuss.' Regina took a sip of coffee and a fastidious mouthful of toast. 'I am only asking you to pop into the village for some ribbon. Have you some other pressing engagement for the morning?'

Kate gazed at her aunt in exasperation. It had been five days since Regina's unfortunate foray into David's bedchamber, and, while she had seemed to accept David and Kate's tangled explanation of how they had come to be embracing each other, Kate had intercepted not a few speculative glances from her in the meantime. Kate felt she ought to be denying something – she was not sure what – and had been made uncomfortable by what she assured herself was a perfectly innocent act of solicitude.

'I have no hesitation in running an errand for you, Aunt. It is simply that I prefer to go alone.'

'But that's nonsense. Lawrence has declared himself most anxious to put himself and his curricle at your disposal for the morning.'

'Anxious, Aunt? That's coming it a bit strong, don't you think?'

Regina's voice sharpened. 'Where do you learn such vulgar language, Kate? Yes, anxious. You know how much Lawrence delights in your company.'

Kate burst into laughter. Really this was too much. It was obvious that Lawrence took no more delight in her company than he would have in that of his old tutor. The next moment, however, she became serious. A jaunt in Lawrence's curricle was obviously to be the latest in a series of incidents engineered by Regina to throw her and her disagreeable cousin together. Yesterday, she had narrowly escaped his company as she rowed across the ornamental lake to the secluded little island at its center.

'Now, then,' the countess continued. 'Lawrence said he would have the curricle brought around in less than an hour, so—'

'Aunt Regina,' Kate interrupted. 'I do not require Lawrence's escort on a simple ride to the village, so please do not coerce him into coming with me. Indeed,' she rushed on as Regina opened her mouth to speak, 'you know very well that Lawrence no more desires my company than I do his, and I wish you would stop trying to bring us together. I will tell you again, Aunt, I have no intention of marrying Lawrence, even should he bring himself to the point of asking me.'

Regina stiffened and dropped her cordial demeanor. 'Then just what are your plans, Kate?' she asked coldly. 'Do you think, perhaps, to relegate me to the position of dowager?'

The silence of the room thrummed in Kate's ears as she regarded her aunt.

'I – I don't know what you mean,' she whispered through lips suddenly dry.

Regina laughed shortly. 'Do you not think I haven't noticed how your eyes fly to David the minute he walks into a room, and how they cling there as though he were your last hope of salvation?'

'You are mistaken.' Kate's voice sounded loud in her ears. 'David and I are – close – because of our childhood association. There is nothing more between us, I assure you.'

'Oh, yes,' Regina smiled slowly. 'I'm sure there is nothing – yet. I am not quite so sure about the future, however. David is in desperate need of funds, as we all know. You, by sheer coincidence are – or will be – in possession of an enticingly large fortune. I should be very much surprised if your old playmate does not soon express an indication that he would like to be so much more to you.'

Kate rose from her seat at the table with such violence that her chair toppled to the floor.

'I will not listen to any more, Aunt Regina! David would not stoop to marrying for money. As for my fortune, it is my intention to use it to live independently as far away from Westerly as possible. Otherwise, I would cheerfully wish it to perdition – particularly if it would spare me Lawrence's ridiculous attentions!'

She whirled and ran from the room, upsetting her coffee cup as she did so, and leaving her aunt to gape after her.

Blindly, Kate fled down the corridor and through the French doors at its far end. She did not stop until she reached an overgrown bower some distance from the house, where she flung herself down on a stone bench stained with bird droppings and chipped on one corner. This had used to be her favorite hiding place as a child. A retreat where she could ponder the problems of her young life or savor its happy occurrences. She had not been here for a long time, and found to her disappointment, that it no longer had the power of solace.

David a fortune hunter? What nonsense. He was far above such greedy machinations. Silently, she cursed Aunt Regina for having put such notions in her head. Yes, he loved Westerly and was in despair over its present degradation, but he would never consider . . . And he had never shown himself to be anything other than her good friend. Never. Her fingers crept up to brush her lips. Yes, there had been that moment when his mouth had covered hers so searchingly – so demandingly. That had not been the kiss of a good friend. She had felt in that moment as though her very soul had been absorbed into his, and – for just that instant – she had been sure he shared that sense of inevitable oneness.

But then he had pulled away, and there was nothing in his eyes that spoke of destiny fulfilled.

She had seen little of him since his surgery, though it was obvious he was doing splendidly. His stride was long and sure now, with the merest trace of the limp that would probably remain with him through his life.

Again, however, he seemed angry with her, as he had after every instance where she had allowed herself to indicate the love she felt for him. When Aunt Regina had intruded on them in David's bedchamber, their embrace had been wholly innocent – an expression of the unbounded gladness each had felt for his release from the prison of pain in which he had languished for so long. Yet, David had behaved as though he had been caught trying to seduce a vestal virgin. And, he had scarcely spoken to her since.

A fortune hunter, indeed. She almost wished he were. It would be nice to know that at least something about her attracted him, she thought sourly.

Rising, she began to make her way back to the house, only to b
brought up short at the sound of running footsteps approaching her
little glade. Curious, she peered around a clump of bushes, only to be
nearly overrun by the master of Falworth, clad only in shirt and
breeches.

'David!' she cried unnecessarily. 'You're running!'

Whereupon, of course, he immediately stopped. He was covered
with perspiration, and panting so hard he could not speak. Grasping
her by the arm, he led her back to the stone bench and sank down on
it.

'Lord,' he gasped. 'I had no idea I had fallen so far out of condition.'

'But. . . .'

He drew a damp sleeve across his streaming face. 'I have been
loping along for a mere hundred yards, and I feel as though I've been
running in a steeplechase.'

'But. . . .'

'But,' continued David, 'you are going to say that I should not be
running at all. Let me tell you, Nurse, that I have Doctor Craven's
permission.' His expression became serious, and he turned to face
her.

God, she was beautiful, he thought, with morning sunlight turning
that glorious mane to fire, and caressing the delicate planes of her
face. His gaze dropped to her softly curved lips, then to where the
lace-covered muslin of her gown fell softly over her breast. His fists
clenched involuntarily as he forced a smile to his lips.

'Under his supervision, I have embarked on a series of exercises, as
suggested by that doctor in Spain – the only one, I might add, for
whom I had an iota of respect. Besides the occasional gallop, the
program calls for calisthenics that can easily be done indoors.'

Kate's eyes shone, not only at his news, but at the fact that the
silence between them was at an end.

'I'm so glad, David, that you have slain at least some of your beasts.
For I'm sure that once you regain your bodily health, that of your
spirit cannot be far behind. I had been sulking over losing my villa,
but if its collapse resulted in your new outlook, I am amply rewarded.'

'Losing your villa? What are you talking about?'

David's tone seemed oddly concerned, and Kate's brows lifted. He laughed in some confusion.

'That is, surely, since the first two rooms are intact . . .' He glanced at her and smiled again. 'You will think I've taken leave of my senses, but your villa has been very much in my mind of late. At least, part of it. Your soldier – the one in the wall painting. . . .'

Kate said nothing, but her gaze remained questioning.

'I keep seeing him before me – I don't know why, but I feel a sort of affinity for him.'

Gently, Kate touched his hand. 'You are both warriors,' she smiled. 'I wonder where his battles were fought? Certainly not in Britain, for the Romans had held undisputed sway here for some time before our friend built his house high above the Avon. Indeed, he may have been a Briton, granted citizenship years before. Perhaps he received his wound in Germany.'

She lowered her eyes, suddenly aware that his strong, brown fingers still lay under hers. She marveled at the power of their touch to warm her, and she longed to stroke them – to feel them respond and lift to caress her.

This time it was she who drew abruptly away, only to find that David was gazing at her with such a very odd expression that she became breathless.

'Kate,' said David tentatively. 'I'd like to ask you a question.'

Kate felt her blood thunder in her ears. 'Yes?' she replied, in what she hoped was a tone of great calm.

'It's about Lawrence.'

Her heart, which a moment ago had threatened to lodge in her throat, now fell precipitously to the toes of her kid slippers.

'I really don't. . . .' she began.

'Please, Kate, for once let me speak to you about him without your flying into the boughs. May I have a round tale please? Just what are your feelings for him?'

Kate could feel her temper rising, and she drew a deep breath as she answered carefully.

'May I ask just what is your concern here?'

David flushed, but he replied coolly. 'I am your guardian, Kate. If you are desirous of marrying Lawrence, I should be made aware of it.'

'Has Lawrence said anything about marriage plans to you?' Kate's fists were clenched into such tight balls she thought she must be drawing blood.

'No, but Regina has spoken fairly plainly on the subject. She says you have an understanding.'

Kate longed to blurt out a fierce denial, but something kept her lips pressed together. She knew an urge to make it perfectly plain to Lord Falworth, that just as he found nothing in her to hold his attention, so then must he be assured that she was equally heart-whole.

'I have not decided,' she said indifferently, 'whether to accept Lawrence's suit. We have known each other for this age, of course, and I naturally feel comfortable with him. However' – she yawned delicately – 'I feel it is rather too soon for me to become betrothed. After all, when I have lived in London for a year or two, I may find someone with whom I can form a real attachment. Don't you think? I mean, since I shall be so very rich, I think I ought to consider carefully on whom I bestow my hand.'

She glanced at him from beneath lowered lashes, and was startled to find her gaze returned with one of blazing fury. His voice, however, when he spoke was rigidly controlled.

'By all means. One cannot be too careful with one's hand, particularly when it clutches such largesse. You must be sure to calculate to a penny the worth of each and every suitor, so that you may not only retain your own fortune, but, oh happy day, combine it with one even greater. Perhaps you should consider the Duke of Grunstable. I hear he is hanging out for a rich wife. Of course, he is small and ugly and very old, but of what significance is that compared to his vast wealth? I bid you good day, Miss Millbank.'

He turned on his heel and strode from the little bower.

By the time he tramped into the house, he was aware that he had probably exceeded Doctor Craven's instructions, for his hip ached abominably, and he fairly trembled with fatigue. He knew, however, that his morning's outing had been good for him.

If only the tearing ache in his heart could be dealt with so easily. He shook his head, his outrage almost palpable. He could not believe the conversation he had just held with Kate. When he had questioned her on her involvement with Lawrence, he had fully expected her to deny the relationship. Incredibly, she had indicated that she was taking that puppy's suit seriously! He had vowed that if Kate and Lawrence were really in love, he would not stand in their way – but 'Miss Moneybags' had certainly not sounded as though her heart were in any way involved. 'One must be careful where one bestows one's hand,' indeed! He could not recall ever having heard her mention the fortune she was to come into one day, even in the days when it was only half the sum she and her brother would inherit together.

'Women!' he muttered to himself as, refurbished in clean shirt, coat, and pantaloons, he hobbled out of his chambers and down the corridor to Lucius's room.

He found his friend at his dressing table amid a welter of discarded neck cloths. Fellowes hovered nearby, dividing his attention between his master and an open portmanteau some feet away, into which he was tenderly placing coats, pantaloons, and breeches.

Lucius merely held up a hand, and did not so much as look away from his mirrored reflection until, some minutes later, he had completed the final fold of his creation. Only then did he rise to face David.

'Lucius, you are a picture of manly perfection,' murmured David.

'One does one's humble best,' his friend acknowledged modestly.

'Are you nearly ready to leave then?' David moved to the portmanteau, absently inspecting its contents. 'Lord, I'll miss you.'

'Well, you seem to be making great progress here – in more ways than one,' he added with a barely perceptible smile. 'And in his note, Father sounded as though he has need for me at home. Besides, dear boy, it's not as though I'm moving to Moscow. It's only a two-day journey from here to Kent, after all.'

The two moved out of the room, leaving the mundane packing details to Fellowes. Downstairs in David's study, they settled down over a last glass of wine.

'I do hope you'll keep me posted as to how matters progress here,' said Lucius, meditatively sipping his excellent Chambertin.

'Matters?' David lifted a questioning brow.

'Oh, the harvest – Lady Falworth's adherence to your neat little schemes for economy – Lawrence's attempts to keep his feet on the straight and narrow. I understand, by the way, that he was involved in a brawl in some stew down on Avon Street recently. Actually,' he continued, in response to David's grimace, 'I'm told by one of the footmen, who witnessed the fracas, that your tiresome little half brother was defending your honor. Yes, indeed, it seems he was airing his grievances to one of his friends, but when the gentleman agreed with all of Lawrence's calumnies, Lawrence immediately reversed his position and took great umbrage.'

David said nothing, but only shook his head in surprised appreciation.

'I'm also,' continued Lucius meditatively, 'curious about how her ladyship's betrothal schemes will work out.' He ignored David's sudden stiffening. 'Her plan to acquire my modest self for her daughter failed, but what of Lawrence and Kate?'

David was about to respond offhandedly, but – this was Lucius, after all. He sighed.

'I believe,' he said slowly, 'that neither one of them has the slightest interest in the other, but I cannot be sure. I wish Kate. . . .'

After a moment's hesitation, he related his earlier conversation with that maddening minx. To his surprise, Lucius threw back his head in laughter.

'It is unfortunate, my lad, that you were raised without older sisters. Had I been there to be asked, I should have told you that nothing so infuriates a female as being told by the man in her life that he is anxious to marry her off to someone else.'

His words produced such an explosion of emotions in David's mind that for a moment he could only stare at his friend.

'The man in her life?' he asked, hitting on the most shattering aspect of the statement. 'Where did you get such a buffleheaded notion? And I am not, for God's sakes, trying to marry her off to anybody – surely she must know that.'

Lucius crossed his legs and inspected the shine on his Hessians before lifting his eyes to David's.

'Tell me, old fellow, does she know you're in love with her?'

An unthinking denial sprang to David's lips, but it died unspoken as Lucius held his gaze with one of understanding. He spoke quietly. 'Have I been so obvious?'

'Only to an intelligent observer, of whom, if I may say, there are damn few around here – with the exception of her ladyship, of course.'

'Regina? You think she suspects that. . . .'

'That your feelings for your little cousin have gone far beyond brotherly affection? *Absolument*.'

David ran strong fingers through his hair. 'Oh, God, you don't suppose she's told Kate of her speculations, do you?'

Lucius laughed derisively. 'I should imagine that Kate is the last person in the world to whom she'd divulge such information. Tell me,' he continued, 'why are you so fearful of Kate discovering the true state of your heart, if you'll forgive the fanciful imagery.'

David glared at him. 'Because I am not worthy of her – if you'll excuse an even more revolting turn of phrase.'

'Because you believe you killed her brother?'

At this, David sprang to his feet. 'How the devil. . . ?' He stopped, and sank slowly back into his chair. 'Are you a mind reader as well as an acute observer?' he asked wearily. 'I've never told anyone – except Kate. . . .'

'During your nightmares, you become quite – voluble, you know. And, do you remember? I was the first to come upon you lying on the edge of that infernal ditch at Badajoz. Before you had completely regained consciousness, you babbled at some length about – about what had occurred during the siege.' Lucius sighed heavily. 'Later, I watched your downward spiral from the finest officer I had ever known to a haunted, reckless care-for-nothing, and there was nothing I could do.'

There was a long silence in the room, broken only by the sigh of the breeze through the window and the ticking of the mantle clock.

'Yet,' murmured David, 'knowing what you did, you remained my friend. For that, I thank you, Lucius.'

'What I know, you bacon-brained clunch, is that if you had been able to save young Philip, you would have.'

David's face hardened. 'Good God, you, too? Lucius, you don't understand—' He broke off.

David swallowed. He had revealed to Kate the fear that had consumed him on that bloody night, but he was damned if he'd discuss it with anyone else, even his best friend. He sighed wearily.

'Let it go, Lucius. Suffice it to say that Kate's misplaced trust makes for the most exquisite punishment I could possibly endure. Besides, you know she looks on me as a surrogate brother – right now, she needs a replacement for Philip, and that's what I'm trying to be.'

Lucius snorted.

'Besides, she's going to be a very wealthy young woman in a few months. I couldn't possibly ask her to settle for me, when she will have half the eligible men in London at her feet.'

Lucius snorted again. 'Lord, I never knew you could be such a gudgeon.' He rose and adjusted his coat and the splendid waistcoat beneath it. 'Never let it be said that I should come between a man and the enjoyment of his guilt, Davey lad, but if you'll take a piece of advice from an old comrade, you'll snap up the matchless Miss Millbank before Regina marries her off to Lawrence. Believe me, as one who knows, that woman's machinations are not to be made light of.'

With that, he hastened from the room, remarking that he must make his farewells to the rest of the family.

For the first few moments after David stalked from the bower, Kate simply sat, wishing she had bitten her tongue – that she had gnawed it through at the roots, for that matter. Would she never learn to control her wretched temper? What must David think of her? She had surely sounded like – well, like a certified bitch. If he never spoke to her again, she would not be surprised.

A fresh horror gripped her. Had she left him with the impression that she was actually in love with Lawrence? He had said he would not stand in her way if she truly wished to marry him. Lord, how unutterably stupid she had been.

She rose slowly, and with dragging steps, made her way back to the house. There, unable to bear her own thoughts, she fled to the library and tried with a notable lack of success to immerse herself in one of Uncle Thomas's volumes on her favorite subject, the Roman occupation of Britain. It was here that Lucius found her some time later.

'You are the last on my list of good-byes,' he sighed as he eased himself into a leather-covered armchair. 'And, I might add, the only one to whom it is truly a hardship to say farewell – other than David, of course.'

'I don't see why you are leaving at all,' Kate said with a smile. 'Westerly will be dull when you are gone.'

'Well, I don't know about that, but Father wants me back home, and when Father speaks, nations listen.' He paused for a moment. 'You're looking remarkably pensive this morning. I'd like to think the shadow on your brow is the result of my departure, but I feel there must be another reason.'

'Oh – no – I've just been so engrossed in this book.' Her eyes fell as she met his gaze, and she amended her statement with a rueful smile. 'If you must know, David and I had another – confrontation, and it was all my fault. Oh, Lucius, why do I behave like such a peagoose when I'm with him?'

'I believe,' he replied after due consideration, 'that it is a failing of women in love.'

'What!' Kate started forward in her chair, causing the heavy tome to fall to the floor with a thump. Oblivious, Kate stared at Lucius. 'What are you talking about?'

'Merely making an observation.'

'But I am not in – that is, of course, I love David. He is my dearest friend, and has been closer than. . . .'

'If you're going to tell me again that you love David like a brother,' said Lucius severely, 'I really shall think you a ninnyhammer. I am not seven, you know.'

'Dear heaven, Lucius,' she breathed in alarm. 'You haven't said anything like that to David have you? For, I'd curl up and die if he even suspected. . . .'

'You impugn the honor of the Pelhams, my good woman. Never let it be said that yours truly would betray the secrets of a maiden's heart. No matter how totty-headed the maiden happens to be.'

'Now, see here. . . .' she began, but was quickly silenced.

'Well, just look at the way you behaved this morning. During your, er, confrontation, was there the slightest hint in your demeanor that would give David the idea that your feeling for him is slightly warmer than that of a spinster aunt for her pet pug?'

'Of course not. Lucius, David thinks of me as nothing more than a bothersome child grown to adulthood. Oh, yes, he loves me, but only. . . .'

'. . . As a sister. Oh, God, spare me.'

'. . . But only,' she finished with great dignity, 'because he has needed a friend, and I am here for him.'

She rose to look, unseeing, out the window.

'And I have been glad of that,' she continued, pleased that her voice remained calm, 'but the time will soon come when he will not need me anymore. He will marry eventually, and by the time that occurs, I shall be gone from Westerly.'

'I see. And who is to be the happy bride? Little Miss Davenport, perhaps, with her fat curls and bouncing bosom?'

'Perhaps,' replied Kate through gritted teeth. 'Although I should think he would look higher. He can, you know. Anyone would wish to m-marry him, after all.' She could feel her eyes filling and brushed her hand angrily against them.

Lucius had also risen, and now he came forward to grasp Kate by the shoulders.

'And you are just going to stand aside and let some other female waltz off with him? My, my, what incredible nobility of soul. Without so much as hinting that he would be so much happier with you, if only he had the sense to see it.'

Kate gazed at him resentfully. 'It's all very well for you to be handing out advice, Lucius. You are not a woman. . . .'

'For which the gods be profoundly thanked.'

'. . . And you do not understand the limitations that are placed on us.'

'Such as those placed on Lady Cilla Merritt?'

Kate was surprised at the bitterness in his tone. He grimaced.

'I had become rather fond of her, you see, and I thought she genuinely liked me. I fear I was shaken in my own estimation after last week's performance – amateurish as it was.'

'Oh, Lucius, surely you realize that Aunt Regina was behind it all?'

'Yes, but, you see . . .' He smiled rather painfully. 'Ah, but I shall recover. You,' he continued seriously, 'will not, I believe.'

He took her hand and bestowed a light kiss upon it.

'I must be off, my dear. David will be waiting in the hall to see me off. Do remember, though, faint heart never won fair gentleman.'

With this, he left the room, Kate following in his wake.

Chapter Twenty

In the hall, they found not only David but Lady Falworth, Crawford, Lawrence, and even Aunt Fred. Only Cilla had failed to join the gathering.

'Good-bye, dear boy,' trilled Regina. 'Do come back to see us soon.'

Aunt Fred chimed in with her own farewell, and Crawford called a genial good-bye. Lawrence stood by somewhat warily. Kate withdrew a little and waited her turn with a smile as Lucius shook hands with the gentlemen and kissed those of the ladies.

When he came to her, he did not take her hand, but reached up to cup her face with both of his and brushed her cheek lightly with his lips.

'Good-bye, Miss Millbank,' he whispered. 'Fare you well.' She smiled mistily.

'And you, Mr Pelham.'

And then he was out the door and leaping into his elegant carriage. The coachman cracked his whip, and in a moment, the vehicle rattled down the long driveway toward the gates of Bath stone.

When David looked around, Kate was gone. His face tightened. As he began to close the great front door, his attention was caught by a flash of something – no someone running across the lawn. Why, it was Cilla! Evidently she had been lying in wait for Lucius's coach to pass, for she reached the driveway just as it sped past her.

To David's dismay, the coach drew to a jarring halt. Good God, was Cilla still up to her tricks? The carriage door opened, and Lucius made as though to step from it. David started to run down the drive-way, but was brought up short as he observed Cilla's gesture of denial. Indeed, she thrust her hands behind her back as she spoke to Lucius, then turned and ran the way she had come, stumbling as she did so.

Lucius stared after her for a long moment, then disappeared again inside the carriage. It sprang into motion once more, and soon vanished behind the trees bordering the drive.

David watched Cilla move slowly across the grass toward the house, and intercepted her as she was about to enter through a terrace door.

'What was the meaning of that, Cilla? Were you determined to have one last stab at Lucius? Have you no shame?'

To his consternation, she burst into tears.

'Cilla,' he cried, his wrath suddenly dissolved. 'Don't do that. Here.' He pulled a handkerchief from his waistcoat pocket and began dabbing ineffectually at her streaming eyes. He led her to a settee placed in one corner of the hall and, with some awkwardness, deposited her upon it.

'Oh, David,' the girl sobbed. 'I didn't waylay him – at least not to serve him any more tricks.'

'Then what was your purpose? Surely, you must know. . . .'

'M-my purpose was to apologize to him.' She straightened, and with an attempt at dignity, she took the handkerchief from him and dried her cheeks. David simply stared at her.

'To what?'

'To tell him I am sorry for my wr-wretched behavior. I have been so ashamed, David! If you could have seen the look on his face – the contempt in his eyes as he withdrew from the conservatory. I simply could not face him afterward – but I couldn't let him leave without explaining.'

'What was there to explain?' David's voice was stern, but not without sympathy. Cilla paled and sank back upon the settee.

'That's what made it so awful. There was nothing I could say to excuse my behavior, so I could only apologize. I'm sure it didn't do a whit of good – his only response was a disdainful stare, but at least I said it.'

'I suppose the whole fiasco was your mother's idea,' said David with a frown.

'Well, yes, it was, but I can't pretend that I didn't throw myself wholeheartedly into her wretched scheme. She wanted Mr Pelham's money, and – I wanted Mr Pelham, and I am so used to falling in with Mama's designs. Indeed,' she hurried on, as though determined to reveal the worst, 'when Kate and Lady Frederica popped up out of nowhere, I was as furious as I was astonished. It was not until I looked into Mr Pelham's eyes that I realized what a truly abominable thing I had done. I learned a great deal about myself that day, you see, and what I discovered was not very pleasing. I shall probably never see him again, but it is no more than I deserve.'

She rose. 'I'll have this laundered' – she indicated the now very damp handkerchief in her hand – 'and will return it to you tomorrow. I must go now.' With a final, faint sniffle, she was gone, leaving David to stare after her in bemusement.

He, too, rose after a moment, and limped from the hall in the direction of his study. Well, well, he reflected, would his family never cease to surprise him? Was it possible that Cilla might escape from her mother's damaging influence? If so, he thought, his lips curving upward, he rather thought that she might see Lucius again sometime, after all.

He entered the study and drew to an immediate halt. Kate stood near his desk, a shaft of sunlight creating a bright aura around her head. She looked up, a diffident expression in her eyes.

'I hope you don't mind my waiting for you here.' Her voice was low and tentative, and it caused a familiar stirring deep in David's stomach. He felt as though all he wanted to do right now was simply stand and look at her for an hour or two. No, what he wanted to do right now was to walk up to her, take her in his arms, and kiss her until she was breathless.

'No, of course not,' he replied in a voice of calm courtesy. 'Will you have some wine?'

'No – no, thank you. I thought we might have a talk, David.'

In answer, he drew up a chair for her, and when she was settled, pulled up another for himself. Kate looked at him for a moment before she began to speak. Dear heaven, she thought, would she ever get over her need of this man?

'It seems,' she began, in a voice of cool reserve, 'that many of our conversations lately have ended in unnecessary confrontation.'

It had taken her some time to compose that little speech, and, while she had been quite proud of it a few moments ago, it now sounded stupid and stilted in her ears. David, however, merely nodded.

'Yes, we seem to have developed a knack for rubbing each other the wrong way.'

This, unfortunately, led Kate's wayward thoughts to the moment outside the villa when David's fingers had stroked her with such shameful results. She blushed.

'This morning, we were discussing my plans for my future.'

David nodded again.

'I thought perhaps I should tell you that, while I have no immediate plans, I shall be coming into my majority in a few months.'

David still said nothing.

'At that time, I believe I shall make plans to remove from Westerly to live in, perhaps Brighton, or Bath, or even London.'

Though she knew she had decided on the correct course, she listened achingly to the silence that yawned between them. He did not say the words she would have given her famous fortune to hear. Indeed, when he finally answered, his voice was harsh.

'A wise decision, Kate. It would be foolish to immure yourself here, for you have your life ahead of you.'

Kate felt almost physically bruised by his words, as though he had just hurled a handful of pebbles at her. The smile she bestowed on him, however, was merely questioning.

'Perhaps Lord and Lady Buckminster would sponsor you for a year or so.' His voice was barely a growl now. 'I know the relationship is quite distant, but surely you must be well acquainted with them.'

'Oh, yes.' Kate marveled at her control. Why, one would think that leaving Westerly was her dearest wish. 'In fact, their daughter, Susan, and I made our come out in the same year. Lady Buckminster and Aunt Regina often gave parties and routs together.'

'Well, then. . . .'

'But I don't need a sponsor, David. It would look absurd for someone of my age to be seen on the catch at Almack's. No, I shall set up my own establishment. I am trying to persuade Aunt Fred to come live with me.'

'I see.' Inside his head, David screamed her name, shouting at her not to leave him. God, how was he going to get through the rest of his life without her? How could she consider leaving Westerly?

'Well,' he concluded, his tone even, 'I expect there is no more to be said, then.'

He began to rise, and Kate knew a moment of panic. Was this all he had to say on the subject of her leaving Westerly forever? *Faint heart never won fair gentleman.* The frivolous words tumbled in her brain. She lifted her hand in an unconscious gesture, and he sank back.

'Is this all right with you, David?' she asked hesitantly. 'I mean, if you'd prefer that I stay here, I would – consider it. At least, until you marry – then I think another woman in the house might be a problem, don't you?'

David had been quite pleased with the control he had exhibited thus far, but at this little speech, he thought he might possibly explode. Prefer that she stay? Until he married? *Married?* The thought of marrying anyone except Kate would have been ludicrous were it not so painful. Yet, he must marry. It was his duty, after all. His duty, as always, was blindingly clear.

'You are quite right. It would no doubt be in both our interests were you to set up house in London as soon as you reach your majority. I'm sure you will make a splendid *parti* – perhaps you will allow me to stand godfather to your first child.' He smiled a smile that he thought would crack his face, and Kate returned it with one that she thought would crack her heart, except that it had already been shattered.

So much for winning the fair gentleman, she thought dully, as she excused herself and made her way from the room. She had practically flung herself at him, and all he had done was make it perfectly plain that he did not care if she left Westerly tomorrow, and worst of all, his primary interest seemed to be in marrying her off to the first eligible male to appear on the horizon.

In the days following, Kate and David maintained a pattern of cordiality, smiling at each other in the corridors, and making civil conversation at dinner. David's strength grew, and he found himself able to attend to matters that had been wholly beyond him before. Kate busied herself with her self-imposed duties around the estate, finding some solace in the welcome she received in the tenants' cottages. To her surprise, Cilla asked if she might accompany her on her visits, and Kate discovered that the flighty young miss possessed a way with very small children, kissing away hurts and inventing nonsensical games that drew gurgles of laughter from them.

David readdressed himself to the mountain on his desk, and found to his relief that it had the power to occupy his mind, at least temporarily. The nights were something else. Kate's voice seemed to fill his mind, and he was tormented by visions of her eyes, laughing into his, of her lips, tantalizingly close. The scent of her hair was almost a physical presence, and end-less, aching hours were spent picturing how it would look spread out on the pillow next to him.

And then, when he finally slept, the old dream would return to torment him.

Kate lay in the darkness, rigid with the effort it took not to leap from her bed and rush to David. The master's suite was some distance away from hers via the corridor, but his window, open to the night breeze, was just across the courtyard from hers. Thus, at his first cry, her eyes had flown open. She clutched her bed covers with both hands as another anguished moan sounded – and one more. Then, silence. She knew Curle must be at his bedside now to minister to his master.

Dear God, would he ever stop punishing himself? Was there noth-ing she could do to free him from the chains of self-hatred he had wound around his soul? A sudden thought sliced into her mind. She had been so absorbed in mourning her unrequited love, she had almost forgotten that David had been her friend before he had become her love. He had once said that he needed her friendship.

She had shown him precious little of that commodity lately – so busy salvaging the shreds of her pride that she treated him now more as a pleasant acquaintance than a friend. Would it be possible to get back to that old, satisfying affinity with him? She had desperately missed the sense of oneness that she had always felt in his presence. How would he respond to an overture of renewed friendship from her?

Well, she thought, as she turned her face into the pillow, she supposed there was only one way to find out.

But when she went to seek him out the next morning, he was

nowhere to be found. He was not in the breakfast room, nor was he in his study. The butler informed her that he had ridden out early, but said he would return in time for a meeting with his bailiff, scheduled at eleven.

David had risen early, greeting the first rays of morning sun that slanted through the windows of his chamber with marked disfavor. He had never fully returned to sleep after he had awakened, sweating and horror-struck, to find Curle at his side, and now he gave up the possibility of further rest as a lost cause.

Stripping off his nightshirt as he emerged from the bedclothes, he moved to the window to greet the day, and his gaze lifted to the distant hills beyond the Home Farm.

There, just in that hazy gap in the sloping landscape above the Avon, overlooking the ancient Roman Road – there lay Kate's villa. There, a painted soldier stared into the darkness of the ages, his tragedy unnamed.

Turning, David swiftly donned shirt, breeches, boots, and coat, and hurried from the room.

The sun had barely risen above the horizon when he approached the entrance to the villa. He scanned the hillside above it and noted that more of the hill surface had sunk into the cavity below. He sighed at the memory of Kate's disappointment, and lighting one of the stored lanterns, he gingerly made his way into the first room. There, he found his pad, lying where the first rumblings of disaster had shaken it from his fingers, and brushing off the accumulated coating of dust, began to complete the work he had started.

Well, old fellow, he thought, as he copied the details of closely cropped curls and arrogantly curved brows, how did you come by that scar? Nasty piece of work. A spear wielded by an agile enemy? Or a sword, in hand-to-hand combat? And tell me, Longinus – or Leonidas – did you dream? Did the faces of dead comrades come to keep you company in the long watches of the night?

A long sigh shuddered through him, and he hurriedly completed the final pencil strokes of his sketch. Moving back outside, he glanced down at the portrait he held in his hands. Kate would be pleased. He riffled through the rest of the pages in the pad, and noted with relief that he had made drawings of all the finds and their locations in the first two rooms, as well as the battle mural in the now-destroyed back room. A pity about the rooms beyond, but perhaps someday a methodical excavation could be made. Someday when there was money for such frivolities.

He looked about him aimlessly. He was loath to return to the house just yet. Something about the solitude of this place appealed to him – that and his speculations about the owner of the villa. He grasped a spade from the little niche near the entrance where Kate kept her tools and moved to the stonework that she had mentioned to him earlier.

She was right, it didn't look very promising, but a little farther beyond – was that a rock over there, or was it a man-made carving? Scrambling to examine it, he discovered that it was indeed a piece of carving, but most of it was submerged in the soil. He worked for some minutes with the spade before he was able to loosen it. When he finally lifted the stone in his hands, he found that it was part of an ornately worked basin.

Was he holding a piece of fountain, he wondered excitedly. He glanced around. Yes, if the little door that Kate had hacked out were indeed part of the main entrance to the villa, this would be the right place for a courtyard, wouldn't it? He began digging in the dirt around the basin. To his delighted astonishment, after a few moments, his spade made the chinking sound of metal striking stone. Carefully, he lifted another few spadefuls of earth, and it was not long before he discerned that he was uncovering row after row of small, colored stones. By God, he thought exultantly, he had discovered a mosaic!

His first thought was to rush back to the house to fetch Kate. She would be beside herself at the news of his discovery. But, no. He would first uncover the mosaic and present it to her whole and beautiful after its fifteen-hundred-year interment.

Carefully he began removing the dirt from the area, pausing every now and then to brush the pavement clean and to examine the picture that was beginning to emerge. He had apparently begun his digging at the bottom of the picture, and as he worked, it soon became apparent that this was not an ordinary mosaic, featuring twining leaves and dancing mythological figures. He was sure, yes – it was another battle scene!

A strange excitement gripped him, and he worked on, almost in a frenzy of impatience. He could see now that he was uncovering the record of an ancient Roman siege. Scaling ladders had been placed against thick fortress walls that loomed over the oncoming force.

Badajoz!

The word seemed to leap into his brain in burning letters. The morning was far advanced now, and his wound was beginning to throb, but he did not – could not stop. In front of the pictured wall was a ditch, deep and treacherous, and atop the ramparts, men flung spears and smoking firebombs down upon the besiegers. A trembling began deep within David. Faster he dug, his arms jerking spasmodically as he tossed spadeful after spadeful of dirt away from the emerging image. The ladders! God, the men straining to reach the top of the walls had no chance. The men above were pushing the ladders away, waiting until they were heavy with climbers. Couldn't they see? Look! that fellow just entering the ditch . . . Suddenly, it seemed to David as though he observed the scene through a spyglass – everything about him fell away, and his whole being focused on that one man. His breath came in painful bursts, and his ears rang with the clash of armor and the screams issuing from a hundred throats.

Look! Could the soldier not see the ladder that was positioned just above him? There must be ten men on it, and, oh God – it was toppling. Jesus! Look out!

David stood swaying over the ancient pavement as the ground seemed to heave beneath him. His head felt as though it would explode, and he couldn't get his breath. A fire burst of – recognition? – exploded in his mind. God, what was happening to him? Sobbing, he fell to his knees and flung his arms over his head to protect him from the onrushing darkness.

Chapter Twenty-one

David had no idea how long he lay sprawled on the rocky ground sloping before the villa. Gradually, he became aware that he could breathe again, and he gulped in great lungfuls of air. He looked down at the pavement beneath him, and almost shouted at the sense of release that swept over him.

He knew now what had happened at Badajoz that night! He remembered everything – and he was not responsible for Philip's death! Those blood-soaked hours were now as clear in his memory as if they had taken place yesterday. How could he have forgotten?

Again, he experienced the fear that had gripped him in the fiery waters of the ditch. Philip's face floated before him, his arms outstretched in dreadful supplication. Must get to him – bring him back safe to Kate. He was nearly there! Nothing had touched him – nothing had exploded beneath his feet – his fingers almost grasped Philip's. Then, a shout above him and a rushing sound.

He looked up, and time seemed to slow as the ladder fell endlessly toward him. In the bloodred glow of the flames, he could see the men clinging to it, arms flailing and mouths open in terror. It was too late for escape. There was only an instant of horrified realization, and then, a sudden blackness.

He had come to moments afterward to find himself imprisoned by the ladder. He was pressed in between it and some object projecting from the surface of the water. The weight of the ladder, and the men who had fallen with it was crushing – he could hardly breathe. He realized that all that had saved him from death was the grass bag one of the men had dropped. It had fallen on him moments before the ladder struck him, thus cushioning him from some of the force of the blow he had sustained. His body was almost completely submerged, his face only inches from the water. The pain of the weight of the ladder was excruciating, and he could not move. Around him he could hear the cries of the wounded. And he could not move. The blackness came again, and he drifted in and out of consciousness all the rest of the night.

Philip's face swam before him, but only as a terrible vision, for he could not see beyond his corpse-laden prison. The noise of the battle quieted at last, and he became aware of exultant cries coming from within the city. Ours, he wondered dully, or theirs? His position had shifted, so that his head was no longer supported by the object against which he was so painfully wedged. It was becoming increasingly difficult to hold himself above the water, and he knew a desperate panic as he felt himself being pushed further toward it by the weight of the ladder.

Just when he had believed himself moments from death, shouts sounded from nearby. With the last of his strength, he uttered a single, hoarse cry before the darkness claimed him again. When he became conscious again, it was full morning and Lucius's anxious face was bent over him.

David shuddered, willing himself to return to the present. He lay still for a moment, savoring the warmth of the late morning sun and knew one more moment of painful grief for his lost friend. It was almost immediately softened, for unknown to him, time had done its work, replacing the anguish with a gentle regret for a young, vibrant life that had been taken too soon.

He rose and looked down again at the battle scene painted in stone. He had cleared away the main section of the mosaic, but there was no doubt much more to be revealed. The little figures seemed insignificant now, fighting their dusty, remote little war.

Kate. He must find Kate. His heart bounded in a great surge of joy. He was innocent of Philip's death! He could grieve with Kate, but he no longer need feel responsible for her tears. He was free to love her honorably – could he teach her to love him? Yes, he had promised to find her a suitable husband – he had given his word that she should have Lawrence if that's who she wanted, but by God he would lay his own heart before her first.

209

Could she ever see him as anything but a beloved friend? He remembered those fleeting seconds when he had covered her mouth with his outside the villa. Had he detected a response in her slender body, or was he the victim of his own heated imaginings? He warmed at the remembered softness of her curves pressed against him. He had sensed an eagerness to match his own, but perhaps . . . No, he must not take his dreams too far. He would be gentle and he would be patient, and in time, God willing, she would come to love him with the same fire she had ignited in him.

He smiled, envisioning the years ahead with Kate at his side. Together, what a paradise they could make of Westerly!

And with whose money will you create this paradise? The thought gnawed at him all the way back to the house. Surely, Kate would not think he wanted her for her fortune. On the other hand, with Regina's greedy ambitions as an example, how could she think anything else? Would he be able to convince her of his love?

Then again, what if he were simply creating a rosy fantasy? What made him think that she could love him, even without the conditioning that made her think of him as her blasted brother? What had he to offer? A face that he could not but consider unprepossessing at best, and a form certainly less than godlike. Ah, he mused, let's not forget the title – females pay attention to that sort of thing. But not, he rather thought, females like his Kate. There was Westerly, of course. Kate loved Westerly, but would she be willing to be saddled with it as it was now – debt-ridden and unproductive?

As he rode, his thoughts grew ever gloomier, but underneath it all, his mind sang of his freedom from guilt. Surely, now he could pursue his dreams. And his love.

He galloped into the stable yard and, leaving his horse in the care of one of the grooms, hurried into the house.

'Kate!' His voice could be heard echoing through the lower floors of the manor. 'Kate!'

But the only response he drew was from a worried Fleming, who hurried into the kitchen wing to greet him.

'Miss Kate isn't here, my lord,' said the butler anxiously. 'She should have returned from the village before lunch, but she and Mr Lawrence have been gone for hours.'

Kate and Lawrence?

'Where is Lady Falworth?' David asked, white-faced.

'Her ladyship is in the green saloon, sir. She is. . . .'

But Fleming was talking to the empty air.

David found Regina engaged at her embroidery. She raised her head as David strode into the room, and at the sight of him, a certain wariness crept into her eyes. She smiled and stretched out a hand to him.

'David! You look as though you'd been digging ditches – I hope you have not overtaxed your strength.'

'Your concern is most gratifying, madam. Now, tell me of this expedition undertaken by Lawrence and Kate.'

'Lawrence and Kate?' She fluttered her eyes in a pretty show of surprise. 'Why, I asked Kate to pick up some things for me in the village, and Lawrence offered to take her in his curricle. I must say, I have been wondering where they could have got to.'

'Just where has he taken her, Regina?' snapped David. 'Someplace, I suppose, where they will not be found until the morrow?'

'Nonsense,' replied her ladyship, a shade uneasily. She attempted to meet his angry gaze, but immediately dropped her eyes. 'Oh, very well, I shall admit I arranged their little, er, jaunt just so that Lawrence and Kate could further their, um, relationship, but it was to be nothing more than a morning's outing. I can't imagine what could have happened to them.'

'I see. And have you sent anyone out to make inquiries?'

'Yes,' she replied calmly. 'When they did not return for luncheon, I sent a footman out, but he says he did not meet them on the road, and no one in the village has seen either of them. I'm sure, however, there must be some simple explanation of their absence, and I've no doubt they will return shortly.'

David eyed her narrowly.

'You have no idea where Lawrence could have taken her?'

'Good gracious, David, you sound as though Lawrence has fashioned some sinister plan to abduct Kate. How perfectly ridiculous! I should imagine they are simply paying visits – or perhaps Kate wished to go to a neighboring village – for some reason.'

'If there are sinister plans afoot, my lady' – David's eyes held an unmistakable menace, and Regina began to pluck nervously at the silk fringe of her shawl – 'I think we know at whose door they can be laid.' He moved forward to take her shoulders in a harsh grip. 'If this is another of your plots, Regina, know that it will be the very last one you fashion.'

He turned and strode from the room, leaving her to stare after him, rigid with shock.

Returning to his study, he stood for a moment, frowning in thought, then betook himself to Lady Frederica's chambers.

He found the elderly artisan hard at work at her loom, and it was with the greatest of difficulty that he was able to disengage her from her new project, a depiction of St George slaying a particularly gruesome dragon.

'Well, I can tell you that he and Crawford were talking about Pucklechurch earlier today,' she said thoughtfully.

'Pucklechurch! That's over three hours from here! It's in the opposite direction from the village.'

Lady Frederica shrugged. 'I understand Lawrence said something about traveling there, although he did not seem to be happy about the project. It seems he carried on at some length about 'Mama's everlasting plotting.' Quite incensed he was. One of the upstairs maids – the youngest Branham girl, I think – told me that he and Regina had a horrendous row over it. Lawrence said he didn't see why he had to ferry Kate about the countryside today – why couldn't he go tomorrow? He whined and blustered at some length, but Regina finally won out, of course. When last seen, Lawrence was stamping down the corridor in the devil's own temper.'

David's fingers raked through his black hair as he paced the floor. ' "Ferry Kate about the countryside"! My God, if he's so much as touched her I'll . . . Did you hear anything further of Regina's plans? Why Pucklechurch for God's sake?'

'Well,' replied Aunt Fred judiciously, as she clipped a strand of wool with her scissors. 'It's quite out of the way, and not a place one would think of looking for them, and it's not too far from Westerly. I expect that tomorrow morning Regina will mysteriously receive word that the unhappy couple has been discovered there. At which point, she will sail off after them and have them back home and formally betrothed before lunch.'

David's enraged response to this was largely unintelligible. He stared at her for a moment, again running his fingers through hair that was already wildly disordered. He groaned, envisioning a terrified Kate being mauled by her loathsome cousin.

'He would not serve Kate such a turn, would he? Or me?'

'People,' murmured Aunt Fred, 'particularly impecunious young men, are apt to do odd things where money is involved.'

'My God!' cried David through clenched teeth as he hurtled out of the room. 'I'll kill him!'

Lady Frederica gazed after her great-nephew for a moment. Then she picked up her bobbin once more and turned back to St George and his dragon, an odd smile curving her lips.

The next few hours seemed to last an eternity to David. Because he rode on horseback, he was able to leave the main road now and then to travel the lanes and byways that provided a shortcut to Pucklechurch. Thus, it was well under the three hours it would have ordinarily taken to make the journey when he spied the square tower of the charming village church.

Within a few minutes, he had arrived at the single inn available to travelers who passed through the town. He was surprised at the bustle of vehicles and horses in the inn yard, and the number of persons, mostly young men, streaming in and out of the doors of the little building. He brushed this circumstance from his mind as he handed a sweating and trembling Barney to the ostler who hurried to greet him, then dashed into the inn.

'Well sir,' said the landlord, a grizzled and somewhat flushed personage, busily removing empty tankards from the tables in his taproom. 'Don't remember the gentleman, partick'aly. The description you give c'd fit almost any of the sprigs who been hoppin' about here today. But the redheaded gal – oh, yes, she's here, right enough.'

'Where?' asked David frantically. 'Which is her room?'

The landlord chuckled. 'Oh, she ain't in no room, sir.'

'Well, private parlor, then.' David was ready to throttle the man.

'Nope. Nor private parlor, neither.' He gazed vaguely around the taproom as though he expected to see the red-headed gal perched on his bar. 'Tell you what, you might find 'er in the stable.'

'The stable?' David's tone was frantic. 'What would she. . . .' But at the landlord's shrug, he turned and ran from the inn.

He checked as he entered the stable, adjusting his gaze from the brightness of the afternoon sun to its shadowy depths. From the far end of the structure he heard voices, and as he made his way toward them, was rewarded by a glimpse of brilliant color at the far end of a stall-bordered corridor.

Yes! It was Kate, and with her . . . David could just make out the dim masculine shape that loomed above her. The shape spoke, and was instantly recognizable.

'Look, here, Kate.' Lawrence's voice was unaccustomedly harsh. 'I'll not put up with this. Come away into the inn. I don't see what you're making such a fuss about, anyway,' he finished, falling into his more familiar whine.

'Just keep your hands off me, Lawrence,' snapped Kate, and now David could see that she stood near one of the pair of chestnuts that pulled Lawrence's curricle. 'If you think I'm going to stay in this benighted village while you – ouch! Lawrence, you're hurting me!'

David hurtled forward, just as Kate gave a vicious twist. With an anguished squeal, Lawrence reeled backward, bent double in pain. David paused, almost laughing aloud in his relief. Good girl! She had apparently remembered the lesson he and Philip had taught her when she was thirteen of how to disable a man with one, quick thrust of the knee – a piece of instruction she had been told never to divulge to any of Westerly's adults on pain of punishment too terrible to mention.

While David watched in appreciation, Kate stood over her victim for a moment, startled at the damage she had inflicted. Then, she whirled to grasp the bridle of the horse she had been saddling.

'I'm sorry, Lawrence,' she said over her shoulder as she worked, 'but you really shouldn't – oh!'

Kate, unfortunately, had overestimated the recovery time on the blow she had dealt, and now Lawrence, with an enraged snarl, had hurled himself on Kate, murder in his eye.

Galvanized into action, David leapt at his half brother, unleashing all the pent-up concern he had endured over the last hours. Staggering back in surprise at the unexpected onslaught, Lawrence's head snapped back as David's fist connected with his nose, producing an immediate and satisfying flow of blood. He slid in an ignominious heap to the floor.

Sparing him not another glance, David opened his arms to Kate, who flew into them and buried her head on his shoulder.

'Kate! My God, are you all right?'

'Oh, David!' she cried joyfully. 'I have never been so glad to see anyone. This has been a perfectly wretched day. You would not believe what this tiresome idiot has been up to.' She cast a disdainful glance at Lawrence, who still lay sprawled atop a malodorous heap of straw.

'Oh, wouldn't I just,' growled David, nudging Lawrence ungently with his toe.

'Why'd you hid be?' whimpered Lawrence. 'I thig you broke by dode,' he finished in some indignation.

'I'll hit you again, you appalling little worm. You've made it quite clear that you hate me, and care nothing for Westerly, but when it comes to abduction. . . .'

'Abduction!' Kate and Lawrence spoke as one.

'Oh, but David,' said Kate. 'Lawrence did not abduct me – at least, not precisely. That is, I went with him quite willingly.'

Motionless, David could only stare at her, for his heart seemed to have stopped beating.

Chapter Twenty-two

'I don't understand,' said David finally, his voice a painful rasp. He turned to Kate. 'Was it an elopement, then? Did you willingly accompany Lawrence here?'

'To Pucklechurch?' replied Kate indignantly. 'Of course not.'

David expelled the breath he had been holding during this entire exchange.

'Then what. . . .' he began.

'Good God!' This from Lawrence, who was struggling to rise, holding a delicately embroidered lawn handkerchief to his streaming nose. 'You dode really thig we were elopig, do you?'

'What else was I to think?' demanded David impatiently. He turned again to Kate. 'Just what the devil is going on?'

But Kate had swung on him, her nose now just inches from his own. 'Do you honestly believe,' she began in a furious tone, 'that I would consider marrying that wretched toad?'

'Here, I say,' interpolated Lawrence weakly.

'And even,' continued Kate, as though he had not spoken, 'if I were to contemplate such a ludicrous step, do you think I am so lost to propriety that I would consider a runaway marriage? Do you?' she repeated, as David showed no inclination to answer.

'Of course not.' David sought for the right words to placate the wrathful figure before him. If he had thought Kate a youthful deity in her gown of amber silk, she looked now like a fully matured avenging goddess, with her hair falling unbound over her shoulders. In the rays of late afternoon sun filtering through the dirty stable windows, it blazed like a bonfire on midsummer's eve. 'I knew you would never go willingly with him – that's why I assumed you'd been abducted –

216

but then you said you weren't, so. . . .'

Kate threw up her arms in a gesture of exasperation.

'Oh, for heaven's sake. Lawrence didn't bring me to Pucklechurch in order to compromise me. He merely wanted to go to a prizefight here.'

For an instant David wondered if he were going irretrievably mad. 'A – a what!?'

'A mill, David,' Lawrence interposed frantically. His nose had stopped bleeding, and apparently had begun functioning in a normal fashion. 'I only wanted to see the mill just outside of town, you know. Been making plans for weeks – had a wager with Crawford – and I was just about to leave, when Mama came up with this confounded idea that I should take Kate to the village. As though she needed me to accompany her.'

'I tried to tell Aunt Regina that I preferred to go alone,' said Kate. 'Frankly, after the episode in the conservatory, I didn't trust her. But – well, you know how she is – she kept going on about it, and since it was only a trip to the village, in broad daylight, I finally agreed.' She glared malevolently at Lawrence. 'Then, as we left the gates, he turned in the opposite direction from the village and sprang his horses! I told him to stop at once, but he wouldn't listen.'

Lawrence shrugged uneasily. 'Well, if I had, I was sure you'd jump out of the curricle, or something stupid.' He turned to David and stretched out his hands placatingly. 'I told her we would probably be back by dark.'

'Probably?' asked David in a strangled voice.

'Well, the thing is. . . .' He stopped and blinked uncertainly.

'Yes, Lawrence?' David's voice was deceptively mild. 'Tell me what the thing is. Did you think Kate would enjoy an afternoon at a prizefight, sitting in an open vehicle surrounded by the raff and skaff of this county and several others?'

'Well, no, of course not.' Lawrence stiffened with self-righteous outrage. 'I planned to leave her here at the Angel.'

'Of course, how stupid of me.' David spoke quietly, but with such menace that Lawrence flinched. 'Much better to leave her unattended and unprotected in a country inn, the target of attention from a flock of taproom habitués.'

'No,' wailed Lawrence, 'you don't understand. I had arranged for Phoebe, her maid, to meet us here. I had bespoken a private room where Kate could wait – she would have been quite comfortable.'

'If you think,' Kate broke in, 'that being held a virtual prisoner for hours in a cramped, smelly little inn with nothing to occupy myself constitutes a comfortable afternoon. . . .'

'But where, then, is Phoebe?' interrupted David.

Lawrence squirmed uncomfortably. 'Well, she never, ah, showed up. Don't know what could have happened to her.'

'And the room, Lawrence,' added Kate poking an angry finger into his chest. 'Tell him what happened to the room.'

'Oh. Yes. Well, it seemed the twit of a landlord rented it to somebody else before we got here. Really, David,' he blustered. 'Somebody ought to launch an investigation into the shoddy practices of today's innkeepers. Some chap offered him more money – rooms devilish hard to come by with the mill scheduled for today, of course – and he just gave my room away.'

'At which point,' said David smoothly, 'you immediately made preparations to return home.'

Lawrence fell silent.

'Return home, indeed,' snapped Kate. 'Oh no, Lord Lawrence proceeded ahead with his plans, blithely assuring me that Phoebe would no doubt show up at any moment. He said he would escort me to the church, and I could just curl up in a pew and wait. Nobody would bother me there, he said.'

As she spoke, Kate's hair seemed to take on an even more brilliant, flame-like hue until it appeared she might simply shoot skyward like a fireworks display.

'And *then*,' she continued, her hazel eyes spitting sparks, 'he complained that if Phoebe did not appear, it would be necessary to drive me home tonight, which was unfortunate, because he had planned on a tight little beefsteak dinner with a few of his cronies, whom he hasn't seen in donkey's years. In fact, he rather thought it would be quite jolly to spend the night here! That's when I finally decided to take matters into my own hands and drive myself back to Westerly. I might have made part of the journey in the dark, but it was better than staying here with this – this devotee of the Fancy.'

'Is this true, Lawrence?' Again, David did not raise his voice.

'Well, she's making too much of the whole thing, of course, but – aaugh!'

Once again, Lawrence found himself stretched out on the stable floor, once again bleeding profusely, this time from his mouth.

David stepped over him and began to draw the chestnuts out of their stalls. When he was able to grasp both leading reins in one hand, he turned to place an arm about Kate's shoulders, and together they made their way into the yard.

'Wha' 'oo hoo'n?' called Lawrence in agonized accents, as he lay among the stable floor litter. 'Oo're nah go' leemee 'ere!'

Gently, David shut the stable door. Turning, he beckoned an ostler and gave instructions for the horses to be hitched to Lawrence's curricle, and for Barney to be given space to rest until someone could be sent for him. Ten minutes later, David and Kate were on their way. The stable door remained closed.

'What a dreadful shame,' said Kate some moments later as they tooled along the road leading from Pucklechurch. 'Lawrence will miss the mill, after all. In fact, I wonder how he will get home?'

'I should imagine he will connect up with friends and beg a ride.'

'I would not mind,' Kate said grimly, 'if he had to crawl to Westerly over broken glass.' She turned to David, her expression lightening. 'But you didn't tell me how you happened, to—' She stopped, an arrested expression on her face.

'David?' The question in her voice was tentative. 'You look – different. Has something happened?'

David returned her gaze seriously, and then pulled off the road into a small spinney. The sun was sinking low in the sky, and if they tarried, they would not get home before dark, but his joy was too great to be contained. He had already waited too long to tell her.

'Yes, my dear, something has happened.' And, his words tumbling over one another, he told her of what had occurred at the villa.

'I am sorry beyond words that I was unable to save Philip,' he concluded. 'But I know now that I was truly unable to do so.'

'Oh, David.' She reached up to smooth a raven lock that had fallen across his forehead. 'I knew that must have been the case – but now

I'm glad that you know it, too. He is at peace now – and I think you are, too. I – I think there will be no more nightmares.'

'No,' he echoed, 'no more nightmares.'

They sat silently for a moment, hands entwined. David knew he should pick up the reins and jog the horses into activity, but he could not bear to break this moment of communion. Unthinking, he lifted his hand to touch Kate's hair, and as he did so, she placed her own on his sleeve. He turned then, and took her in his arms, burying his face in that glorious mane.

Kate uttered a small sob of joy and pressed her face into David's chest. She knew his embrace was merely a release from the burden he had carried for so long, but it felt wonderful beyond imagining. Dear Lord, how could she leave him to go to live in Brighton, or London, or some other awful place? She should push away from him now. Yes, in just one more sweet moment she would remove herself from his strong arms, and they would continue on their way. One more earth-shattering moment. But, what was he murmuring against her hair, and why were his lips moving to her face – brushing so softly against her cheek?

She could feel the pulse thundering in his throat. Then, she could no more have stopped herself from raising her lips to his than she could have stopped breathing in the scented summer air that flowed about them in magical currents.

David's last thought before his mouth came down on Kate's was a reminder of his promise to himself to be slow and gentle in his wooing of her, but it was instantly drowned in the heady sensation of her closeness. His lips moved softly on hers, and as he tasted the tender warmth there, his kiss became urgent and demanding.

Kate felt as though she were drowning in her love for him, and she lost herself in the dizzying wonder of his touch. Her hands reached up to stroke the dark curls at the nape of his neck, and he groaned, clasping her as though he would draw her into him. Her lips parted to welcome him, the heat of his passion creating a running fire in her veins.

He drew back from her at last, and took her face in both his hands, looking at her with a hunger too long denied.

'But why didn't you tell me,' Kate said at last, smiling with the brilliance of the sun at noon.

'Tell you. . . ?' he whispered harshly.

'That you love me, of course.' She laughed aloud. 'That you love me just as much as I love you.'

'You do?' he asked incredulously. 'You do love me? I mean really love me – not as your friend – or your big brother?'

'David, it's been so long since I had any sisterly feelings for you – well, I'm embarrassed to tell you how they have changed.'

He pulled her to him and kissed her again, stroking her until she thought she would go wild with wanting him. When his hands brushed the curve of her breasts, a gasp escaped her, and she shifted slightly so that his fingers could mold themselves against her.

He stilled and, after a long moment, straightened. His breathing rasped in his throat as he pressed her hands against his lips.

'May I take it, Miss Millbank, that your would-be betrothal to Mr Lawrence Merritt is no longer a consideration?'

'Be – Lawrence?' She jerked upright. 'David, how can you ask?'

'Just getting everything in order. If you're sure there is no other claim to your affections, Miss Millbank, may I offer – that is, would you do me the honor. . . ?' He drew her into his arms again for one more, searing kiss. 'Oh, God, Kate,' he breathed roughly, 'will you marry me?'

Her gaze, as she looked into his eyes, brimmed with laughter and love as she replied softly, 'Of course, I will. I thought you would never, ever in this lifetime, ask.'

This, of course, called for another long kiss that sent Kate into another spiral of wanting, and it was some moments before she emerged, flushed and breathless to gaze into his eyes. To her surprise, she found there a look of concern.

'Kate,' he began hesitantly. 'There is something we should discuss before – that is. . . .' He stopped.

'Why, what is it, love?' queried Kate playfully. 'Don't tell me you are having second thoughts already. I promise you, I shall take action for breach of promise.'

David's expression did not lighten, and Kate's immediately became serious as well.

'David?' she said slowly.

He put her gently from him and withdrew to the far edge of his seat.

'You will shortly be a very wealthy woman, Kate.'

She said nothing, but watched him from beneath lifted brows.

'I, on the other hand, can offer you nothing. At least, for now. I – I would not. . . .'

'Did you not just offer me your love? And do you not think that is all I want from you – that, and a nursery full of children?' She smiled wickedly, preparing to nestle once more into his embrace.

But David remained rigid. 'I would not,' he plunged on determinedly, 'want you to think. . . .'

'That you are marrying me for my money? David, you are being incredibly mutton-headed,' said his beloved. 'Do you think I am unaware that my wealth is a lure for fortune hunters? And do you think I do not know you better than to suspect you of evil designs on my fortune?'

'But everyone will assume. . . .'

'Not that I care, but I expect all the world will congratulate you on having made an advantageous marriage.'

'Yes, but. . . .'

'And just think, my very dearest love, what we can do for Westerly now! You must admit, having all the funds you need to restore the estate will be a splendid thing.'

David sighed. 'You are eminently correct, my practical little darling. And my first project, after I have acquired all your lovely money, is to begin a methodical excavation of your villa, starting from the top down.'

'Oh, David!' Kate breathed ecstatically. 'That would be. . . .'

'Followed by the establishment of two or three schools, set up on the estate and in the village. Do you think you could manage their supervision?'

'Oh, David!' she sighed again, looking so beautiful that he was obliged to draw her into his arms once more.

It was another long moment before the curricle at last was set into motion. Conscious of other vehicles on the road, Kate did not ride, as she would have liked, with her head on David's shoulder, but her fingers frequently went to his to be clasped possessively.

'Aunt Regina may be a little put out at this turn of events,' said Kate, at last.

David laughed. 'She will be absolutely livid. At least, I certainly hope she will. I think we'll have to do something about the soon-to-be Dowager Countess of Falworth.'

'That sounds rather sinister.'

'Don't think I haven't considered from time to time pushing her off the handiest cliff, but what I meant was, I believe I shall suggest rather strongly that she remove to the dower house after we're married. After we're married,' he repeated happily. 'I do like the sound of that.'

Kate wriggled closer to him, and there being no other riders on the road, she brushed her lips against the tip of one ear.

'Mmm. If you do that anymore, the wedding ceremony may become redundant.'

She laughed. 'You did not tell me how you came to know where to find me,' she said.

He related the sequence of events that had occurred on his return that morning from the villa.

'I'll have to thank Aunt Fred when we get home,' he concluded, 'for without her, I should not have known where to start.'

'But,' said Kate in puzzlement, 'Aunt Fred knew about the mill. I was with her last night when she and one of the footmen were discussing the odds-on favorite. She must have guessed what was in Lawrence's mind today – why in the world do you suppose she didn't tell you?'

David grinned slowly. 'Because she's a supremely crafty old file, that's why. She knew that the thought of you forced into a betrothal with Lawrence was likely to drive me into my own declaration. I have even more to thank her for than I realized,' he said with a chuckle.

'And what about Lawrence?'

'You know,' replied David meditatively. 'I begin to think that, despite his general lack of anything approaching common sense, there may be some hope for him. I believe I shall install Lawrence at the River Farm, with Pettigrew's son as his bailiff. I am quite impressed with that young man. Any profits the farm produces will go to augment Lawrence's allowance, and if, in the fullness of time it looks as though he has taken hold of the place, I'll deed it to him.'

'Oh, very well,' sighed Kate. Then, she smiled roguishly. 'I was rather hoping you'd send *him* to the West Indies. It made a man out of Uncle Thomas, after all.'

David, his eyes alight, replied, 'But who knows what – or who, he might bring back with him?'

'Very true,' she agreed solemnly. 'What would the neighbors think of another black-mopped infant roaming the stately halls of Westerly?'

At this appalling piece of irreverence, David had no choice but to stop the curricle and silence his betrothed, very slowly and thoroughly, and most pleasurably.